THE CLIFFSIDE INN

FIVE ISLAND COVE, BOOK 3

JESSIE NEWTON

COPYRIGHT

CHAPTER ONE

E loise Hall stood and shook the dean's hand. "Thank you, Donald." She wasn't sure what she'd just done, but as she left his office, she knew she'd left her keys behind.

She wouldn't be able to get in her office again. It wasn't her office anymore.

Eloise walked down the hall, a path she'd tread many times over the past twenty years. She remembered the first time she'd made the trek from the human resources office on campus to Dr. Donald Travis's office. He'd been Dean of Life Sciences for two years before Eloise had started, and he'd hired her, fresh out of Harvard, no other teaching experience.

They'd always worked well together, and Eloise's mouth turned down into a frown as the bright rectangle of light up ahead signaled the exit from the building. Once she left...she wouldn't be coming back.

Her steps slowed as her mind sped. What had she been thinking? She'd just quit her job.

She'd made a terrible mistake.

She slowed further, refusing to let herself stop. She looked over her shoulder, as if everyone she'd come in contact with over the past two decades would be there, suddenly lining the halls and applauding as she walked out of the biology building for the last time.

There was no one there. No one clapping.

Eloise did stop then, and she turned back fully, her heart taking on a new brand of courage. She began a slow clap for herself, a smile filling her soul as it took over her face.

She'd done it.

She'd quit her job to move to Five Island Cove, date her serious boyfriend full-time, and restore the Cliffside Inn, a building she'd owned for about as long as she'd been a professor here at Boston University.

Her self-applause sounded loud in the summer silence of the building, and Eloise knew that in just two weeks, these halls would be full of students and teachers, aides and secretaries. She always called these last couple weeks of August the calm before the storm, and she took one last moment to envision this building, her office, her classroom, the way she always wanted to think of them—full of life, chattering students excited to learn, and the energy only a college campus could possess.

Then she turned and walked out the doors.

The heat of the season hit her straight in the chest, but she took a deep breath of the too-hot and too-muggy air anyway. As she blew it out, she heard the voices she'd spent every day talking to over the phone or video chat since she'd left Five Island Cove in June.

"She's probably not done," Aaron said. "She said it could—"

"Eloise!" Grace said, catching sight of her first. She skipped toward Eloise, who grinned down at the girl. She laced her fingers through Eloise's when she arrived and said, "I knew you wouldn't take long."

"How could I?" Eloise asked her. "It's your birthday, and we have some very important celebrating to do." She smiled at Grace and lifted her eyes to Aaron as she approached. He swept one arm around her waist and pressed a kiss to the soft, delicate spot on her throat just below her jaw and ear.

"Hey, sweetheart," he said, his voice already throaty to go with the deep quality.

Eloise giggled at the way his hand moved up her back, and she stepped sideways to greet Billie too. "Wow, Billie," she said, taking her all in. "You talked your father into the mascara."

"I told you she'd notice," Aaron said.

"Is it too much?" Billie asked, shooting her dad a dirty look.

"I don't think so," Eloise said, bending down to peer at the girl closer. She was a stunning child—and Eloise knew she wouldn't be a child for much longer. Billie started seventh grade this year, and that meant junior high. No single teacher in charge of her, and multiple classes, and all those boys...

No wonder Aaron didn't want her to wear makeup. The mascara made her eyelashes look a league long, and since Billie was somewhat of a sober child, she had the starving model look down pat.

"You look very pretty," Eloise added.

"I told you it wasn't too much," Billie said to Aaron, who seriously looked like he might stick his tongue out at her. She'd certainly used that sassy tone of voice with him.

"Billie," he warned. "Watch your attitude."

Eloise looked back and forth between them, the battle silent but raging. "Am I going to have to separate you two?" She did step between them, taking Aaron's hand in her free one and releasing Grace's so she could hold Billie's. "Come on. Let's make a pact that we won't fight today. It's Grace's birthday, and she's turning eleven. I have eleven of the most fun things to do in Boston planned for us, and eleven movies to choose from for tonight, and eleven different kinds of ice cream bars."

She first looked at Aaron, who she could count on to

be the most mature. He still wore a storm on his face, but he nodded. "I can commit to that," he said.

Eloise looked at Billie, who stood nearly as tall as Eloise now. "Bills?"

"Yes," she said, though plenty of surliness rode in her tone.

Eloise smiled at her and drew her into a hug. The girl relaxed then, and Eloise whispered, "Hey, he let you wear it."

"I know." Billie sighed and stepped back. "Do you really think it looks pretty?"

"Yes," Eloise said. "You did just what I said too. Not too clumpy on the bottom." She looked over her shoulder for Grace, who'd wandered off after a butterfly during the battle of the wills. "Come on, Grace. If we don't get going, we won't be able to do everything for your birthday."

She'd shown Billie how to apply the mascara over a video chat several days ago. She'd bought Billie the mascara, along with an excellent makeup remover wipe, and had them both shipped to Aaron's house the next day. Billie had called her when she'd opened the package, and Eloise swore it was one of the only times she'd heard Billie laugh.

"What's the first thing?" Aaron asked as they strolled toward the parking lot. "And are we taking my car or yours?"

"Yours won't be full of residual cat hair," she said. "And it's an SUV." She knew the red vehicle parked next to her car in the lot was his, because the only other one belonged to Dr. Travis. "Let's take yours."

Aaron clicked the button on the fob to unlock it, and everyone piled in. "All right," Eloise said. "I have a few ground rules for today." She surveyed the group, twisting as far as her spine would allow to meet Grace's eyes. "Okay?"

"Okay," they all said.

"First, not everything we do will be everyone's favorite. I know that, but I still expect everyone to have a good attitude and not to complain. I went to a lot of effort to find the things we're doing, and I expect you to be kind and thoughtful of my feelings."

She glanced at Aaron, who simply looked at her with wide eyes. She wondered if anyone had ever spoken to him like that—or to his girls. "Of everyone's feelings."

"Yes, ma'am," Aaron said, reaching for and taking her hand in his.

"Second, you have to eat some real food today, or you can't have any of the birthday cake and ice cream I have at my house." Eloise smiled, raising her eyebrows at Grace, who giggled. Billie nodded, taking everything super seriously.

"Third, let's have fun today," she said. "You've never been to Boston, and it's a fabulous city." She nodded and looked at Aaron. "We're ready, Captain."

"I don't know where we're going," he said.

"Oh, right." Eloise sprang from the SUV and opened

her car's back door. She pulled out her giant bag that she took everywhere with her and turned back to knock on the window. "Pop the back," she said, through the glass.

Aaron got the message, and she began to move the eleven gifts she'd bought for Grace from her trunk to the back of the SUV.

"El," Aaron said, his voice halfway between disapproval and awe.

"Can I open one now?" Grace asked, as she'd knelt up on the seat and had seen what Eloise was doing.

"That's going to be rule number four," Eloise said. "You don't get to ask for the presents. I will give them to you when you should have them."

Grace's face fell, and Eloise's heart rebounded too. She picked up the gift she'd wrapped in pale pink paper and took it Grace's side of the car. "You get this one right now."

"Thank you, Eloise," Grace said, and she opened the present with the light of joy in her eyes. She took out the stuffed terrier and looked up at Eloise.

"That's Rhett the Boston Terrier," she said. "He's my school's mascot." The stuffed animal wore a BU jersey, but he was snarling like he might rip someone's face off if he came to life. "You have all those stuffed animals in your room, and I thought you might like one to remember your trip here."

"I do." Grace reached for her and wrapped her skinny arms around Eloise's neck. "Thank you, Eloise."

"Of course, Gracie-Lou." Eloise squeezed her tight,

closing her eyes the same way as she hugged the girl, and then stepped back. With the door closed, she took a moment to clear her throat and shake off the emotion. When she got in the front seat again, she said, "New England Aquarium, here we come."

———

SEVERAL DAYS LATER, THE HIGH FROM A GRAND adventure for Grace's birthday had worn way off. Eloise had been working like a dog, getting everything she owned packed, thrown away, or donated to the Salvation Army.

Aaron, Billie, and Grace had helped every single day, and then she'd take them to one of her favorite restaurants in town.

She stretched the tape over another box and took it into the front entry of the brownstone. She seemed to have come miles already, and yet, she still had many more to go. She put the thought out of her mind, because if she focused too hard on what she had left to do, she'd give up right now.

Aaron came through the front door and picked up the box she'd just set down. "Morning, El." He grinned at her, switched the box to the side and leaned in to kiss her.

"Hey." She kissed him back, glad to see him here so early. "Just you?" Usually, Billie and Grace crowded into the house behind him, and she didn't hear their footsteps or their voices.

"I told the girls they could sleep in and stay at the hotel if they promised not to leave the room or call me until noon." He grinned at her. "I'll get this loaded and come help you keep packing. Getting close?"

"I think so," she said, turning to survey the hall that led into the living area and kitchen. She had to be getting close, because they were all leaving Massachusetts tomorrow morning, on the same flight. Alice had been a great help to her in arranging to have the things she'd accumulated in the first forty-five years of her life moved across the water to the cove.

Eloise owned way too much to keep in the caretaker's apartment at the inn, and she'd already arranged for a storage unit on Sanctuary Island. She'd be staying with her mother just down the cliff until she cleaned up the apartment enough for her to live in, and Eloise knew she wouldn't have a day off of packing—or unpacking—and cleaning for a while.

For a brief moment, she couldn't believe she'd traded her gorgeous brownstone and her prestigious job at BU for a moldy, one-bedroom apartment at an inn that likely wouldn't open for many months.

By then, it would be the off-season, and Eloise didn't expect a lot of business to come pouring through the doors of the Cliffside Inn.

She turned when Aaron set the box down, surprise flowing through her veins when he took her into his arms and kissed her like he meant it. "I just realized we're alone for the whole morning," he said, his lips sliding down the curve of her neck.

"Mm." She melted into his touch and didn't protest when he took her upstairs to her bedroom.

THE NEXT MORNING, ELOISE DID INDEED HAVE THE brownstone ready to be vacated. She, Aaron, and the girls had worked until just after ten last night, and all she had to do this morning was shower, get dressed, and take her suitcase downstairs to her car. With that done, she sat on the steps and waited. She needed to drive her car to the dock, where she'd actually park it in a shipping container. That, and the one she'd filled with boxes and furniture, would arrive in the cove on a boat in ten to fourteen days.

She'd fly to Five Island Cove with Aaron and the girls, and she'd live out of her suitcase and use RideShare until her vehicle arrived.

Her stomach knotted, because Eloise Hall didn't do things like this. She stood as a couple came down the sidewalk. The man, Jacob, lifted his hand, his face already set in a permanent smile.

"Eloise," he said as he passed the gate and turned down her sidewalk.

"Hey." She embraced him and then Millie. "All right." She exhaled heavily and took the key out of her pocket. "Here's the key. She's cleaned out and ready for you."

She hadn't sold the brownstone, because they were extremely valuable, and she hadn't wanted to. She practically owned it, and she'd found a research assistant and his wife who were willing to sublet it from her.

"Thank you, Eloise," Millie said, and she hugged Eloise again. "This has been such an answer to our prayers."

"Mine too," Eloise said, nodding. She had to cling to that, otherwise, she might not be able to get herself to walk away.

Aaron rolled up to the curb in his red SUV, and Eloise felt like the sunshine broke through the clouds in her whole life. "Let me know if there's anything you need," she said. "Or if something breaks down or anything like that." She lifted her hand to let Aaron know she needed another moment. He did the same, and she focused on Jacob and Millie again. "Really. It's a good place, though."

"We're very excited," Jacob said.

"The shipping container will be gone on Saturday," she said. "Maybe sooner."

"No problem."

"Okay." Eloise turned and looked back at the thick, black door, and then faced Aaron, Billie, and Grace. "Okay." She nodded, tucked her hair behind her ears, and went down the sidewalk.

Aaron rolled down his window and said, "All good?"

"All good," she repeated. "So you'll follow me to the dock?"

"Yep." He chin-nodded to his phone in his cupholder. "I have it on the maps, and Billie is my navigator." He smiled at his daughter in the passenger seat, and Eloise couldn't wait to be in this car with them.

"Perfect," she said, and she went to her car, got behind the wheel, and drove away from the house she'd lived in for twenty years.

CHAPTER TWO

Kelli Thompson had just set a bowl of macaroni and cheese with seared hot dogs in front of Parker when her husband walked in through the garage entrance. They couldn't park in the garage, because Julian had stacks and stacks of things he needed for the courier business. Bike chains, and boxes, and tubes for papers. Backpacks for his riders, bike racks, a few filing cabinets, and literally everything else under the sun.

"Hey," he said, anxiety instantly present in his expression.

"Hey." She turned away from him, coaching herself to stand straight and tall. She did not need to cower under this man's gaze anymore. She picked up the wooden spoon she'd used to stir the dinner she'd made, and one Julian would never approve of.

Well, in Kelli's opinion, he could ask his girlfriend to

make the type of dinner he wanted. Kelli wasn't going to do it, she knew that. She wished she had someone she could tell about this situation, but she hadn't been able to bring herself to put anything on the group text with her friends in Five Island Cove.

She didn't share things like this with her mother, and Julian had asked her not to say anything to his mother.

For a few weeks after she'd returned to Newark, she and Zach had communicated regularly, but their texts and messages had dwindled to only a few each week now, if that. She felt completely alone in a city of hundreds of thousands.

She spooned herself some of the macaroni and cheese and joined her son at the table, refusing to look at Julian. "What are you doing tonight?" she asked. Since he'd had his assistant over—Tiffany Mullinax—and they'd revealed the fact that yes, they were a couple. They were dating. They were together, Kelli hadn't been able to think further ahead than five minutes.

Julian and Tiffany didn't want Kelli to leave. He wasn't asking for a divorce. He wanted both of them.

The word that had come out of his mouth had sent Kelli into a tailspin. She hadn't even known what it meant.

Throuple.

He wanted to have the three of them have an open, emotional, close, and sexual relationship.

The *three* of them.

Julian put his messenger bag on the sideboard and

eased past Parker and into the kitchen. Kelli had never minded the small house where they lived—until now. She'd never minded how much Julian worked—until now. She'd never minded how his whole life and what he wanted had dominated her entire existence—until now.

"I don't know," he said. "What are you doing?"

"I think Parker and I are going to go to the park," she said.

"Tiffany wondered if she—" He cut off as Kelli lifted her head and glared him into silence. "Okay." He lifted his hand in surrender, something she'd literally never seen him do. At least not for her. "You need more time."

"You sprung this on me six days ago," she said, glancing at Parker. He wasn't a baby, and he listened to every word his parents said. "So yes, Julian, I need more time." She looked down into her bowl, her appetite gone. She glanced at Parker. "Finish up, bud," she said. "We'll go to the park and maybe a movie."

If she left the house, then Julian could have his other woman over. She'd suspected he'd been cheating on her since her last trip to Five Island Cove, but he'd been denying it for two months. He denied it when he met her at the airport. He denied it when she'd walked into his office and found "Tiff" leaning over him as they both looked at something on his computer.

The way she'd been standing, and the look on her husband's face... Kelli had asked. Julian had denied it.

Over and over, he'd denied it.

Until six days ago.

Kelli was still reeling from the conversation, and it had literally lasted fifteen minutes from beginning to end. She'd left the house immediately afterward, and she hadn't come back until after midnight. Julian had put Parker to bed himself, and Tiffany hadn't been in the house. Kelli had stood in the darkness, the light above the stove the only way she could see anything in the room.

She'd felt outside of her skin, outside of her own reality. She still did.

"Okay." Julian put a couple twenty-dollar bills on the table. "Text me if you want us to come."

Kelli bristled at the word *us*, and she took the money and stood up in a fluid motion. She stuffed the bills in her pocket and left her nearly-full bowl of food on the table. "You ready, Parker?"

"Yeah," he said. He left his bowl on the table too, and Kelli was glad. Julian's eyebrows drew down, but Kelli didn't want to have this conversation right now. Kelli put a protective arm around her son and walked out the door her husband had come in only five minutes ago.

The stress and tension in her shoulders deflated the moment the door closed behind her, and then the tears came. She wasn't sad, and she wasn't nervous, and she wasn't anxious. Crying was simply her way to release all of the negative emotions she had. Positive ones too.

She put on a brave face, complete with a smile, and opened the passenger door for her son.

A FEW HOURS LATER, SHE REACHED FOR THE HALF-
empty bucket of popcorn she and Parker had shared, and
the weight of the world started to descend on Kelli's shoulders. Home used to be a place of safety for her, and if she
didn't have that, she didn't have anything.

Her lungs quivered, because she really didn't want to
go home. "Want to take this?" she asked her son.

"Can you make caramel popcorn with it tomorrow?"

"Sure," she said. "And we get a refill, so let's have them
fill it up on the way out, and we'll have lots. We can take
some to my friends at the gym, and you can take some to
your party."

Parker grinned at her. "I forgot about the party."

"You did?" Kelli stood as the lights started to come up.
"I can't believe that. You've been so excited about it."

"Yeah." Parker didn't say anything else, and Kelli
knew he had to be thinking something. She had no idea
how to get his thoughts out of his head, and she often got
one-word answers from him and not much else.

She stopped by to get the extra popcorn, and she
herded Parker through the teenage crowd loitering in the
lobby to the parking lot. Her phone rang, and she juggled
the full popcorn bucket and her purse to get her
phone out.

Her mother's name sat on the screen, and Kelli's heart
sent out a few extra beats.

She managed to tap the call open and put the phone to her ear while holding onto everything. "Hey, Mom," she said, nodding for Parker to keep going.

"Hey," her mother said, her voice sounding small and very far away. Kelli could never judge the mood her mom was in, because she said everything in about the same, even tone. "What are you up to?"

"Just leaving a movie," Kelli said, walking through the twilight. School started in a few weeks, and the days would get shorter and shorter until it would be full dark at this time of night. She mourned the passing of summer already, and she still had more time to enjoy it.

"Okay," her mom said.

Kelli gestured for Parker to come get the keys out of her purse. "Mom?" she asked. "Are you still there?"

"Yes," her mom said. "I just—" She cleared her throat. "I have to ask you something, and I'm a little nervous." She gave an anxious chuckle, and Kelli's stomach tightened. Her fingers ached as she pinched the very edge of the popcorn bucket.

"Just say it, Mom," Kelli said as Parker unlocked the car and got in the front seat.

"Have you heard from Zach at all this summer?"

"Yeah, sure," Kelli said, her voice automatically moving into a false zone. Truthfully, her last few texts to her half-brother had gone unanswered. She missed him, because they'd really connected in Five Island Cove in

June, and she'd thought she meant more to him than just a couple of weeks of interaction.

"He's been coming by the house," her mom said.

Kelli froze. "He has?"

"Yeah, a few times." Her mom sounded stressed, and Kelli didn't like that.

"Well, what does he want?"

"Money," her mom blurted. "He keeps asking me for money, Kelli, and I don't have anything to give him." She spoke in a huge rush of words now. "Last time he came, the only reason I didn't just give him what I had in my purse was because Devon was with me." She let out a breath that shook over the line.

Kelli didn't know what to say or do. Her first instinct was to rush home, pack a bag, and get on the first flight to Five Island Cove. She could comfort her mother and confront Zach about his behavior. Didn't he know that her mother wouldn't want to meet him, ever? It would be like looking into the face of her husband's betrayal.

In that moment, Kelli knew exactly how her mother felt. Back then, when her husband had cheated on her, and now, as she had to deal with the aftermath of it many years later.

Kelli did not want to be that woman. She didn't want to walk through her front door after a morning at the gym and see Tiffany sitting at the table. She didn't want another woman in her family, in her marriage, in any of it.

She hadn't wanted to lose Julian, and he claimed to love them both. He wanted them both. He said lots of couples did things like this, because it kept things interesting at a time in their marriage where things sometimes got stale.

Kelli didn't understand that. Her life with Julian hadn't been stale. She'd felt distant from him, because he'd started sharing parts of himself with another woman.

"I'm coming to the cove," she said, making up her mind on the spot. She moved toward the car and put the popcorn in the back seat. It would probably spill all over the place by the time she got home, but that wasn't her primary concern right now.

"I'll call him too," she said. "Don't worry, Mom. I'll take care of Zach."

"Okay," her mom said, her voice shaky. "Sorry, Kelli. I know you two are friends."

"Yeah," Kelli said, climbing into the front seat. "Okay, bye, Mom. I'll keep you updated." She hung up, her fingers shaking. Friends.

She didn't think she and Zach were that close of friends anymore, despite her best efforts. She didn't want to call him in front of Parker, as her son had really liked Zach.

She also didn't want to wait. Her fingers flexed around the wheel, and she forced herself to wait, because the last thing she needed on top of everything else was a citation for using her phone while driving.

At home, instant annoyance shot through her when

she saw Tiffany's car parked in her driveway. "Go on inside," she said. "Tell them I have to make a call, okay?"

"Okay," Parker said. "You can get the popcorn?"

"Yep." Kelli painted a smile on her face and watched her son go through the garage and inside the house. She quickly dialed Zach then and listened to the phone ring and ring.

He didn't pick up, and Kelli ended the call. Immediately, she dialed him again, muttering some choice words for him under her breath. When he didn't answer the second time, she barked into the phone, "Zach, it's Kelli. How dare you go to my mother's house and ask her for money? Stay away from her."

Her mind raced as fast as her heart. What was she going to do about it from so far away? Zach would likely scoff when he got the message.

Kelli's mind cleared, and she zeroed in on one thing: Aaron Sherman.

"I know the Chief of Police," she said, much smoother and much quieter. Much more deadly. "If I hear that you've even visited Bell Island, I will have you picked up and held in jail until I can get to the cove and figure out what you're doing and what you want."

She was surprised by the vitriol inside her. She hadn't asked him if the allegations were true or what he needed money for. She knew her mother wouldn't call her and lie about that, and Kelli didn't have any money to give Zach anyway.

"And call me back," she said. "I'd love to hear a good explanation for why you did this." She hung up then and almost tossed her phone in the cup holder.

Another ray of light touched her mind, and Kelli got out of the car before she lost her nerve. It had been sticking around longer and longer, and for that, Kelli was grateful.

She marched into the house, where the kitchen sat in darkness, as did the living room and dining room. She expected to see Julian and Tiff on the couch, possibly holding hands, while they watched a movie.

They weren't there.

"Parker?" she asked, heading for the stairs. Up she went, and she found her son in his bedroom, already in his pajamas. "Ready for bed?"

"Yeah," he said. "I can help with the popcorn in the morning."

"Sure," Kelli said, smoothing back his hair. She'd let it grow long in the front, and she smiled at him. "Maybe we should go get haircuts in the morning."

"All right," Parker said.

"Then it won't be too short when school starts."

He nodded and climbed into bed. She tucked him in and kissed him goodnight. In the hall, she looked toward the guest bedroom and the bathroom. No sound. The master suite was downstairs, but she was terrified to go inside.

She knew how Julian made love, and she did not want

to see him do it with someone else. Her lungs felt like someone had cast them in plaster when they were empty, and she couldn't get enough air.

Her feet simply moved, her muscle memory taking her from tucking in her son to her own bedroom, where she normally changed into her pajamas and went to bed, intending to wait up for Julian, and only making it about half the time. ·

She pushed open the door to the bedroom, and sure enough, Tiff and Julian were there. They both lay in bed —*her* bed—fully clothed, the TV flickering against the lamplight. Both lamps on either side of the bed were lit, and the three of them looked at one another.

Tiffany was on the edge of Julian's side of the bed, and he lay closer to the middle. He looked at her, begging her. Kelli could feel it from across the room. "There's room over here," he said.

Kelli could not fathom climbing into that bed with the two of them and giving her permission for this outside relationship to be brought inside. How would she explain it to her friends and co-workers? Her mother? Her son?

Herself?

She shook her head, decisions being made left and right in the few moments she stood there. "Tomorrow, Parker has a birthday party. We're making caramel popcorn for him to take."

"Okay," Julian said. "I can probably give him a ride. Or Tiff can." He looked at the brunette, and Kelli wondered what he'd seen in her that he hadn't found in Kelli. Did it really take two women to satisfy a man like Julian?

"I'll do it," Kelli said. "On Saturday, I'm going to teach my last class at the gym, and Parker and I are going to Five Island Cove to visit my mother."

Julian's eyebrows shot toward the sky. "Really, Kel? Your mother?"

"And Eloise needs help with the inn," Kelli said, refusing to let him mock her and make her second-guess herself. She'd done that for far too long in her life, and she was ready to take the reins and direct the horse where it needed to go.

She gazed evenly at Julian, her eyes flickering to Tiff for only a second. "I can't do it, Julian," she said. "I'm sorry, but I can't do it." She started to move toward the master closet, where her luggage was.

"Parker and I are going to the cove, and we aren't coming back."

CHAPTER THREE

R obin Grover pulled open the doors at the surf shop and reached up to push her sunglasses on top of her head. She wasn't there to find a new surfboard or a bathing suit. The very idea of wearing what the twenty-something's wore to the beach was laughable, though she'd been running this summer like she had a banshee on her tail.

She turned right almost immediately and headed for the door in the corner, which led to the fish and chips shop on the outdoor patio. She had to go into the shop to get the patio, and the noise increased as she approached the doorway.

Plenty of people knew about Ron's Catch of the Day, from locals to tourists. Thankfully, Alice had texted to say she'd mistaken the time, and she'd been here for thirty minutes. Robin stepped up onto her tiptoes to try to find the taller woman past the people blocking the entrance, but it was a fruitless endeavor.

Settling back onto her feet, she pulled out her phone to check if Alice had said she'd been seated yet. No texts. She was probably plastered against the wall in there, trying to stay out of the way of the press of bodies.

Robin inched past a man talking to another gentleman. "Excuse me," she said, and with her petite frame, she managed to slink by a few other people too.

"Robin," Alice called from down the long counter, and relief filled Robin as she caught sight of her best friend.

"Hey," Robin said when she arrived at Alice's side. She had to turn sideways to fit between the stool and another man, and she really just wanted to go home. She had plenty of work to do for an upcoming wedding that weekend, and then she and the girls would be entrenched in back-to-school shopping next week.

Then school finally started, and Robin had been hoping and praying for some sense of normalcy to return to her life.

Duke would be home in only ten days.

Robin's breath caught in her throat at the thought of that, and she covered her emotion with a smile. "Not seated yet, huh?"

"He just came by and said I'm next," Alice said. "Did you see Kristen on the way in?"

"No." Robin twisted and looked back through the jungle of people. "When we get a table, and I know where it is, I'll go out and wait for her. She'll never survive this."

Alice chuckled, but she didn't argue. Robin was right, and they both knew it.

"How are the twins?" Robin asked. She wasn't really curious about Ginny, because Alice's daughter was practically perfect in every way. It was Charlie who concerned Robin.

"They're still alive," Alice said with a hint of darkness in her tone. "Driving me to drink, as usual. Yours?"

Robin grinned, though she knew Alice didn't drink anymore. She nodded and said, "About the same." She didn't have twins, but her oldest daughter was more than a handful. Jamie was still a pre-teen, and she didn't give Robin any trouble—other than Robin couldn't get her to leave the house. She'd rather sunbathe on the back deck with a book, shower at odd hours, and curl up in front of the TV with Robin than go out with her friends.

Robin was concerned that Jamie didn't have friends, and she'd be going into eighth grade, which was a really hard year for girls—especially if they had to eat lunch alone. She'd tried to get her into an acting camp this summer.

Jamie said no.

Music? No. Cooking class? No. Seafaring girls? *Double no, Mom.*

Robin supposed Jamie could be doing worse things than reading fantasy novels, and she'd let the topic drop after that. Besides, the town of Five Island Cove had cancelled the Seafaring Girls program.

"Good," she said. "Jamie is ready for school to start, and Mandie is going to die a slow death if she doesn't go to school soon." She put a smile on her face that stretched tightly, and met Alice's eye.

They burst out laughing, and most of Robin's tension left her body.

"They're really challenging us, aren't they?" Alice asked.

"It's all new for me," Robin admitted. "The first time I sent her to Rocky Ridge alone, I was freaking out."

"I know," Alice said dryly. "I was on the other end of those forty-one thousand texts."

"Oh, it wasn't that many," Robin said, giggling. But Mandie was flirtatious, and cute, and she'd developed a lot in the past nine months. Boys noticed her a lot more now, and she'd been flitting around from boy to boy in the spring.

When she'd met Charlie, though...

Robin suppressed another wave of worry. "I asked her about sex," she said, wishing she had something to drink.

"Alice," a man called, and Alice held up her hand.

"Hold that thought," she said. "Let's get our table."

"I don't want to talk about this with Kristen," Robin said.

Alice turned to follow the guy with the menus, though

Robin didn't need one of those. She'd eaten here dozens of times, and there was nothing better than the fish and chips. They got a table along the railing, with the ocean breeze billowing up from the water. Robin put her purse on one of the chairs while Alice settled in on the other side.

"She acted like the very idea of doing that was disgusting."

"Charlie acts like that too."

"So you don't think...?" Robin let her words hang there. She wasn't sure why she was so worried about Mandie getting pregnant, only that she was. Intellectually, she knew it wouldn't be the end of the world. But she also knew having a baby so young would make it that much harder for Mandie to achieve her dreams.

"No," Alice said. "I don't think they're sleeping together."

Robin nodded, trying to take Alice's belief and make it hers. "Okay, I'm going to go find Kristen."

Alice's phone chimed, and she picked it up. "This is her. She said she just walked in."

"Be right back." Robin wove through the crowd again, easily dodging around people now. She wasn't worried about getting told she couldn't skip to the front of the line, and she found Kristen standing just inside the doorway that led back into the surf shop.

"Kristen." She hugged the older woman, a warm love spreading through her. Kristen was like the mother Robin had never had, and she loved her with every fiber of her being. "How are you?"

"It's so busy here," Kristen said as she drew back. "But I'm good. How are you, dear?" She smiled at Robin, and Robin wondered what it would be like to have her own mother look at her with such acceptance. She couldn't believe that she still wanted that, as she was forty-five years old and didn't need her mother's approval anymore.

Or maybe she did.

No matter what, when her own mother looked at her, it was with a critical gaze. Sharp eyes that saw every flaw. She always had something demeaning to say, and Robin felt like she had never done anything right in her whole life.

"This way," she said, pushing her mother out of her mind. "We just sat down." She kept hold of Kristen's hand as she maneuvered back to Alice, who stood to hug the woman who had simply accepted them as they were since the moment they'd met, over thirty years ago.

Kristen sat on the same side of the table as Alice, and Robin faced them both. "Updates," she said, ignoring Alice's disgusted look. She even rolled her eyes, but Robin didn't care. She couldn't help it if she loved the games and rituals they'd been using since they were teens. "I have something really good."

"You go first then," Alice said.

"No," Robin said, grinning at her as a woman appeared with glasses of water. "I'm going last." She looked up at Laura-Ann. "Hey, Annie." She smiled at the woman. "How's that boyfriend of yours?"

Annie, a tall brown-haired woman, grinned down at Robin as she held out her left hand. "He's my fiancé now."

Robin gave a little shriek as she bolted to her feet and grabbed Annie's hand to examine the diamond. "Annie. Oh my goodness." She looked up into the other woman's eyes, hers wide. "You have to let me plan the wedding. Please, please, Annie."

"Didn't you get my message?" Annie asked with a laugh. "I called last night, literally ten minutes after he asked me."

"I haven't checked my business line since lunch yesterday." Robin hugged the woman she'd known for seemingly ever. "I'm so happy for you. Congratulations."

"Thank you, Robin. We don't have a date yet, but I'm hoping to nail it down with my mother this weekend."

"Just let me know as soon as you can, so I can see if I can schedule it."

"I will."

Robin re-took her seat and said, "I'll have the fish and chips and a strawberry lemonade." Real strawberries came in the lemonade, with a dash of puree and syrup, and Robin loved it with every taste bud she owned.

"Cod, right?" Annie asked.

"Yep."

She went around and took the rest of the orders—

everyone got the cod fish and chips—and then Robin looked at Alice. "You go first."

"Believe it or not, I have something exciting too," Alice said, drawing her slight shoulders back into that power stance Robin was well-acquainted with. "Frank didn't contest any of the addendums to the divorce, and I'm expecting to hear from Susan by Friday. If not then, on Monday for sure."

"And it'll be final?" Kristen asked. "Over?"

"It'll be final and over," Alice said, and Robin could practically see the weight of the world lift from her countenance.

"That's amazing," she said. "Text me the moment you know."

"I will," Alice said. "It'll be on the group." She turned to Kristen and covered her hand. "And I'll call you, Kristen. Okay?"

"Thank you, dear." She smiled and when she looked at Robin again, Robin saw her age for maybe the first time. Kristen had lines around her eyes from years of laughing, and far more gray hair than Robin remembered. When she lifted her water glass to her lips, her hand shook slightly. A movement there, then steadiness.

Robin had no trouble seeing her own age every time she looked in the mirror. She worked hard to keep the extra hairs off her chin and the wrinkles between her eyes from getting too deep. But she'd never seen Kristen quite this old.

Shock traveled through her system, and thankfully, Annie returned with their cold drinks. "Fish is coming, ladies."

"Your turn," Robin said after she'd unwrapped her straw and taken a long drink of the sweet and sour lemonade. The stuff personified summer for Robin, and while a hint of sadness accompanied the thought of another summer coming to a close, she couldn't wait for this one to be over.

Then she'd have her husband back. Her daughters off to school. She could work during the day without having to worry about where Mandie was and if she'd lied about who she'd be with so she could sneak across the channels to Rocky Ridge to kiss Charlie.

She had never done that, but it was the kind of thing Robin would've done—and had done—and she wasn't so far out of touch that she didn't suspect her daughter of doing something devious like that.

"No real update," Kristen said. "Rueben and Jean are looking to adopt a new dog. Clara actually called on Sunday night to tell me she and Lena have decided that Lena is ready to live on her own." She wore a proud smile, and Robin had no idea what it would be like to parent a child with Down Syndrome.

Kristen only had one granddaughter, and that was Lena. Reuben and Jean had never had children, though they had plenty of fur babies.

"That's amazing," Robin said, beaming at Kristen too.

"Good for her," Alice said.

"Clara's a mess," Kristen said. "I'm considering flying to Vermont to be with her for a couple of weeks." Pure indecision raged with fear in her expression.

"You are?" Alice asked, shooting a glance at Robin.

The news surprised her too. Clara and Kristen didn't particularly get along. Things had been better since Joel's funeral—at least according to Kristen.

"Yes," Kristen said. "I asked her about it, but she had to get to work."

"What would you do in Vermont?" Robin exchanged another look with Alice.

"You know it gets cold there, right?" Alice asked.

"It gets cold here," Kristen said, waving her hand. "I wouldn't go for months or anything. I'm thinking maybe once school starts, and there are less tourists taking up the flights. Then I'll go."

"I think you should," Robin said, her own mother right at the forefront of her mind again. "She'd probably appreciate it."

"I think she would too," Kristen said. "So it's not about me. It's about her." She nodded, and Robin took that as an indication that her update was over.

Annie arrived with blue baskets of fried fish and French fries, and Robin's mouth watered. She reached for the vinegar and salt and doused everything though the chef here seasoned his food perfectly.

"Robin, you didn't even taste it."

"I know what I like." She shot Alice a look that said, *I'm not twelve and you're not my mother*. "Okay, my update is that I got the name of AJ's boyfriend."

"No, you did not," Alice said, her voice awed. "What is it?"

"And," Robin said. "Eloise is due back in the cove this weekend." She grinned at the two women across the table from her. "I can't wait. I can't believe she's moving here."

"That inn is going to need a lot of work," Kristen said.

"It sure is," Robin agreed.

"What's his name?" Alice asked again.

Robin leaned forward, sparks dancing through her veins. She *loved* a good secret. "Peterson. His name is Peterson." She looked between Kristen and Alice, pure life dancing within her. "Now we just need to find a reason AJ needs to come to Five Island Cove—with him."

CHAPTER FOUR

Alice Kelton hummed to herself as she moved around her office. She liked to keep things fresh by getting up and analyzing them from different angles. She often found that she could see solutions easier that way.

She only had a few clients, and they didn't need anything too terribly difficult from her. One had asked her to review a couple of contracts she'd received from a publisher, just to make sure she wasn't being taken for a ride. Another had asked her to help settle a property line dispute. That was the one Alice was currently researching, as she didn't know everything there was to know about property law in Five Island Cove.

She'd studied family law the most, and she'd intended to help women with divorces, parents with custody issues, legal guardianship issues, as well as family estates and trusts.

Her knowledge of most of that had been rusty, but Alice had dedicated a few hours every day over the past two months to brushing up on her skills in the legal system in Five Island Cove.

She currently had one client that fit exactly what she'd studied in school, and it was a case where a twenty-year-old daughter had filed a protective order against her stepfather. In Alice's mind, and for the only year she'd practiced law, she'd have represented the daughter. But this time, her client was Bruce Rogers, a forty-seven-year-old single father who lived on Rocky Ridge—right next door to Alice's father.

Alice didn't care how the clients came to her, as long as they kept coming. To her surprise, the moment she'd set up a rudimentary website and put one notice on The Islands, which was basically an online classifieds section for Five Island Cove, she'd had a fairly steady stream of clients.

She could work on eight or nine cases if they were as small as the ones she had now. Bigger cases took more time, but earned her more money.

Frank had been true to the agreement they'd made in June, and Alice still had access to the bank accounts. The mortgage on the beach house—her real house now—had been paid every month on time. She drew money for groceries and activities, and she'd just texted Frank about the school shopping she'd do with the children next week.

The following week, school would start, and Alice

wasn't sure she was ready for her kids to leave the house early in the morning, travel by ferry to Diamond Island, and attend tenth grade. At the same time, she remembered how incredibly grown-up she'd felt doing exactly that, and she reminded herself that Charlie and Ginny had been ferrying themselves all over the cove for the majority of the summer.

Today, they'd gone to Friendship Island, as the rumors circulating around the cove were that someone had bought the old inn there and was reopening everything. Alice actually wanted to see that come true, as she had some good memories of Friendship Island. It was actually the closest island to Rocky Ridge, and when she'd been a teenager, a short, ten-minute clipper ride would get her to the sister island.

It too had black sand beaches and white sand beaches. The tropical feel on one side, and sheer black cliffs on the other. Alice liked the juxtaposition of Friendship and Rocky Ridge, because so much of the world seemed to exist in opposites like the islands did.

Her phone rang, and Alice knew it would be a client before she even looked down. She'd gotten a special number just for business, and her second cell phone never left the office. She picked it up, unsurprised by the "unknown" sitting on the screen.

"Alice Kelton," she said, making her voice professional and polite at the same time. *Friendly*, she reminded herself. Robin had called her on the business line once, and she'd said Alice came across a little cold. "How can I help you?" she added in a chirp.

"Ms. Kelton?" a woman said, and Alice immediately moved her fingers to increase the call volume.

It was already all the way up, and she switched it to speakerphone as she said, "Yes, ma'am."

"I'm wondering—this is Louise Harrison."

"Hello, Louise." Alice moved around the desk to her chair and sat down. She could hear something tumultuous in the woman's voice. But more than that, Alice could *feel* the unrest, even through the phone line.

"I feel like I need a lawyer," the woman said. "Someone mentioned you grew up here, and that you could maybe help me."

"I'm happy to have a quick conversation now," Alice said. "To let you know. I am a lawyer, but I don't know everything. There are different branches of the law, and there are some things I simply don't have experience with." Alice had vowed to be completely transparent with herself and her clients, no matter what. "Or we can meet. I can come to you. You can come to me. I know some people would rather discuss personal things in person. Then I can give you an idea if I can help you or not."

"It's my husband," she said.

"Okay," Alice said when Louise didn't continue. Anything could come after that, and Alice didn't want to assume anything.

"He's very sick, and we need help with a will. Power

of attorney." Louise's voice broke, and Alice frowned as she struggled to keep her own emotions in check. She wished she would be devastated if Frank became ill enough to warrant worrying about what was in their will. At this point, though, Alice was barely getting to the point where she could get a text from him that didn't send her into an ornery mood.

"I can help with that," Alice said very quietly. "Why don't you give me your address, Louise, and I'll come Monday morning." Alice puttered around the office on the weekends, and she'd meet with clients if she had to. She wasn't sure this warranted taking her from her children on Sunday, though, and Saturday was practically over.

"That's fine," Louise said. She rattled off an address on Sanctuary Island that Alice struggled to write down fast enough. She repeated it back to Louise, who confirmed it. Then she said, "Oh, my daughter's coming. I have to go. Nine o'clock?"

"See you then," Alice said, but Louise was already gone.

Alice set the phone on the desk and tapped the space bar on her keyboard to wake her computer. If there was one thing she loved, it was making a new file for a new client. She loved printing out consent forms and making notes for herself and the initial research she needed to do. She'd done a couple dozen wills in the years she'd been with her firm in New York, and while it had been sixteen years, she felt confident she could help Louise Harrison.

With everything printed, a folder properly labeled and ready for Monday morning, Alice decided she'd done enough for one day. She went into the master bedroom and changed from her shorts and tank top into a bathing suit. It wouldn't get wet, but wearing a swimming suit by the pool made her feel like she was truly experiencing summer.

Thankfully, she'd put on ten pounds since her friends had stayed in the house with her, and Alice thought it was probably all the lunches she, Robin, and Kristen had attended together. She wasn't nearly as stressed, and she'd been sleeping better than ever.

"Once the divorce is final, everything will be even better." She made herself a non-alcoholic drink, picked up her sunglasses, and went outside to the pool deck. Charlie had talked her into buying a Wi-Fi speaker, and he'd hooked her phone to it. All Alice had to do was open her music app and tap on what she wanted, and before she knew it, her jazzy songs came through the speaker on the table down on the end of the row of chaises.

She relaxed into the chaise behind her, a sigh leaking from her lips. She was slowly making her way toward being able to pay her own bills, and if there was one thing Alice wanted more than anything, it was to be completely free from Frank.

Right now, she had to rely on him, but one day—one day soon—she wouldn't.

With that thought in her head, Alice closed her eyes

and enjoyed the warmth of the summer sun on her skin. She soaked up the vitamin D, feeling her cells rejoice that she'd gotten them out of the house for a little bit.

"Mom," Charlie said sometime later. "How long have you been out here?"

Alice blinked as she came to full consciousness very rapidly. Her head still felt fuzzy, but she couldn't remember the last time she'd taken a nap that hadn't stemmed from trying to shut the world out.

"Hey," she said, smiling at her handsome son. "You're back." She sat up, feeling some of the grogginess start to fade. "What time is it?"

"A little after four," he said. "Have you been out here long? You always tell me to put on sunscreen." He cocked one eyebrow at her, and Alice laughed.

"Thanks, Dad," she said, teasing him. "I've been out here maybe fifteen minutes." She glanced at her mocktail, and sure enough, it still had tiny chunks of the ice cubes she'd used. She reached for it, her mouth suddenly very dry. The cranberry and ginger exploded against her tongue, and her stomach growled.

"I brought Robbie back with me," Charlie said. "Will too."

"Okay," Alice said, swinging her legs over the side of the chaise as Charlie stood. "I'll get some dinner going.

Hot dogs and hamburgers?" If she did a barbecue, Charlie would cook the meat. All Alice would have to do is prepare the toppings and open the pantry to find a bag of chips. "We have a watermelon too," Alice added, just remembering that she'd bought the fruit a few days ago.

"Sounds good," Charlie said. "I'll get the grill going."

"Thanks." Alice followed him inside to find his two friends sitting at the dining room table. Five Island Cove wasn't huge, and it was spread out over five islands. Charlie had always been exceptionally gifted at finding and making new friends, while Ginny usually suffered a little bit. She really liked to trust someone before she told them too much about her life, as she'd had some problems with betrayal and gossip in the past.

Today, she sat at the table too, something on her phone that both boys were leaning in to see. The three of them exploded into laughter, and Alice's parental instincts fired. "What are we watching?" she asked.

"The guy who does those pet tricks gone wrong," Ginny said, still giggling. She handed her phone to Alice, who didn't really want to see the video. She only watched them to make sure her children weren't viewing something they shouldn't.

Even she laughed when the little white dog that was trying to jump through the hoop stumbled and fell off the length of fence it had been running along. "Oh, that poor thing," she said with a small giggle as she passed the phone back.

"You should see the horse one, Mrs. Kelton," Robbie said. He was older than Charlie by two years, and Alice had worried about that for a day or two—until she'd realized how much of a teddy bear Robbie was. He was tall and dark, like Charlie, and they both loved to get up early and go surfing in the morning.

Robbie came to Rocky Ridge on the first ferry over, and Alice much preferred her son spending his first hours of the day with Robbie over Mandie Grover, his girlfriend. It had been official for at least a month now, and that was definitely still something Alice worried about on a minute-to-minute basis.

Thankfully, she had Robin on the other end of the relationship, trying to keep her daughter in line too. Alice wouldn't even know what to do if she didn't.

Will was a year younger than Charlie, and they'd met on Diamond Island when Charlie had gone to see Mandie once. He lived around the corner from her, and he was the youngest in his family. The only child left at home, and Alice got the impression his parents didn't really care what he did as long as he came home at night.

She'd asked for his mother's number once she'd realized that, and Alice quickly pulled out her phone and texted Rita. *Will is here for dinner tonight. I'll make sure he gets back to you soon.*

Thanks, Alice, Rita answered, as she usually did. As Alice got out a couple packages of hot dogs and one of premade hamburgers, she tried to envision her life in a few years, when she would have an empty nest.

The first thing she needed to do was get rid of this huge house. It was ridiculous for just the three of them as it was. She'd tried to get Eloise to stay with her while she worked on the inn, but Eloise didn't want to have to deal with the ferry. She'd opted to stay with her mother, and as she'd put it, "that will motivate me to get the caretaker's suite done quickly."

Alice couldn't even imagine moving back in with her father at her age, and she turned away from the thought as she moved to get the lettuce out of the fridge. Something caught her eye and made her pause.

No, it couldn't be...

Alice turned back to the counter as if she were simply going to continue laying out cheese slices. Instead, she stared at where Ginny and Robbie sat at the table. Will had gotten up and gone off with Charlie somewhere, and Alice wished the older boy had gone too.

She knew why he hadn't though—he was currently holding Ginny's hand right there on the table. Alice's pulse hammered in her chest, then moved up into her neck and the back of her throat.

"Ginny," she said, well-aware that her voice sounded like a bark.

The two teens jumped and simultaneously looked at her. Alice blinked and tried to pull back on her tone. "Can you come help with the condiments? I'm going to go see what we have in the storage room by the way of chips."

"Sure," Ginny said, standing up and joining Alice in the kitchen.

"Thanks, sweetie." Alice stepped past her, saying, "We have avocados too. And maybe you could make that special sauce with the mayo, mustard, and ketchup."

"All right."

Alice passed the dining room table, where Robbie still sat. "Where did Charlie and Will go?"

Robbie jumped to his feet, his eyes a little frantic. "I think to Charlie's room. I'll head up."

Alice nodded as the boy scampered past her and up the steps leading to the twins' rooms. They'd moved out of the one across the hall from her now that the house was empty, and Alice liked having the whole wing to herself.

She deliberately forced herself not to turn around and march right back to Ginny to ask her what was going on with her and Robbie. "Be right back," she said, moving toward the steps that went down instead of up. Before she could get there, the doorbell rang.

Alice detoured toward the foyer and the huge, wooden door she rarely used. It took her a moment to figure out how to unlock it, and most of her strength to heave it open. She could hardly think, because how was she going to deal with both of her twins in their first real, romantic relationship? How could she protect Ginny when she didn't go to lunch with Robbie's mom every week?

Because her thoughts took so much of her mental energy, it took several seconds for Alice to realize who stood on her front porch. "Kelli?"

The honey blonde woman lived far, far away in New Jersey. She shouldn't be here.

She wore a nervous look on her face that faded as pure determination took over. She put one hand protectively on her son's shoulder. "Hey, Alice," she said. "Sorry to just show up like this. I'm wondering if we can stay with you for a day or two."

CHAPTER FIVE

Eloise entered the kitchen where she'd grown up, so many memories streaming through her head. "Morning, Mom," she said, reaching for the coffee pot.

"Morning, dear," her mother said back. This was also typical of what happened in the Hall household. Nobody ever spoke about anything hard. Whatever had happened the night before was in the past. Even if her father had hit her mother or her, and they'd both left the house and then cowered in the car for an hour.

Nothing was ever said.

More often than not, it was her father who'd fled the house, leaving Eloise and her mother to deal with whatever he'd left behind. Broken Glass. Damaged items, and the walls full of shouting and his breath that smelled like whiskey.

Eloise pushed against the memories. She'd stayed with

her mother before, but never for very long. She'd only been here for two nights now as it was. But she had many more in front of her.

As she stirred a spoonful of sugar into her coffee and turned to the fridge to get out a carton of cream, her determination to get the inn livable renewed. She just needed to get the caretaker suite livable as quickly as possible, not the whole inn.

She'd only been up there once since she'd arrived back in the cove. She'd rationalized that she had so much to do, but she couldn't just jump right into the complete renovation that the Cliffside Inn needed. She was planning to take the next six months to do the renovations, and then spend the next few months after that getting her marketing in place, her social media in line, her website perfect, and things booked for the summer.

She knew that she could start booking as early as February, if she could attract the right crowd to the inn. Her father had often run Valentine's Day specials, and something like a spring vacation getaway.

Eloise knew those events brought in some good revenue in the offseason. Her summer months would be the where she made the bulk of her money. As early as mid-May, people would start coming, and if she could keep them here until mid-September, she believed she could turn a profit with the inn.

She'd had it for so long, that the monthly payments were quite low. She'd been able to secure additional funding for the renovations, and she'd rolled that into the original loan.

She'd made a list of things that needed to be done, and every day, more got added to it. In another page in the notebook where she'd been keeping track of what she needed to do, she'd started a list of contractors, merchants, suppliers, handymen, and other people that could come help with things that she simply couldn't do herself.

For example, Eloise had no idea what needed to happen to make sure that the swimming pool in the back yard of the Cliffside Inn would be at the right pH for guests. She wanted everything about the inn to be an oasis, and that required a professional to come clean the pool and make sure that it was properly filled and chlorinated.

She'd added the name of a guy who could come do that for her, but he was very busy around Five Island Cove. The pool at Cliffside wasn't the only pool in the cove, and she had to get on Mitch Hancock's schedule if she wanted the pool to get serviced. Luckily for her, she wasn't trying to get it ready for the winter. She was trying to get it ready for next summer.

Either way, she had a list of people that she'd be relying on. For one, there was a ton of mold in the caretaker's suite. That would be the first call that she made on her first Monday morning in Five Island Cove. There was only one more week until the kids would start school, and she wanted to be able to spend time with Aaron and his girls before they would be entrenched fully in a new routine.

Billie was entering junior high, and Eloise wanted to be there for her as she made the transition. She always made sure to talk to Aaron first, so he wouldn't be upset about what she was doing with his children. At the same time, her maternal bonds to both Billie and Grace was growing day by day, and she was starting to think of them as hers. It was easy for Eloise to step into that role, since their mother was not in the picture at all.

She was very careful not to call herself their mother, and she was also mindful about asking each of them questions about their mother, so that they would feel comfortable talking to her about their mom.

When she'd asked Aaron about her tactics, he'd said that she really didn't need to bother with that. That Carol was completely out of the picture. She'd made it clear that she was not interested in being Billie or Grace's mother. He wasn't even sure where she was, and she had not sent cards for their birthday nor called them in the last two years.

Eloise could not understand the woman. She had spent most of her adult life wanting children and coming to the realization through therapy and meditation that she would not be a biological mother herself.

She thought she was too old to have children now, but she hadn't been to a doctor to find out. It didn't really matter because she and Aaron had talked about having more children, and he didn't particularly want them. Grace was eleven years old now, and having a baby would be a huge age gap for him.

Eloise completely understood. She was in her mid-forties anyway, and there were plenty of complications for having a baby at that age. Still, she'd heard that fifty was the new forty for motherhood, and the idea lingered in her mind.

"I don't know what you're worried about," she told herself. "Aaron isn't any closer to asking you to marry him."

They talked about marriage, sure. He hadn't done anything beyond that, at least to her knowledge. There'd been no ring shopping. There'd been no mention of where or when. There'd been no discussion about if the girls would participate or not.

She adored Aaron, and she knew she was only one step away from being fully in love with him. In her mind, an engagement would solidify that, and she could start to make a plan for what she wanted to have happen next.

Frustration filled her as she poured a little bit of cream into her mug and turned toward her mother, who sat at the small kitchen table crammed against the wall. Everything about this house was too small for Eloise. Everything she looked at held a memory, and most of them were not good.

"What's on your agenda for today, Mom?" she asked.

"Oh, a little bit of this and a little bit of that," her

mother said, which was about what her mother did every day since her father had left and then passed away.

She'd been working from home, doing what she knew how to do. She had a sewing studio that took up two of the bedrooms in the house, and Eloise slept among spools of thread and a half-dozen machines. Everything from sergers to sewing machines to an electronic quilting arm whenever she came to visit.

"How are the cats treating you?" Eloise asked. She'd given her mother her two cats several months ago, when it became too difficult for her to travel back and forth between Boston and the cove and keep the felines happy.

"Just great. Eloise," her mom said, glancing up with a smile. She actually loved the cats, and Eloise knew it. She pampered them with plush beds in her sewing studio so that they could sit in there with her while she altered dresses. She seemed to have a very steady stream of work, especially in the summer, when there were dozens upon dozens of weddings in the cove.

Around the holiday season, when the rich and famous came to have their holiday parties, she sewed her fingers to the bone, and then again in the spring for the prom season, when all the girls were buying beautiful ball gowns that needed to be hemmed, needed to have the waists taken in or back out, or to have the shoulders adjusted so that they wouldn't fall out of their dresses.

Eloise was glad that her mother was able to support herself with something as simple as sewing. She was beyond happy that they'd both been able to carve out a life from so much ugliness.

"Are you seeing anyone?" Eloise asked, not quite sure where the words came from. She knew Kelly's mother had started to date a little bit, so it wasn't completely uncommon for older women to have a date.

Her mother, though, gave her a look that said, yes, it would be completely uncommon for her to have a date.

"Sorry, I don't know why I asked that."

Her mother nodded and said, "I suppose women my age date."

"Are you lonely, Mom?" Eloise, asked, deciding that sometimes hard conversations needed to be had. In her family, she'd never really had them, and that was one of the reasons her first marriage had failed so spectacularly. That, and the fact that Wes had been a complete jerk. She'd known he was bad for her from the beginning, but she'd been so desperate to have the wedding and family she'd thought she should have.

There'd been so much surrounding her telling her what she should want, what she should do, and what life should be like for a woman. She'd bought into it, and she'd been unhappy for years.

For several years after her divorce, she'd attended therapy, trying to recover and find her own way in the world. She'd become a professor at Boston University, and everything had fallen in line for her then.

She thought she'd found her true calling, something

that was at the root of who she was. As a biology professor, she became someone who had the answers for people who didn't. Someone who knew science and could reference it. Someone who didn't have questions or if they did, the answers were easily obtained through research and study.

When she'd found her true LSAT scores in Joel Shields' office five months ago, Eloise's foundation had cracked. Her relationship with Aaron had contributed to the ultimate ending of her career at Boston University, sure, but the real reason was that perhaps she'd been wrong for the past twenty years. Perhaps at the root of her soul was *not* a biology professor.

She'd been trying to figure out who lived there since she'd learned that Joel had doctored her scores. Eloise had always been smart. She did very well in school and, out of her Seafaring Girls friends, she scored the highest on tests and got the best grades. For whatever reason, her test scores had not reflected that.

She'd thought they'd been good enough, and she'd never taken the test again. Had she known her real scores had been too low, she would've studied harder, she would've tried again, she would've *earned* her way into the universities.

She pushed away the feelings of fraud, wishing she could eliminate them completely. But she never could. They always came creeping back, especially in the quiet moments, when nothing was happening.

"Well, I'm going to be up at the inn today," Eloise said, standing up.

"You're not going to have breakfast?" her mom asked.

"I don't eat breakfast, Mom," Eloise said not for the first time. She wasn't sure why she expected her mother to remember these things, but she did. It wasn't like her mom had a lot of people to keep track of as Eloise only had one brother, and he came around less than Eloise did.

"I'm going to see what I need to do," Eloise said. "I've got a lot of phone calls to make. I should have a big dumpster up there, so I have somewhere to put all the garbage." She kept talking to herself, outlining what she needed to do that day. Her mother never stopped or interrupted her.

Up at the inn, she stood in the driveway as she'd done many times before, and she looked at the magnificent building that she'd loved so dearly as a teenager. She wasn't here to reminisce though. She wasn't here to lead Aaron on a tour. She wasn't here to show her friends what she'd bought and what she hoped it would become.

No, today was the day that the work started. She would have plenty of time to dream big dreams and fantasize about full rooms and money in the bank—once the work was done.

Eloise had dressed in a plain grey T-shirt and a pair of cutoff shorts, and she was ready to get sweaty and dirty. Anything she could get done today, she would.

Aaron had to work this whole week, and he'd taken two days off to take his girls back-to-school shopping, and then take them to the parent night. She'd not been invited along for any of the activities dealing with school, though she wanted to go. She wondered if she should say something to Aaron about it.

She quickly pulled out her phone to send him a text. *I'm up at the inn today working,* she said. *I was just wondering if you wouldn't mind if I tagged along with you and the girls as you go shopping this week.*

She looked at the words and read them over, trying to decide if she needed to add anything else. In the end she did typing out quickly, *If you don't want me to come, I completely understand.*

She sent the whole lot of words to him, knowing that he was very busy this week. He'd hired two new cops for the force, as he'd lost a couple of men in the last month or so. He'd also applied for and received a grant for two canine dogs, the first to ever come to Five Island Cove.

He'd been very excited about it, but he also needed a new officer to work with the dogs, train the dogs, and then get the dogs out on the streets where he wanted them to be. There'd been a bit of an increase in the drugs coming through Five Island Cove on their way to the East Coast.

Aaron wanted to clear his streets and keep the cove safe. That was the reason he'd gotten the dogs from the canine program operating out of Savannah, Georgia. Eloise had helped him research the facility and then apply for the grant. She'd coached Aaron through the process and told him not to be too disappointed if they said no.

However, everything Aaron Sherman touched seemed to turn to gold, and nobody ever seemed to tell him no, including Eloise. He was made of muscle from the time he spent running on the beach, lifting weights, and dealing with over thirty men who kept the cove safe.

He had a no-nonsense personality with his girls and his men, but when he was alone with Eloise, the vulnerable, shy and quiet Aaron Sherman manifested himself. He was service oriented; he was helpful. He paid attention to her needs, and he listened to what she said. He was an excellent lover, and Eloise wanted to wake up every morning in his bed and go to sleep every night in the cradle of his arms.

She realized as she unlocked the caretaker's suite that it wasn't the size of her childhood home that bothered her. It was that she'd felt like she'd grown up inside a prison cell and that she would never get out. The day she'd left Five Island Cove had been one of the best and worst days of her life.

The scent of mustiness hit her nose, and Eloise reached into her purse and pulled out the mask that she'd bought at the hardware store. She strapped the mask into place and stepped inside the caretaker's suite to look around. The water had been off at the Cliffside Inn since she brought her friends to look at the place in June, so hopefully there was no new water damage.

Eloise decided to start at the very beginning, and that was right inside the door. She pulled the plastic garbage cans that she'd purchased into the suite and started loading trash inside.

She didn't want to keep anything in here. It had all been sitting here for twenty-seven years since her father had abandoned the Cliffside Inn, abandoned his family, and abandoned the life he'd built in Five Island Cove.

He'd kept it from her, even in death, but even he couldn't control the bank. She'd bought the inn when it had been repossessed and put up on an auction.

Eloise wished she could turn off her mind and shutter the memories behind the closed doors where she'd kept them for so long. As it was, it seemed like she had no control over her mind, which used to be ironclad and unstoppable.

She wondered if she even knew what was important to her anymore. "Of course you do," she said to herself as she picked up a stack of old, moldy National Geographic magazines. Her father had loved the National Geographic, and the sight of the iconic yellow volumes hit her straight in the chest. She could see her father sitting in his recliner, leafing through the National Geographic to look at the photos and read the articles. He'd told her once that that was how he experienced the world.

He'd also fancied himself a bit of a photographer, and he adored the photos in the magazine, talking about how if he could travel to Egypt, he would take a photo from this angle.

Eloise had loved listening to her father talk about the

photos, his ideas, and his wishes to travel. She loved coming to the Cliffside Inn during the summer to work with him and the guests. He came alive behind the pages of a National Geographic and inside the doors of the Cliffside Inn. It was who he was at his core. Eloise wondered if she'd inherited that from him, and if she would be able to find herself within these walls, small as they were.

She'd hauled out two trash cans full of garbage to the Dumpster before her phone buzzed. Aaron's name flashed on the screen and he said, *Of course you can come school shopping with us. We're going Wednesday and Thursday. Tell me what time you want to come and we'll go together.*

A smile filled Eloise's face. He wanted her to be with them. It was as important to Aaron that she had a relationship with his children as it was to Eloise. He'd told her that he was falling in love with her.

When they made love, he was gentle and kind. In those moments, she believed him. In moments where she hadn't been invited to go school shopping, her doubts started to take over.

Eloise was still quite good at pruning her doubts and making sure that she asked the right questions to get the answers that she needed.

She worked steadily throughout the morning, only stopping when her stomach practically screamed at her to get something to eat. She hadn't brought anything to the inn with her. Not that there was any way to keep it refrigerated or heat anything up if she had. She drove her mother's down the winding road from the cliffs on Sanctuary Island to the beach.

Summer was still in full swing, and there were several permanent food stands setup on the most popular beach on the island. Dozens of sunshades kept the sand cool and the picnic tables out of the direct light. People of all ages filled the tables as it was definitely lunchtime, but the lines moved quickly and the food came out at lightning speed.

Eloise waited in line for a seafood wrap—one of her favorite foods that came from Sanctuary Island. Everybody on the islands put seafood in everything: tacos, salads, rolls. But this stand was known for its wraps. Her favorite was the salmon wrap with plenty of romaine lettuce, lemon butter, garlic mayo, and capers.

She always ordered the jumbo, because that came with double fish and double the sauce. They cut it in half for her and she had enough food for two meals.

As she returned to the inn an hour later, Eloise faced another mountain of work. Instead of diving right back into the work that needed doing, she decided to call Robin.

Robin picked up the call on the first ring and said, "Eloise, I've been waiting for you to call."

"I'm surprised you haven't called yet, Robin," she said dryly.

"Yes. Well, I knew you were busy getting settled in," Robin said. Robin knew everything, it seemed. Eloise also knew that there was a struggling woman inside Robin that she wrestled with every day. She didn't let very many people see that woman, and in fact, Eloise thought only she, Alice, AJ, and Kelli knew of Robin's internal war.

"I'm wondering how busy you're going to be over the next few weeks," Eloise said, deciding to do some of that insertion that she had done with Aaron earlier. "I need help at the inn. I know Alice has a few clients now. I know you're busy with the wedding planning. I know Duke will be home soon. But I'm wondering if you could perhaps fit me in a couple days a week. It's easy stuff. It's hauling trash and cleaning things out. I have masks to protect against the mold."

Eloise forced herself to stop talking, because she didn't need to lay out all the problems the inn had.

"I have a wedding this weekend," Robin said. "After that, my next event isn't until the third week of September. Duke will be home right after the wedding. The girls start school, and life should settle down once we're more routined," Robin said. "I can definitely come help you with the inn, Eloise."

"Really?" Eloise asked. "Really, could you?" She didn't dare hope that she could gather her friends around her for moral support. More hands meant more got done in less time.

"Absolutely," Robin said. "Alice would too, you know. She does have a few clients, but once her twins go to school, there's no way she's going to be busy all day long."

"I'll ask her," Eloise said.

"You know what? I got a weird text from Alice this

morning," Robin said thoughtfully. "She said there was a visitor in town who might need a job, and she wondered if I had anything for her to do."

"Who is it?" Eloise asked.

"I don't know," Robin said. "I was going to call her, and then my client stopped by. She just barely left, and then you called and I haven't been able to get to it yet."

Eloise said, "I'm going to call her right now. I'll ask her about the visitor."

"Sounds great," Robin said.

"Are you sure?" Eloise asked, with a laugh. "You're the one who likes to know the inside scoop before everyone else."

Robin giggled, but she didn't deny it. "You know what, Eloise? I'll pass you the baton. You call and get the gossip and then let me know what it is."

"I don't even know who I'm talking to," Eloise said, they laughed together. The call ended, and Eloise immediately dialed Alice. The woman didn't pick up on the first ring or the second. She did on the third and she said, "Eloise, I'm on another call. I'll call you right back."

She watched the phone screen darken, and she worked against the twinge of self-consciousness. She decided she would work until Alice called back, and she opened all the cupboards in the small kitchen in the care-taker's suite and emptied everything into a bin.

She took it out to the dumpster and made three trips before everything was gone. She pulled the fridge out from the wall, and then the range and she got them as close to the door as she could. Aaron would come and help her move them to the driveway, where the recycled appliance center would come pick them up.

Eloise moved on to the living room, which had one wall of built-in bookcases. A television could be housed there, but there was none. She pulled out the books and threw them all away. Deciding to take a break, she sat down on the dilapidated bench that overlooked the island.

She had loved this spot as a teen. She could see her house from here, as well as the beach. She felt like she could see the whole world from right here. As a teenager, the whole world had been wide open, ready for her to experience it, ready for her to come see what it held.

Her phone rang, and Alice's name sat there. "Alice, hey," she said. "You must be really busy. I'm sorry to bother you."

"Not at all," she said. "I'm a little bit busy this morning, but just because I picked up a new client and I..." Her voice trailed off, and Eloise's curiosity jumped to a new level.

"I actually picked up two new clients," Alice said, her voice strong and confident, the way Alice always seemed to be.

At the same time, Eloise had seen Alice break down too. She'd watched her marriage dissolve over the summer, and she'd watched Alice get to a state where she was not eating or sleeping.

"I'm up at the inn today, working, and it's a mess, Alice. A huge mess. And I know I'm asking a lot, especially if you just got two new clients." Eloise stalled, because she didn't want to add more to Alice's plate.

"You need help," Alice said, not asking. "I can come help, Eloise."

"Can you, Alice? I hate to ask."

"You didn't ask. I just offered," Alice said. "And yes, I can. Now this week, I'm really busy this week. But once the twins start school, they'll leave the house by 6:45 am, and I can't do any lawyering until at least ten, when all the offices are open. I can definitely come help."

"That would be so amazing," Eloise said. "I think if you and Robin came, the three of us could really get the inn cleaned out in no time at all." Then she could get the repairman in. She could get things ordered, and maybe she could have the inn done by Christmas.

"Maybe we can have Christmas here at the inn," she said.

"Christmas in the cove does sound amazing," Alice said.

"I know you're the one who always entertains," Eloise said. "I would hate to take that from you." Her mind started to work. Could she hope to host guests for Christmas at the Cliffside Inn?

Her desires and dreams for herself seemed to have no limit. They reached the atmosphere and then they pushed through, going on and up into outer space, where they could not be contained.

"I don't have to entertain," Alice said. "I really don't, Eloise. That was the old Alice. The new Alice is perfectly happy letting someone else clean up after everyone is gone."

They laughed together and Alice said, "Eloise, you'll have four sets of hands, because Kelli showed up on Saturday night."

"What?" Eloise asked. "Showed up? What do you mean *showed up?*"

"I mean she showed up," Alice said. "My doorbell rang, and I opened the door and Kelli stood there with Parker."

"Why?" Eloise asked. "What's going on?"

"I don't know," Alice said. "She wouldn't say."

"Is she staying with you?" Eloise asked, her pulse pouncing for some reason.

"Yes," Alice said. "She said she didn't want to talk about it right now. She had some things she needed to do at her mother's. So she took Parker out there yesterday, and I haven't seen them since."

"She didn't say anything?" Eloise asked.

"Nothing," Alice said.

"Time for a dinnervention," Eloise said.

She could envision Alice nodding, as she said, "Absolutely. Do you want to set it up?"

Eloise wondered what had happened to her friends in

the last couple of months. They had a group text going, and all five of them contributed to it.

But Robin had told Eloise to call and get the gossip, and now Alice was asking her to set up the dinnervention.

That was something Alice did. In fact, Alice had coined the term *dinnervention*, where they could have a good meal together while getting out hard things. That was *her* definition.

She should be the one setting up the dinnervention, but Eloise heard herself say, "Sure. I'll set up the dinnervention. Is this something I need to get AJ here for?"

"I don't think so," Alice said. "I saw her social media last night, and it says she's in Denver, covering a story with the basketball team there. I don't think we'll be able to get her, and even if we could, it will be a while."

"We don't have a while," Eloise said nodding. "I'll call you with the details as soon as I have them."

CHAPTER SIX

Kelli had been gone too long. She couldn't rush the process of finding somewhere she and Parker could live, though. She'd been forced to show up on Alice's doorstep unannounced, and thankfully, her friend had been kind enough not to ask any questions. Alice had let Kelli and Parker in the house. She'd fed them, along with a few teenagers, and given them a bedroom to sleep in.

Kelli had left with Parker bright and early the next morning, taking only half of the luggage they'd brought with them to Five Island Cove. She'd gone straight to Bell Island, but the ferry ride from Rocky Ridge took over forty-five minutes.

Her mother, a ball of nerves, had met her, and Kelli had declined breakfast out in favor of hiding in the house. They'd talked a lot about Zach, and Kelli's relationship with him. He had not called or texted her back, and thankfully, her mother hadn't seen him again either. Perhaps her threats had prompted him to leave the cove and go back to his life in Maine.

"Should we head over to our last one for today?"

Kelli shook the past couple of days out of her head. Blinking, she focused on the real estate agent she'd contacted, Shane Rogers. "Yes, please," she said, holding her head high. She hadn't done anything wrong. She knew that, and she'd been telling herself that it didn't matter who else knew it.

She knew it.

She followed the dark-haired man that was probably a decade older than her out of the rental house she'd been looking at. She couldn't stay with Alice forever, and she'd managed to get Shane to take her house-hunting within twenty-four hours. It helped that she didn't need to get a mortgage loan. She was simply going to rent.

Nerves flittered through her stomach like hummingbird wings. She had no idea how she could possible afford to pay the rent on any of the places she'd looked at that day. She felt like she was on the bottom of the ocean, drowning. No matter how hard she kicked, or how vigorously she swam, she couldn't reach the surface.

The water pressed down on her lungs, filling them with the wrong substance until she was left gasping and choking for air.

"Thanks for driving," she said as she buckled her seat belt. She glanced at Shane, who smiled back at her.

"I'm used to it," he said. "With our ferry system, I can't expect people to be able to drive themselves. And the RideShare fee would be astronomical." He chuckled as he pulled away from the curb in front of the simple, two-bedroom home she'd just toured.

It had been nice enough, but it needed new windows, a new yard in the front and back, and an appliance update.

Kelli told herself she couldn't afford to be picky. All she needed was somewhere to harbor her son, and somewhere she could find enough clarity of mind to see why she hadn't noticed the changes in Julian that had led her to this house hunting endeavor.

Down the street and around a bend in Sanctuary Island, and Shane pulled up to a row of homes that looked like they bordered the beach. "Is this in my budget?" Kelli asked, peering at the individual structures that stood only a few feet from each other.

"Yes," Shane said simply. "I know these don't have yards, and that was a must for you." He unbuckled his seatbelt. "But you're literally on the beach here, Miss Thompson. That is your whole back yard." He grinned at the row of brightly colored houses and got out of the sedan.

Kelli pressed her eyes closed and said a quick prayer before she joined him near the hood. The breeze blowing off the water cooled the hot air. She didn't think there was a better scent on earth than the salty, sea air. She took a long breath and held it for a second, trying to decide if the *for rent* sign was in front of the green house or the yellow one. The sign seemed to be planted smack dab between the two—but that was why she'd hired Shane.

"These are two bedrooms, one bath," he said. "These are reclaimed beach houses, and they've been remodeled for upscale living."

"I can't afford upscale living," Kelli said as they stepped off the main sidewalk and onto the one that led up to the quad of beach homes.

"You can afford this," he said. "It's eight-eighty per month, and that includes all utilities except garbage." Shane continued to rattle off stats and features of the home, but Kelli found that she simply needed to be in the space. It would speak to her if she gave it a chance, and the moment she started up the steps of the yellow beach house, she knew she needed to be here.

She could run yoga classes right in her own front yard. People would pay for them—and pay well. She was a certified yoga instructor, and she had plenty of experience in leading workouts from her job in New Jersey.

"Eight-eighty," she mused as he put in the code and opened the lockbox. Inside, the living room spread before her, stretching from the front door all the way to the back wall. The kitchen sat in the corner and along part of that wall, and then another door led out of the house.

"It's nicer than I thought it would be," she said.

"All of these have been completely remodeled. The bones were there, and they simply enhanced them." He pointed to the ground. "There's no carpet, because the sand would be a nightmare. You've got waterproof and scratch-resistant wood-like tiles here. Very durable for kids...pets..."

Kelli listened to him detail the breakfast bar, and then she followed him into the bedrooms, which took up the other half of the house. They were nothing to write home about. Instead, they were functional, a queen-sized bed in both of them. Parker wouldn't like that, but Kelli didn't have a lot of choices in her price range.

She turned on every light and checked to make sure all the blinds lifted and lowered. There would be no inspection here like there was when buying a new property, and she wanted to make sure she wasn't getting a lemon.

When she stepped onto the deck that spanned the width of the house, she asked, "First and last month's rent?"

"This is the one, huh?" Shane asked with a big grin.

"Yes," Kelli said. "This is the one." She faced the ocean, which came ashore only about fifty yards away. Julian hadn't frozen her out of their accounts yet, but as soon as she wrote a nineteen-hundred-dollar check, he likely would.

He had a mean streak, and Kelli had always tried very hard not to awaken the beast. *He did this*, she told herself as her real estate agent made a few phone calls, and thirty minutes later, he said, "This place is yours, Miss Thompson. All we need to do get some paperwork signed and collect your payment."

A hint of guilt stole through her as she wrote the check and signed the papers. She should've gotten a house on Bell Island to be closer to her mother. Parker would love that, and so would her mother.

Kelli hadn't been able to bring herself to do it. She needed a buffer zone, and hers had just shrunk considerably. She handed Shane his pen. "When can we occupy it?"

"How about right now?" He grinned and handed her the keys he'd gotten out of the lockbox. "Someone will come take the key box off your front door, and all the furniture stays. Do you have pets?"

"No," she said, her mind still stuck on the fact that she didn't have anything to move in. Not really. She'd brought mostly clothes from New Jersey, and she obviously didn't need furniture if this rental came with it.

"Good, we can skip this form," he murmured, almost to himself. "No smoking, drinking, or alcohol?"

"I drink socially," Kelli said. "Mocktails mostly, with the occasional alcoholic drink. Is that a problem?"

"No," Shane said. "The owner just doesn't want these to be turned into party houses." He glanced up from his tablet, where he'd been looking to ask her these questions. "He lives in the red one on the end."

Kelli looked down from her end with the yellow house, to the other end, where the red on stood. It had lawn ornaments stabbed into the sand, and it was semi-disturbing to see a dolphin leaping out of anything but water.

"All right," Shane said a moment later. "This is all yours. I can take you back to the ferry station? Or do you want to stay here?"

"I'll stay for a few minutes," she said. "Thank you so much, Shane."

"You betcha," he said, and he walked back to his car. Kelli stood on the sand and admired the yellow house. It had the most potential to get dirty, but someone had obviously been taking care of these four cabins.

She'd just climbed the steps to go inside her new place when her phone rang. Eloise's name sat on the screen, and Kelli's heartbeat started tap dancing, the staccato beats sending shockwaves through her whole body.

"Hey," a man called, his voice friendly.

Kelli looked up from the phone call that was still coming in. She looked down the row of homes to find a tall, tan man striding toward her. He had blonde hair that he probably put some sort of spray in to make it that light, a wide smile with a dimple in his right cheek, and an amazing positive energy flowing around him.

"Did you get the place?" he asked.

"Yes," Kelli said.

The man laughed, tipping his head back so his face was toward the sky and everything. "I'm glad. I'm Jackson Bybee. I own all four of these." He stuck his hand out for her to shake.

Kelli went back down the steps. "Kelli Thompson," she said, giving his hand a couple of good pumps. "I have an eight-year-old son who'll be living with me."

"That's great," he said. "Old Grandpa Henry right next door has his grandkids over quite often."

"Great," Kelli said, because it *was* great. Maybe Parker would have a playmate. She needed to register him for school today too, but she had a feeling that wasn't going to get done.

"Well, I'll let you explore," Jackson said. "I'm right down the row if you need anything."

"Thanks," she said to his retreating back. That was how Kelli felt about everything in her life. Things were going great—and then just when she thought she had dating and relationships figured out, life would throw her a curveball.

That was all this was. Julian trying to be cute, trying to get attention. She honestly didn't know how he could be starved for it. She was the one who asked him about his day and had dinner ready when he deemed his family important enough to visit from time to time.

She stepped inside her new home and looked up at the vaulted ceilings. This place was far nicer than any of the others she'd looked at today, and she liked the walls of windows in the back.

Before she could even so much as sit on the couch, Kelli's phone rang again. This time, she connected Eloise's call and said, "What's going on?"

"You tell me," Eloise said. "You're on Sanctuary Island and you didn't tell me?"

Kelli took a couple of seconds to get over the shock of Eloise's question. "How did you know I was on Sanctuary Island?"

Eloise sent a peal of laughter up, but Kelli didn't understand what was so funny. "I didn't," she said between the giggles. "I guessed, but now I know where you are."

"I just..." Kelli trailed off, because she hadn't told anyone the reason she'd returned to the cove, not even Alice. She felt like she owed an explanation to her first.

"I just talked to Alice," Eloise said. "She said you showed up a couple of nights ago, and she hadn't seen you since."

"I need to call her."

"Let's have dinner," Eloise said. "Tonight. Is Parker at your mother's?"

"Yes," Kelli said, eyeing the front window. She was starting to think Eloise was nearby, watching her every move. She still didn't want to go to dinner with Eloise.

"Great," Eloise said. "You, me, Alice, and Robin. Right here on Sanctuary."

"I don't think—"

"It's a dinnervention, Kel. We can meet at seven at a restaurant of your choice."

"I can't," Kelli said, annoyance rising through her. She paced toward the back of the house and looked out the window above the sink. She'd always had a window above her kitchen sink, but the home where she and Julian lived had the sink on an inside wall.

"Kelli," Eloise said, her voice kind but completely strong. "We love you, and we know there's something going on."

Kelli watched the waves as they lapped against the shore. They soothed her, even though she really didn't like water all that much. That wasn't true. She loved the ocean and the waves. She just didn't want to experience them while on a boat.

"I can't tonight," Kelli said.

"Why not?"

"I already have a dinner appointment."

"With who?" Eloise asked.

Kelli pressed her eyes closed, her stomach vibrating violently. "I'll tell everyone at dinner tomorrow," she said. "I'll need to call my mother, but tomorrow should work." She turned away from the ocean and leaned into the counter behind her. "Okay?"

"Name the restaurant," Eloise said.

"Coddington's," Kelli said. She'd need a lot of crab cakes and lobster rolls to get the truth out.

"Six? Or seven?"

"Let's do six," Kelli said, because she couldn't think of a reason she'd be later than that. The utilities would need to be turned on, and she'd have to figure out how to get Internet in the beach house. She'd have to get Parker registered for school and buy more clothes than what she could pack in a single suitcase.

Utility companies and elementary schools closed way before six, and she could buy clothes any time.

She drew in a deep breath as Eloise confirmed with her. "'Bye, Eloise."

She faced the water again, a swarm of snakes in her stomach. The phone in her hand didn't yield under her pythonic grip, and she finally tore her gaze from the undulating water and the blue sky above it.

She heard the waves when she stepped outside and turned back to lock the door behind her. After tapping to call a RideShare, she scrolled through her texts to find the string she'd sent to Zach.

He hadn't answered any of them, but Kelli wasn't going to give up. She knew a couple of people around the cove, and she'd been able to get his license plate number. From there, she'd figured out where he lived.

Zach had a studio apartment above a Chinese restaurant, on the block just down the street from Coddington's. She had no idea if he'd be home or not, but she'd called his landlord as if the rental listing was still open, and the woman who'd answered had said, "I wish it still was. The guy who lives there now is this unemployed loser who yelled at some customers last week."

Kelli hadn't even known what to say. She hadn't known Zach to yell at anyone. She'd never thought he'd approach her mother either, and Kelli had started to learn that she didn't know Zach Watkins at all.

Her ride pulled up, and Kelli got in the back seat and gave him the address to the Chinese restaurant. Her heart pounded in her chest, the rhythm of it getting harder and harder with every passing second.

An alarm went off in her mind, and she had the distinct thought that she shouldn't approach Zach alone. With a couple of blocks to go, she texted Eloise. *I need some help tonight. Can you come to The Mandarin Garden?*

Kelli took a deep breath and quickly tapped out another text. *And can you call Aaron and ask him to send an officer to the same place?*

She shouldn't have been surprised when Eloise called and demanded to know what was going on. Kelli took a breath and said, "It's about my half-brother, Zach…"

She didn't even know if he was her half-brother, and Kelli disliked all of this sudden uncertainty in her life. Eloise confirmed that she was on her way, but she was up at the inn, and it would take her about twenty minutes to get down from the cliffs.

"Okay," Kelli said. "I'll wait for you." She ended the call and pressed her phone to her lips, her mind revolving around what she wanted to say to Zach.

"Mandarin Garden," the RideShare driver said, and Kelli snapped herself back to the present. She quickly pressed her card to the payment sensor and waited for the green light. The few seconds it took to register felt like years, but she finally spilled from the car and onto the sidewalk.

She turned to the left and then the right, as if she wasn't sure where she was or how she got there. She shouldn't have come alone, she knew that. She didn't want to go into the restaurant, and the door beside it—which she knew led up to the apartment where Zach lived—had a keypad above the doorknob. She'd have to know that to get to his front door.

Kelli looked at her phone and took a few steps away from the blue door. She turned around and glanced up— right into the blazing blue eyes of Zach Watkins.

CHAPTER SEVEN

L aurel Baker had heard the chirp of the radio on her shoulder hundreds of times. When the Chief's voice came over it, she listened, because he rarely came on to say anything. Dispatch did that.

"Unit to The Mandarin Garden on Sanctuary," he said. "Come back with location and ETA."

Laurel glanced at her partner, Connor Hatch, and he nodded. He reached up and pressed the button on his radio. "Unit S-12 on Blackbird Avenue. ETA, four minutes."

Another chirp, but this one didn't go up as high, which meant the words didn't go out to everyone. "Siren and lights. Get there now," the Chief said.

Laurel didn't waste another second. She flipped on the two switches that started the siren and the lights, and she pressed on the accelerator.

She loved being a cop, but not many interesting things happened in Five Island Cove. Routine traffic stops and the occasional shoplifting offense. Some rowdiness on the beach when too much alcohol got involved, and as the tourists got younger and younger, Chief Sherman had brought on more and more cops.

He'd been busy dealing with his new K9 dogs, and Laure did not envy the amount of work on the man's desk.

"I see them," Connor said. "Two people—one man, and one woman. Oh! He just took a swing at her."

Laurel's pulse crashed against her ribs, and she drove right up onto the sidewalk. In her adrenaline-fueled state, she wasn't sure how she got her seat belt off and the door open.

"Freeze!" she yelled. "Police. Do not hit that woman, sir."

Connor approached the front of the police car. "Step away from her."

The ginger-haired man turned around, and the honey-blonde woman's sobs reached Laurel's ears. Her blood burned hotly through her veins, and she blinked to stay focused on the situation.

She wasn't back in that abusive relationship. Her boyfriend had dark hair, not reddish-blonde. And he wasn't her boyfriend anymore.

"Step back," she said again, rounding the open door of the police car. "Hands above your head."

The man raised his hands slowly as he turned fully toward her and Connor. He wore a smirk on his face that angered Laurel, and she gritted her teeth as Connor handcuffed him and started leading him to the back seat.

Laurel went to the woman sitting on the ground, her hands in her hair as she ducked her head toward her knees. "Ma'am," she said as gently as she could. "Do we need to call an ambulance?"

"No," the woman said, lifting her head. Her eyes held nothing but panic and tears, and she seemed like she might jump to her feet and bolt at any moment. "I'm fine."

"Did he hit you?"

"No," she said.

"Who was he?" Laurel asked, taking in this woman's distress and making it hers. She knew exactly what she felt, and she hated seeing it on another woman's face.

"My half-brother." The woman wiped her face. "Maybe. I'm not sure about that, actually."

"What's his name?"

"Zach Watkins."

"And yours?"

"Kelli Thompson."

Laurel was starting to get too much information, and she pulled out a notebook and started scratching notes in it. "Did you arrange to meet him?"

"No." Kelli got to her feet, and Laurel straightened too, keeping her eyes on Kelli. She didn't get the sense that this woman was lying to her, but Laurel knew that people had all kinds of reasons to lie, and a lot of them were very good at it.

"I—I was just here to get some food, and I ran into him."

"Kelli," another woman called, and Laurel turned to find her. A dark-haired woman hurried toward them, and Laurel already knew her.

"Eloise," Kelli said, sobbing as she grabbed onto the Chief's girlfriend. Laurel watched them, her curiosity at an all-time high.

"What happened?" Eloise asked, stepping back and holding onto Kelli's shoulders. She wore pure concern and shock in her expression, and that felt very genuine to Laurel.

"I came, because—" She cut her eyes to Laurel, who lifted her eyebrows.

Kelli sighed and dropped her chin to her chest. "I've been trying to get in touch with Zach. He's been hassling my mother for money, and I called and left him a message to leave her alone. Then I came to the cove, and I kept asking him to meet me. He never responded."

Eloise looked from Laurel to Kelli and back, recognition lighting her face. "Laurel, thanks for coming so fast." She stepped toward Laurel and embraced her, and all the jealous feelings Laurel had ever had because of Eloise's and Chief Sherman's relationship only turned to guilt.

Eloise pulled back. "Aaron called you, right?"

"Yes," Laurel said, shifting her feet. Eloise Hall was the nicest person on the planet, and she was beautiful and kind, and of course she deserved Chief Sherman. Laurel couldn't help thinking the man was as handsome as the day was long. He was good with his kids, and fair with his staff, and any woman who said she hadn't thought about kissing him was simply a liar.

She cleared her throat and looked at Kelli again. "He never responded..." she prompted.

"Right," Kelli said. "But I figured out where he lived, and I came to talk to him. But I got a bad feeling on the way here, and I texted Eloise to come meet me."

"And she asked me to call Aaron," Eloise said. "I did, and I got in my car and came straight down."

"So you went to his house unannounced?" Laurel asked, making a quick note. She lifted her eyes to watch Kelli's reaction.

"No," she said. "I'd just gotten out of the car. He lives above the Chinese restaurant, and it has a keypad. I can't get up there. So I started walking down the street, and when I turned around, he was just there."

"Then what?" Connor asked, stepping to Laurel's side. He glanced at her notebook, which she tilted toward him. It didn't have all the details, but enough for him to know the man in the back of their car wasn't Kelli's boyfriend.

"He asked me what I was doing here," Kelli said. "I've been practicing this speech for him, and I started to tell him to stay away from my mother, that she didn't have any money, and that he should leave the cove and go back to Maine."

She visibly shook, and Eloise put her arm around her. They exchanged a glance, and then Kelli looked at Laurel again. These two had been friends for a very long time, if Laurel had to guess. "He wasn't happy with that, and I told him I was going to look into everything about him, including the birth certificate he'd shown me a few months ago. I said I was going to find out about his mother, and his aunt, and that was when he started yelling."

"I'll go see if we have other witnesses," Laurel said. "Connor?"

"Yep," he said, and he stepped in front of the two women. He asked her something else, but Laurel needed to get away from the situation. She moved through the people standing on the sidewalk, asking for anyone who'd seen anything to come forward.

A woman wearing an apron lifted her hand and said, "I heard yelling, so I came outside. He had her backed up against the building, and he was about four inches from her face."

"Did she yell back?"

"No, she was already crying."

"Did he hit her?"

"We all heard the sirens, and he looked over his shoulder." She pressed her palms together, clearly nervous. "He turned back and yelled something about calling the cops, and he tried to swing at her. I mean, he did swing at her, but the guy's drunk as a skunk, and he almost fell down."

"Thank you," Laurel said. "What's your name?"

She gave it and said she worked at The Mandarin Garden, and Laurel moved on to find another version of the story. Everyone she found gave a very similar rendition of the story. Zach had been yelling, with Kelli pinned up against the building.

Twenty minutes later, she met up with Connor again, and they conferred. "We've got the guy we need," Connor concluded. "I'll call it in. You want to give her our contact information?"

"Sure." Laurel stepped back over to Eloise and Kelli and pulled a card from the back of her notebook. "We're taking him to the station. Do you both have somewhere safe to stay tonight?"

"Yes," they said together, and Laurel nodded.

"We might have to contact you again," she said, handing Kelli the card. "My advice? Stay away from this guy. Since he didn't actually touch you, I'm not sure we'll be able to do more than question him and warn him to stay away from you too." Laurel smiled the best she could and turned back to her patrol car.

She ignored the man in the back seat who kept yelling

about his rights being violated, and by the time she and Connor got him back to the station, she had a splitting headache. "I need a break," she told Connor as they went to file the paperwork to keep Zach Watkins in holding until he wasn't drunk and they could interview him.

"Baker and Hatch," the Chief barked from his door-way. "My office, please."

"Oh, boy," Connor muttered under his breath, but everything inside Laurel's soul lit up the moment she laid eyes on Aaron Sherman.

Stop it, she told herself. *He has a girlfriend, and she's amazing.* She stuffed away her silly crush and stepped into the Chief's office.

He closed the door behind them and said, "Thank you for getting there so quickly. Kelli Thompson is one of Eloise's very best friends." He sighed as he went past them. "Sit, sit. Tell me what the situation is."

Laurel sat, and Connor looked at her. She was the senior partner, and she detailed everything for Aaron, who kept his mouth shut and nodded throughout the story. "Okay," he said when she finished. "We need to look into Zach's background. Find out if the birth certificate is real, and who he really is."

"Sir?" Connor asked. "Is that...?" He looked at Laurel, who also thought that would be taking this case a bit farther than they needed to.

"He didn't actually touch her, sir," Laurel said much

more diplomatically. "I'm not sure we can hold him once he's sober."

Aaron frowned and then nodded. "Of course. You're both right." He smiled and stood, which caused both of them to jump to their feet too. Connor reached the door first, and he opened it and left the office without breaking stride.

"Laurel," Chief Sherman said, his voice low and husky. It sent shivers through her whole body.

She turned back to him. "Yes, sir?"

He gestured her back into the office and let the door settle almost all the way closed. It wasn't all the way closed, but it might as well have been. Her heart raced through her veins, and her blood pressure felt like it might shoot through the roof.

"I'm swamped here," he said. "But I need to follow up on this on my own time."

"Sir?"

"Would you be willing to work with me on this? On our own time, of course. No police department resources. Just me and you and our best minds at work."

Surprise filled Laurel. She couldn't see anything unethical about following up on a birth certificate on her own time, with her own resources. "Okay," she said.

A smile filled his face, and the tension in the room disappeared. "Thank you, Laurel." He opened the door, and Laurel ducked out, too much giddiness running through her.

She couldn't feel like this about the man. She simply couldn't.

On her way to her desk, she caught sight of Paul Leyhe, and she made a quick detour. "Hey," she said when she arrived.

Paul looked up, his dark eyes full of surprise. He'd asked her out—more than once—but Laurel had still been healing from her disastrous break-up. "Laurel." He leaned back in his chair and smiled at her.

He was good-looking and smart. His sideburns had a hint of gray growing in them, and Laurel liked a more mature man.

"I was just..." She glanced at the desk across from his, where his partner gazed at a computer screen as if hit held the most fascinating information on it. "Can I talk to you for a second?"

"Sure." Paul stood up and Laurel led him toward a back hallway that led to a conference room. She ducked down it and turned back to him. "What's going on?" Paul asked, concern in his voice now. "Something with that guy you just brought in?"

"No," Laurel said. "Nothing like that." She put her bravery in place and looked right into his eyes. "I was just wondering if you're seeing anyone, and if maybe the invitation to dinner is still open?"

Surprise filled Paul's face, and a slow smile spread across his face. "I'm not seeing anyone."

"I was in a bad place when you asked," she said. "I'd

just gotten out of this...abusive relationship, and I needed some time."

"I understand," Paul said, his voice kind and deep, just like Aaron's. "I'd absolutely love to take you to dinner."

"Great," Laurel said, and she meant it. She smiled too. "Can't wait."

CHAPTER EIGHT

AJ Proctor walked past all the other researcher desks, her heels making plenty of noise on the practically flat carpet. She probably didn't need to wear heels at all, because she still hadn't earned her spot on the air.

She carried a couple of folders in her hand, and she'd deliver them to the on-air talent for that evening's broadcast. She'd be back at the hotel by then, eating by herself and watching someone else deliver the facts and narrating the clips that she researched and then wrote.

She didn't hate the job, but it wasn't what she was used to. She'd managed to get selected for this trip to Denver, but she'd thought she'd be the one to be at the basketball arena, interviewing the players and coaches, as well as their representatives.

Instead, she'd been two steps behind Eddie

Winchester as he asked all the questions. She recorded the interview and took notes, and then she typed everything up for him. He had an office with real walls in the building where their studio had been assigned, while she had a desk crammed in between two others.

"Here's the transcripts, Eddie," she said, smiling for all she was worth as she entered the man's office.

"Thanks, AJ." He didn't look away from his laptop. "Hey, we got the early slot in the morning. They start practice at eight-fifteen. We need to be at the arena by seven, so we get at least an hour before they kick us out."

"Seven," she confirmed, though a small part of her died. To get her hair shiny and straight, her makeup just right, and her lips glossed, AJ had to get up five to make a seven a.m. meeting at the basketball arena in downtown Denver.

She did love the mountains, as she'd never seen anything like them before. There was no water here, no shore, and no scent of salt in the air. The Rocky Mountains had a charm all their own though, and AJ wished she'd had more opportunities to travel.

On her way back to her desk, AJ's phone chimed. She pulled it out of the pocket in her slacks and saw it was Eloise on the group text. She loved her friends from Five Island Cove, and she quickly swiped the text open.

Dinnervention with Kelli at six tomorrow, the text read. *Coddington's.*

AJ's chest pinched, and she hated that she hadn't

known about this sooner. There was no way she could get from Denver to Five Island Cove by six tomorrow night. She hadn't even known Kelli was in the cove, and she wondered what had happened to bring her back so soon. They hadn't had plans to meet, and the texts had been how they'd been keeping in touch.

When Robin had asked if AJ had met anyone interesting in New York, she'd told them no one. They hadn't believed her, so AJ had simply said, *Peterson*.

No one had asked specific questions, and AJ hadn't had to lie to them. Peterson was the name of the goldfish she'd gotten on her second day in New York, because her apartment in Brooklynn depressed her. It was a studio, and she barely had room to sit, let alone think.

She'd needed something else to focus on, and there'd been a pet store down the block on the corner. She'd ducked in there one afternoon after buying groceries, and the next thing she knew she had Peterson to talk to at night.

She'd made a pact with herself not to start dating the moment she landed in New York, and to her great surprise, she'd kept that vow. It helped that she worked at least twelve hours each day.

She sat at her desk and looked at her phone. *A dinner-vention*, she thought. *Must be serious.*

Out of all the women, she was the closest to Kelli, and she hadn't heard anything from her friend. She didn't want to ask all of her questions on the group text, so she just sent them to Kelli. It wasn't all that surprising that she didn't answer, but frustration still threaded through AJ.

She reminded herself of the time difference, and then she stood up. She still had a couple of things to do, but she could complete them from the hotel room. She gathered the tape and the folders she needed, and with her laptop, put everything in her bag.

"AJ," Mike said as she went past his desk. "A bunch of us are going to dinner at The Roost. You in?"

"Oh, I don't think so," she said with a smile. "I still have a few things to do tonight, and I need to call my friend." She kept walking, because she knew better than to let Mike get a real conversation going.

She hadn't forgotten that he'd asked her out on the very first day she'd arrived in the office. She didn't normally say no when a man asked her out, but she'd had the pact, and she wasn't all that attracted to Mike. He had a loud laugh, and she stood taller than him.

AJ reminded herself that she wasn't a twenty-some-thing anymore, and she probably should've simply said she'd love to go to dinner once she got settled in her apartment in Brooklyn.

She wasn't sure how anyone in the office managed a relationship, because she worked more here than she had anywhere else. She didn't hate it, but she wasn't used to being the low man on the totem pole. She'd had to learn to like the taste of humble pie, and she thought she'd done a pretty good job in the past two months.

She drove her rental back to the hotel, where she ordered something from room service, spread out her work, and turned on the sports syndicate channel. Her prediction that she'd eat alone in her hotel room came true before her very eyes when the room service attendant arrived with her pasta with chicken and pesto.

As she ate, she allowed herself to feel the range of her emotions. She hadn't been on her anti-depressants for a couple of years now, but she considered it from time to time. One of those times had arrived, because a shroud of darkness descended on her as she considered her meal.

Her phone chimed again, and Kelli's name sat on the screen. A bright ray of hope shone from the phone, and AJ abandoned her fork in favor of her device. She tapped on Kelli's name and quickly read her response.

Too much to type out.

"Then I'm going to call you," AJ muttered, and she tapped the green phone icon and listened to the line ring.

"It's late here," Kelli hissed instead of hello.

"You said it was too much to type out," AJ said. "What did you think I would do?"

Kelli sighed, and she added, "Let me go in the other room."

"Where are you?"

Kelli's breathing came through the line, but she didn't answer right away. A few seconds later, she said, "Believe it or not, Alice's."

"What's going on?"

Kelli sighed again, this time longer and with more frustration in the sound. "I should've known better than to come back to the cove. No one can keep a secret here."

"You don't need to keep secrets from me," AJ said. "Besides, I'm not in the cove."

"Everyone else is," she said. "Eloise moved here over the weekend, and I came because...because...well, Julian and I are separating."

Shock moved through AJ, and she sat back in the desk chair. "You are?"

"Yes," Kelli said, her voice clipped and short. "I really don't want to explain everything."

"Why not?" AJ asked. "It's me, and I'm not even there. You can't even see my face."

"I can picture it right now," Kelli said. "I'm just embarrassed, AJ."

"Why? Is this your fault?"

"No," Kelli whispered.

AJ cocked her head, because she had always been able to hear things in Kelli's voice she didn't want to give away. "Tell me what happened."

"Julian had a girlfriend in our house when I got back," Kelli said. "Well, not right away. But he's been dating his new assistant."

"That snake," AJ said. There were a lot of things she could tolerate, but cheating wasn't one of them.

"It gets worse."

"How?"

"He doesn't want a divorce. He wants...both of us."

AJ had heard of this kind of alternative relationship, and there was no way Kelli would ever participate in it. Her husband should know that about her. AJ had never met Julian, but he must not know Kelli at all.

"I'm so sorry," AJ said.

"So I packed a few things, and Parker and I are back in the cove. I just found somewhere to rent today, and Parker and I will be there tomorrow. I should've just gotten a hotel."

"It's still tourist season," AJ said.

"I didn't even try," Kelli said. "Julian and I—" Her voice muted for a moment, and AJ could imagine the way she'd be trying to swallow back her emotion. "We never had much money to begin with, so my first thought wasn't to get a hotel. It was to come to Alice's."

"And she told Robin, and now there's a dinnervention."

"I think she told Eloise, actually," Kelli said. "How can anyone say no to Eloise? She's, like, the nicest person ever."

AJ laughed, glad when Kelli joined in for a couple of seconds. "It is easier to say no to Robin or Alice, isn't it?"

"I have a hard time saying no to anyone," Kelli said. "But I did it with Julian. I told him no while he was lying in our bed with his girlfriend. I said no, AJ."

"I'm proud of you, Kel. You know I'd be there tomorrow night if I could, right?"

"Of course you would," Kelli said. "I know that, AJ."

"I love you, Kel."

"There's more," she said, and she went on to detail an encounter with her half-brother in front of a Chinese restaurant on Sanctuary Island.

AJ sat there in a state of shock, trying to make what she knew about Zach line up with what Kelli was saying. "I don't even...this is wild."

"I've got to get some answers about him," Kelli said. "I need to talk to my mom, and I need to register Parker for school." She exhaled, and AJ could hear her spiraling.

"One day at a time," AJ said. "You've got time for all of that."

"I need a job," she said. "I need a ton of stuff for my house. It's furnished, but I don't want to sleep on someone else's sheets." She sniffled, and AJ wished she was there so she could hug her best friend.

They'd spent so many nights together, looking up at the stars and talking about their families, their grades, or their hopes for things. Never once had AJ said she wanted to get married, but now it seemed to be the only thing she thought about.

Kelli had always wanted to be a mother, but she'd had trouble getting pregnant, and she just had the one son.

"I feel like my life is falling apart," Kelli said.

"At least you had something put together that could fall apart," AJ said.

"Tell me about Peterson," Kelli said.

AJ didn't want to lie to her, nor did she want to admit that Peterson was a goldfish. She said, "I'm too tired tonight. Another time."

"Okay," Kelli said.

"Love you, Kel. Don't let this define you."

"You always tell me that," Kelli said. "I'm grateful and glad, but I don't know what defines me. If the experiences I have don't define me, what does?"

"I have no idea," AJ said. "I just don't want you to let his decision change who you are."

"I don't have a clue who I am."

"You're Kelli Thompson," AJ said. "And I'm AJ Proctor, and..." She waited for Kelli to start, and then she joined in with, "No one can tell us what to do."

AJ smiled, because she could see herself and Kelli, riding their bikes as fast as they could down the steepest hill on Bell Island, shouting those words to the world. AJ had felt completely free during those times, with the wind in her face and her thoughts racing so fast that she didn't have to dwell on any one of them.

"Text me tomorrow," AJ said. "Let the others pamper you. Don't be embarrassed. This doesn't say anything about you."

"Doesn't it?" Kelli asked. "I think it says I'm such a bad wife that Julian needs two women to keep him satisfied."

"No," AJ said. "Not at all. It's nothing like that. It's just a sexual preference."

"Feels like I'm not good enough," Kelli said. She drew

in a deep breath. "I'm so tired. I love you, AJ. I'll text you tomorrow."

"Love you, Kel." The call ended, and AJ put her phone on the desk and stared at the wall. She wanted to go to New Jersey now, hunt down Julian, and ask him if he knew what he was giving up.

Kelli was such an amazing woman. She'd overcome so much in her life already, and AJ had no doubt she could weather this storm too. In June, when they'd all gathered for the summer sand pact, Kelli had really come alive. She'd been so different from the time they'd spent together for Joel's funeral, and she was starting to act more like the person she'd been in high school.

AJ clicked to brighten her laptop again, and instead of going back to work, she started searching for airplane tickets from Denver to Five Island Cove. She couldn't go, but she could dream.

She felt like she'd been doing that a lot lately. Dreaming for a chance to get on-air. Dreaming to meet that perfect man that would sweep her off her feet. Always dreaming, that was AJ, and she wished they'd start to replace the nightmare that was her reality.

CHAPTER NINE

Robin thanked the RideShare driver and got out of the car, her calves already cramping in these wedged sandals. She was far too old to wear shoes like this, but she'd wanted to wear them at least twice before she made a final determination on them.

Mandie and Jamie had both said they looked amazing, and Robin agreed. The problem was, looking amazing wasn't worth the price of constantly aching feet or spasming muscles for the next week.

She loved to run in the morning, but by the time she'd get home, Robin doubted that she'd even be able to walk.

She entered Coddington's, her chest already tight. Eloise had managed to get Kelli to agree to meet them for a dinnervention, and that alone was a miracle. It was also why Robin had suggested that Eloise talk to Kelli.

She'd shown up at Alice's, so that suggested Kelli trusted Alice. The airport was on Diamond, though, and Robin had plenty of guest rooms too. In fact, Kelli had stayed with her when she'd come for Joel's funeral.

Yet, Kelli hadn't come to Robin.

She'd been telling herself it was nothing for two days. Alice had an enormous house on Rocky Ridge, and Robin's husband would be home on Saturday. Kelli had probably wanted to intrude as little as possible.

Although...

Robin pushed the thoughts away. She hated the second-guessing. She hated that she was still unsure of her place in the group, and she reminded herself she didn't need a place. She was perfectly secure in her marriage and her place as Duke's wife, her kid's mom, and the best wedding planner in the cove.

Her stomach swooped at the thought of her upcoming wedding. The Burke's were a high-profile family out of Nantucket, and Robin wanted everything to go as smoothly as possible for the wedding. She wanted that for all of her clients, of course, but Lily Burke had the ability to bring a lot of business to Robin, and while Duke had made twice as much money this summer while in Alaska, Robin always wanted to build her business.

"How many?" a woman asked, and Robin hadn't even realized it was her turn. She quickly scanned the lobby and didn't see anyone she was meeting.

"Uh, four," she said. "But they might already be here."

The woman looked down at her podium, which was covered with colored squares of paper, sheaves of notes, and buzzers. Robin wanted to wash her hands just looking at all of the things that could carry germs.

"Hailey?" she asked.

"No," Robin said. "It's probably under Eloise."

"I don't have an Eloise."

"Alice?"

The woman looked up. "I have a Hailey."

"Okay," Robin said. "Then four."

The woman handed her a buzzer and said, "Fifteen or twenty minutes."

Robin took the buzzer and got out of the way for the next patron. She felt like she was in the way, something she'd been feeling more and more lately. Kristen had told her that was simply what happened as children got older. Robin wasn't as relevant as she'd once been. Her kids didn't need her as much, though they needed her more in some ways.

She didn't have to drive them all over the island or go with them on the ferries to the neighboring islands. But she expended at least ten times that amount of energy worrying about them. Was Mandie really where she said she'd be? What if she got into a situation on Rocky Ridge she couldn't get out of? The ferry ride to the northernmost island took forty minutes, and that was from shore to shore.

"There she is."

Robin turned at the sound of Alice's voice, and she faced all three of her friends as they came in together.

"Hey, friend," Alice said with a smile. She folded Robin into a hug that didn't hurt as much as it had even two months ago. Alice wasn't all bones anymore, and Robin thought she looked better than she had in years.

"Eloise," Robin said, grinning at her. "I'm so glad you're here."

Eloise smiled back and hugged Robin. "I'm glad too, funnily enough."

"How's life at your mother's?"

"It's...different," Eloise said. She side-stepped, and Robin faced Kelli. The woman wore a look of pure fear on her face, which she smoothed away in the next moment.

"Hey, Robin." Kelli flashed a brief smile and hugged Robin too. She took a deep breath and faced the fray that was the restaurant. "How long?"

"She said fifteen or twenty minutes," Robin said.

"It's never that long," Alice said.

"I hope not," Eloise said. "I can't stand here for very long. I worked myself hard at the inn today."

"I want to hear all about the inn," Robin said, shifting her purse on her shoulder.

"There's not much to tell right now," Eloise said. "I'm basically throwing away everything I touch." She heaved a great sigh, and Robin believed the exhaustion she heard in the noise.

She'd been up to the Cliffside Inn with Eloise in June, and it had been one big mess. She almost thought it would be easier and take less time to knock the whole thing down and start over. It wouldn't be nearly as cheap though, and though Eloise had bought the inn a long time ago, Robin assumed she still had a budget.

"And I'm taking tomorrow and Thursday off," she said, glancing around. Her eyes skirted away from Robin's as she added, "To go school shopping with Aaron and the girls."

"Aaron's going back to school?" Alice asked.

Robin rolled her eyes, and when Eloise did too, Robin couldn't contain her giggle. Alice had an interesting sense of humor, that was for sure. Robin was just glad to hear her attempting to joke at all, as she hadn't been in a place to do that for a while now.

"That's a big deal," Robin said. "I don't want to pry, but—"

"Yes, you do," Eloise said with a smile. She swatted playfully at Robin's shoulder. "No, there's been no talk of a wedding."

"Dang it," Robin said. "I really want to put you on my schedule, and I'm terrified I'll book someone else, and you'll hire someone else." It really was a real fear she had too.

"I'm not going to do that," Eloise said. "I'll set the date with you, not Aaron."

Kelli smiled—finally—and Robin wondered how hard

they'd have to pry that evening to get the truth from her. Eloise had specifically used the word "dinnervention" in her text, so everyone knew what was happening tonight.

"Remember, some of us haven't been planning our weddings since we were eight." Eloise giggled. "Besides, I've been married before. So has he. We don't want anything big." Her eyes widened. "I mean, at least I don't. We haven't...really talked about it."

"I'm surprised by that," Alice said. "The man knows you gave up your whole career to move here, right?"

"Yes," Eloise said quickly, already on the defensive. "It's...he's very busy."

"El," Robin said, and her friend's eyes came back to hers. "Two things, and then I swear I will not say another word about you and Aaron for...a week."

"Wow, a whole week?" Eloise asked dryly. She folded her arms, her dark eyes sparkling with an emotion halfway between annoyance and laughter.

Robin grinned at her. "Probably eight days, because we'll get together next Wednesday for lunch." She looked around at everyone. "All of us, okay?"

"I love the Wednesday lunch," Alice said. "And the twins will be at school, so I'm definitely in."

"Kelli?"

"Maybe," Kelli said, looking away. "I don't really know what will be happening in eight days."

"She has a good point," Eloise said. "I should be available. I'm just trying to get the caretaker's suite as livable as possible, as fast as possible."

"Robin," the hostess called, and Robin looked down at her buzzer. It hadn't gone off. She honestly wasn't sure why she'd been holding it all this time. She stepped over to the hostess, the other ladies in her wake.

"Right here," she said, handing the buzzer back. "That didn't go off."

"Yeah, about half of them are broken." The woman just took it back and put it in the same stack she'd taken it from. "This way."

She led them through the crowded seafood joint to a table crammed in the back corner. Robin didn't mind, because then she wouldn't be bumped a bunch of times as other people got up and left or new people came in and took seats.

"I can't wait for school to start," Alice grumbled as she took the seat next to Robin. "Then maybe some of these people will leave the cove." She glared around at the packed and busy restaurant.

Robin looked at her, realizations manifesting themselves in her mind.

"Alice," Eloise said, drawing out the name into more than two syllables. "Did you hear what you just said?"

Alice froze, her eyes widening. "Oh, no," she moaned. "I just sounded like my mother."

"No," Robin said, working hard to hold back the giggle. "You sounded like *my* mother."

Alice swung her attention to Robin, clear horror in her eyes. Robin couldn't help laughing then, because it had been Alice and not her who'd said that.

She knew she could have just as easily. It also reminded her that even if she didn't want to be like her mother at all—even if Alice didn't—it was almost impossible to escape that possibility.

They ordered drinks, and Robin folded her arms on the checkered tablecloth. "All right, Kelli. Let's get this dinnervention started."

"Wait," Eloise said. "I need to call AJ. She wanted to be here." She tapped and got the call open, and Robin smiled at AJ on the video chat.

She waved to everyone and said, "I'm going to be on mute," she said. "I'm still at work." She put her finger to her lips, her eyes sparkling, and Robin really wanted to ask her about Peterson too.

AJ seemed so different than she'd been only two months ago. She probably wasn't drinking at all, and she actually looked younger and more relaxed, so the new job must be going well. AJ didn't say much about it. She mainly sent texts about New York City and pictures of the architecture there.

Robin loved every picture, and when Duke got home on Saturday, she was going first welcome him home with his favorite meal. They'd spend time together as a family. She'd make love to him, and then the next thing on her list was to ask him to take her to New York City.

She'd never been away from Five Island Cove, as her parents didn't have an inclination to travel, and the family business kept them chained to the islands. Once her parents had divorced, there was even less opportunity to leave the cove, and she alone had stayed after high school. She'd met Duke, and he fished the seas around the islands, and there was no reason for her to go anywhere.

"Okay," Eloise said. "You're up, Kel."

They had to pause once while they put in their orders, but otherwise Kelli talked and talked. And talked. By the time she stopped, Robin had eaten her soft-shell crabs and chips. Her stomach felt just as hollow as before though, because of Kelli's story.

Kelli finally picked up her lobster roll and took a bite.

"That's unbelievable," Alice said. She met Robin's eye, and Robin saw rage in Alice's expression. She wasn't sure if she was more angry or more disgusted.

"You know," Eloise said. "The Hillstone's have that sort of alternative relationship in their marriage. It's not that uncommon."

"Sure," Alice said. "I'm sure there were tons of swingers in the Hamptons too. I saw the lawn ornaments. What I'm saying is, it's unbelievable for Julian to think *Kelli* would be interested in that lifestyle."

Robin nodded, because Alice had hit that one on the nose.

"That's what I thought," AJ said, and Eloise jumped.

"Oh, my goodness, AJ," she said, picking up the phone. "I forgot you were there."

"Yeah, I've been looking at the ceiling for half an hour. Thanks, Eloise." She laughed, and everyone at the table did too.

Once that settled, Robin couldn't help looking at Kelli. She reached across the table to her and covered her hand with hers. "Tell us what you need, Kelli. Someone to help babysit while you get moved into your new place? Someone to help you register Parker for school? What do you need for the rental? Towels? Soap?"

"I have a ton of laundry detergent pods," Alice said. "I ordered one container, but the girl who did the grocery delivery thought it was a seven, and they wouldn't take them back."

"They wouldn't take them back?" Robin looked at Alice. "That's insane. Those are expensive."

"I guess they've been having kids buy them and open them, take a few out, and then return them." Alice shook her head. "Whatever. I literally have enough to do laundry for the next decade."

"Everything I own is coming from Boston," Eloise said. "Literally, a whole brownstone full of furniture, appliances, toiletries. I'm living with my mother. So." She shrugged, and the message was clear. She wasn't going to be using any of that stuff.

"I have a ton of sheets we're not using," Robin said. "And my mother just cleaned out her basement, and she had some of my old toys down there. Like, from thirty-five years ago."

Kelli looked around the table, and while she'd been steady and strong through a quick recap of what had happened with Zach last night, and then the reason she'd left New Jersey and come back to Five Island Cove, now her lower jaw trembled.

"Oh, don't cry," Eloise said, reaching over and putting her arm around Kelli. "You'll make me cry."

"You guys are amazing," Kelli whispered, and yet Robin could still hear it in the crowded restaurant. She could *feel* Kelli's gratitude way down deep in her soul. "I love you all so much." She nodded and quickly wiped her face. "I'm not going to cry. I'm not."

She met Robin's eye, and Robin swore she saw a brand-new version of Kelli Watkins being born from the ashes of her life, right there in the restaurant. "I will take your help with registering Parker for school. It's on Diamond Island, and it'll save me two ferry rides."

"Done," Robin said, mentally adding it to her to-do list for the following day.

Kelli looked at Alice. "I'll take your laundry pods."

Alice smiled and nodded, and she added her hand to the stack in the middle of the table.

Kelli swiveled her head to Eloise. "And I'll take whatever you're willing to give me from your brownstone in Boston."

"Honestly, you can probably have it all," Eloise said.

She put her hand on the stack in the middle too, and they looked around at one another.

"I wish I was there," AJ said, and Alice gasped. She met Robin's gaze with her own startled eyes, and that set everyone laughing again.

***

ROBIN TIPPED UP ONTO HER TOES, THE DESPERATION inside her at a breaking point. It had been since she'd woken that morning. Where was Duke? Why hadn't he been with Bryan?

The man who had recruited Duke to Alaska for the summer fishing season had disembarked from the plane ten minutes ago, and his family was already leaving the staging area.

She wanted to see her husband right now.

"There he is," Mandie said, and Robin craned her neck to the left.

Mandie moved that way, and Robin grabbed her youngest daughter's hand. "Come on, Jamie." She followed Mandie, and they edged around the crowd still waiting for their loved ones.

Robin spotted Duke instantly, because the man called to her in a way no one else ever had. Tears sprang to her eyes, especially when both girls called, "Dad!" and started toward him. He laughed and scooped them both into a big bear hug while Robin wept several paces behind them.

His eyes met hers over the tops of the girls' heads, and an entire electrical storm began brewing between them. She lifted her hand to wipe her eyes and turned it into a wave.

He started toward her, and she took in the broad, boxy shoulders. The dark hair salted with gray now. And the beard.

Oh, dear, the beard.

"That's a sexy look," she said, reaching up to trace her fingers along his jawline. The hair there was softer than she expected, and when he took her in his arms and kissed her, there was no scratching from it.

She melted into him and kissed him back, trying to communicate to him how much she'd missed him and how happy she was to have him home.

"Ew, stop making out," Mandie said, and Duke pulled away.

He gaped at Mandie, which caused Robin to burst out laughing. "See what I've been dealing with alone?" she asked between her giggles.

"I always kiss your mother like this," Duke said. "It's not making out."

"It's gross," Mandie said, glancing around as if any of her friends would be there and see Robin and Duke kissing.

Duke looked at Robin, his eyes wide and filled with shock. "She's still your daughter," Robin said. "She's just... a teenager now."

Mandie rolled her eyes and walked away, but Robin just gazed up at Duke. "I don't care what she thinks," she said. "Kiss me again, baby. I'm so glad you're home." He did what she asked, and Robin didn't care if she made out with her husband. She hadn't seen him for four and a half months, and she just did not care.

CHAPTER TEN

"Eloise, will you come in with me?" Billie asked, and a healthy dose of surprise shot through Eloise.

She forced herself not to look at Aaron as she said, "Sure thing." She adjusted the strap of her purse and looked at Grace. "Do you have anything to try on?"

"Nope."

"Just me and you, Bills." Eloise smiled at the teenager, hoping she didn't mess this up. She went into the dressing room with the girl and turned to lock the door behind her.

Billie slipped her pants off as Eloise sat on the bench at the back of the booth. She picked up one of the pairs of shorts for the girl and handed them to her. "Do you like this type of fabric?" she asked.

"Better than jeans," Billie said. "No one's wearing jeans this year."

"No?" Eloise looked down at her denim shorts. "Good

to know." She knew Billie hadn't commented on her personal style. Besides, Eloise wasn't thirteen and didn't need to fit in with the cool kids at the junior high. She could wear her mom jeans all she wanted.

Billie buttoned the navy blue shorts that barely covered her behind and turned to look at the sides and back. "My dad will never let me wear these."

"Will they let you wear them to school?" Eloise asked as delicately as she could. "What's the dress code?"

"No," Billie said, putting her hands in the pockets. "They have to go down farther than this." She faced Eloise. "What do you think?"

Eloise thought she'd like to be thirteen again to have a slim, tight body like Billie's. She smiled at the shorts and then at Billie. "They're super cute."

Billie had wide, beautiful eyes that stayed open when she smiled, and her dirty blonde hair fell halfway down her back. She'd straightened it today, and with the little mascara she wore, Eloise knew she was going to turn a lot of heads and break a lot of hearts.

She reminded Eloise of AJ in so many ways, though Billie didn't like sports. Aaron had told her she had to find a group at school, and Billie had steadfastly refused band and orchestra, soccer and swimming, debate and chess.

She'd finally settled on art and musical theater, though the last one had come about after an argument between her and Aaron. The two were like oil and water, though they were nearly the same person. Aaron loved Billie fiercely, though, and Billie loved her father too. Teenage years were simply hard, and Eloise anticipated the next several years would be trying for Aaron.

For her, too, she hoped.

Billie started to step out of the shorts, and Billie took them from her and handed her the next pair. "Those look like they might meet the dress code," she said as Billie pulled them on.

The light pink shorts covered Billie's legs to mid-thigh, and she stood straight and tall, her arms down at her sides. "Yep," she said. "They go past my fingertips."

"Is that the rule?"

"Yes," she said. "But it's stupid. No one follows it, and they don't even make people change."

"Oh, then the blue ones should be fine."

"It'll be a miracle if I can get Dad to buy those," Billie said. "Let alone leaving the house in them."

"You're a pretty girl," Eloise said. "He's probably worried about what the boys will think."

Billie met Eloise's eyes in the mirror. "I'm pretty?"

"Beautiful," Eloise said with a smile. "Gorgeous—have you seen your hair? And when you smile, there's this light in your eyes." She tucked her own hair behind her ears so she wouldn't embarrass herself or Billie. "Trust me, you're going to make some boys go crazy."

A flush immediately started to creep into Billie's face.

"What's his name?" Eloise asked.

"Who?"

"The boy whose eye you're hoping to catch."

Billie started unbuttoning the pink shorts, and Eloise folded the pair she'd already tried on. "Promise not to tell my dad?"

"You think there's anything on these islands your dad doesn't know?" Eloise asked with a light laugh.

"He doesn't know all the kids at the junior high," Billie said, handing back the shorts.

Eloise gave her the last pair—a white pair with an overlay of lace. They had an elastic waistband, and Billie just pulled them on. They were too big, and they sat way down on her hips in a way Eloise didn't like.

"His name is Jake," Billie said as she twisted and turned to look at the shorts in the mirror. "These aren't right."

"They're too big," Eloise said. "I can get a smaller size."

"No, it's okay," Billie said. "I don't like them very much." She slipped out of them and put on her own pair of black shorts that went to the dress code level of mid-thigh. Eloise needed to start paying attention to the length of shorts other teens wore so she could see if Billie fit in or not.

"So these two?" Eloise asked, picking up the blue and pink pairs as she stood.

"If we can," Billie said. "Let me see the prices." She took the shorts and looked at the tags while Eloise stooped to get the white shorts from the floor. She folded them as Billie asked, "What's thirty percent off of thirty-six?"

"Almost eleven dollars," Eloise said almost immediately.

"How do you do that so fast?" Billie asked, shaking her head. "I'm not great at math."

"I'm sure you're fine at math," Eloise said, though she had no way of knowing. Aaron hadn't told her about his children's grades. "I just do ten percent, because that's easy. Move the decimal and get three-sixty. Then multiply that by three." She stopped talking, because it didn't really matter how she'd done the mental math. "It's actually ten-eighty off. So those will be just over twenty-five dollars."

"I'll almost be out of money," Billie said, as Aaron gave his girls a budget for their school clothes. Three hundred dollars each. Billie had been buying things at a faster rate than Grace, as Grace didn't even really seem to care what she wore to school.

In fact, Billie had been picking out all of her T-shirts and shorts that day.

"What else do you need?" Eloise asked.

"I want some of those sandals that look like beach shoes," she said. "Everyone has them." She opened the dressing room door, and Aaron looked up from his phone.

"How'd it go?" He pocketed his phone and stood. "Find anything good?"

"These," Billie said, handing him the shorts, the pink

pair on top. "Should be about forty dollars, with the discounts."

"You'll have eighteen dollars left," he said, taking the clothes. He lifted the pink shorts to look at the blue ones beneath. "Bills. You can't wear these to school." He looked up, his dark eyes sparking with several things at once. Slight irritation mixed with compassion.

"I know," Billie said. "But I can wear them to parties and the mall and stuff."

"Parties?" Aaron sounded like he'd just inhaled anything but air into his lungs. He coughed, and he looked at Eloise.

She tried to give him an encouraging look. Surely he remembered going to parties as a teenager. Eloise keenly knew he'd gone. She wanted everyone to be happy, and she wanted to volunteer to pay for Billie's shorts. Her shoes too, because she didn't think eighteen dollars would cover them.

"Maybe I could have the rest of Grace's money," Billie said, sidestepping the topic of going to parties. "She has seventy-two dollars left, and she's done."

Grace looked up from her book at the mention of her name.

"That's not how it works, Billie," Aaron said.

"Why not?" Billie asked. "I still need shoes too. Eighteen dollars isn't enough for shoes."

Aaron started toward the check-out counter. "How much are these shorts you can't wear to school?"

"Twenty-five," Billie said, going with him. Eloise extended her hand to Grace, who closed her book and hopped off the chair. She slipped her hand into Eloise's, and they followed too.

She kept one ear on the argument in front of her, hating it. Contention made her so uncomfortable, and she just wanted everyone to be happy. They'd had such a good day so far, and she didn't want to end it on a low note.

Aaron turned to her, and Eloise could hardly believe she was here with him, doing this. It almost felt like a dream.

"What do you think, Eloise?" he asked.

Eloise's pulse got another shot of adrenaline, and her throat turned dry. She looked at Billie, who wore such a look of hope. She knew she couldn't always side with the girls just to get them to like her.

"I don't know," she said, watching Billie's face fall.

Aaron looked at the shorts again. "What kind of shoes, Bills?"

"I need sneakers," she said, still silently pleading with Eloise. "And I want those sandals I've told you about."

Aaron frowned. "Can you get this stuff and both of those with ninety dollars?"

Billie swung her gaze to her father. "You'll give me Grace's money?"

"Both of these?" the clerk asked, and Eloise held her breath.

"Yes," Aaron said, pushing the shorts across the

counter. He turned toward Billie. "I'll give you Grace's money. I can see the two of you have different needs."

"Thanks, Dad." She grabbed onto her father and hugged him, and he met Eloise's eyes over the top of Billie's head.

Eloise smiled and touched her heart with her hand, and Aaron grinned back at her. She loved the silent conversations they could have, and she determined to have a real, out-loud conversation with him later that night, after the girls went to bed.

It would take all of her courage, but as Eloise stood in the clothing store while Aaron handed the clerk his credit card, she fell down the last step of being all the way in love with him.

LATER THAT NIGHT, SHE HELPED HIM WASH THE dishes they'd dirtied by making dinner. Grace skipped down the hall to take a bath. Billie thanked Aaron for the clothes and shoes again and said she was going to go unpack it all and call Addie, her best friend.

Prince had just gone outside, and Eloise felt very much like she would like this to be her reality. A husband. Kids. Even a dog. It was the American dream—and one she'd never thought she'd have, especially with a man like Aaron Sherman.

She linked her arm through his, hoping to let him

know she was interested in spending the night with him. He glanced at her, and she smiled.

"What's in that head of yours, Eloise?" he asked quietly.

She'd never spent the night with him, and she wasn't sure she would tonight either. She'd definitely like to make love to him tonight, even if she had to slip out the door and catch the last ferry back to Sanctuary Island.

It wouldn't be the first time they'd been intimate, but they'd only managed to find a time when the girls weren't around a few times. Eloise wanted more, but she wasn't great at communicating what that was to a man.

"I'm thinking about us," Eloise said. "What are you thinking?"

"About us?"

"Yes." She put the last plate in the dish drainer.

"I like where we are," he said, leaning over to kiss her. The union was quick, and Eloise went back to the sudsy water.

"I'm thinking a little further down the line," she said carefully. She glanced over her shoulder to make sure they were still alone, though both Grace and Billie would be occupied for a while. She handed him the last glass and rinsed her hands in the warm water. "I'm thinking about marriage, Aaron."

He visibly flinched, and that didn't settle Eloise's nerves any.

"Okay," he said slowly.

"Aren't you?" she asked.

"It's crossed my mind," he said, adjusting some dishes in the drainer to make room for the glass. He reached for the towel and dried his hands before facing her. "I just haven't gone too far down that road."

"Why not?" She sincerely hoped it wasn't something they could never achieve.

"My first marriage wasn't great," he said, and she knew that. "I'm not eager to get into something like that again."

Eloise tried not to let the words sting, but they did. The pain of it radiated through her whole body. "I'm not Carol. It wouldn't be the same at all."

"I know," he said, but she didn't think he did. He wrapped her in his arms and lowered his head to kiss her neck. Eloise pressed into the touch, letting her hands drift down his strong arms to his waist. She slid her fingers along the top of his jeans, her message as clear as she could make it.

She brought her mouth to his, and kissing him in the kitchen while his girls were still awake felt scandalous and exciting.

She pulled away, because she wasn't finished talking yet and they couldn't go to bed together right now anyway.

Her courage peaked, and she had to say what was on her mind now or she never would. "I'm in love with you, Aaron. I want to get married." She opened her eyes and met his. They sparkled and flickered with desire, but there was some hesitation and something negative there too.

"Could you think about it a little more? Please?" She pressed her cheek to his so she wouldn't have to keep looking into those eyes and that commanding gaze.

"Yes," he whispered. "I can do that."

"Okay," she said. "One more thing." She drew in a breath, held it for a moment, and then released it. "Do you think it's time for me to stay the night? Or too soon still?"

He pulled away, the surprise in his expression now. "You want to stay the night?"

Eloise practically burned for him, but his surprise shot down her hopes. "Too soon," she said, stepping back. "Okay, let me see what the ferry schedule is." She stepped out of his arms, wishing he'd tell her she didn't need to do that, that of course she should stay with him, and he'd make love to her all night long.

Instead, he stepped over to the sliding glass door and let Prince back inside. He went down the hall to check on Grace. When he came back into the kitchen, he came right over to her and took her phone from her hands.

"The last ferry is at ten-fifty," she said. "I need to leave here at ten-twenty-five."

"No." He took her into his arms and kissed her. This touch had a brand-new feeling to it, and she matched him stroke for stroke as he deepened the kiss, almost fighting him for control of it.

He pulled away and sucked in a breath, then said, "You're staying right here with me tonight." He moved his delicious, powerful mouth to her neck, and Eloise leaned her head back and held onto his shoulders as he kissed her.

He growled and lifted her onto the counter behind her, and she whispered, "Your kids." Aaron brought his head up. Their eyes met, and Eloise giggled as he smiled, the look in his eyes absolute perfection.

He was hungry for her, and Eloise couldn't wait until Billie and Grace went to bed.

"Dad," Billie said, and Aaron spun around. Eloise slipped off the counter, turned back to the sink, and ran her hand through her hair in one fluid motion.

"Yeah?" Aaron left the kitchen in a hurry as Billie asked him about going to get ice cream with Addie and Brandon the following night.

Hours later, she felt cherished under his touch, and he whispered, "Eloise?"

"Hmm?"

"I love you."

She stilled, and when he kissed her this time, it was a whole new type of kiss that reminded Eloise of a slow, summer evening, where nothing could be rushed and there was nothing to do but make love to a beautiful man.

CHAPTER ELEVEN

Kelli tugged at the bottom of her blouse, her nerves like a tangible being in front of her. They sounded like the beating of insect wings inside her head, and she hoped she'd hear the secretary call her name when it was her turn to interview for the teacher's aide position.

Robin had gotten Parker registered for school last week, and he'd gone to his first day that morning. She'd been looking for a job since the dinnervention, as the cove had beach yoga studios that were sitting empty. She didn't want to wait for the business license and then start drumming up her own business.

She just needed a job, and she needed one face. She'd already had a couple of other interviews, which meant she'd missed the Wednesday lunch with Robin, Alice, Eloise last week, and she'd told Eloise she couldn't come help with the inn that day because of this interview.

She really wanted to help her friend with the Cliffside Inn, and she'd been up there once for about an hour to help Eloise hang the curtains in the caretaker's suite.

But she really needed a job, and Eloise had said to take care of herself first. Kelli was trying to do that, despite the number of times Julian had called since she'd left New Jersey.

Apparently, he'd thought she'd only been kidding. He'd been surprised when she hadn't returned last weekend so Parker could start fourth grade at the elementary school he'd been attending since kindergarten.

She'd asked him if he was going to break-up with Tiffany, and when he'd said no, she'd said, "Then I'm staying in Five Island Cove. That is not a lifestyle I'm interested in, Julian."

"You're giving up on us," he'd said.

Those words had ignited an anger in her that still burned even now, days later. *She* was not the one who'd gone out and found someone else to love. Julian had dictated everything in their marriage from the very first day they'd said I-do, and Kelli hadn't had any power over her own life in far too long.

"Kelli Watkins?" the secretary called, and Kelli pushed her thoughts away. They only poisoned her mind and heart, and that was the last thing she needed right now.

She put a smile on her face, stood, and shouldered her

purse. "Good morning," she said to the woman, though she'd checked in with her twenty minutes ago.

"Dr. Pratt is ready for you." She led Kelli through the door and down a short hall to the principal's office. Everything in the junior high felt clinical. There were no posters like she'd seen in the elementary school. Even the people seemed more serious, and Kelli wiped the smile from her face as she entered the office.

Dr. Pratt was a tall woman, easily a size ten, and Kelli connected to her immediately because she wasn't rail-thin. "Good morning," the woman said, though she didn't stand or really look at Kelli at all.

"Kelli Watkins for the English attendant," the secretary said, placing a paper on Dr. Pratt's desk.

"Thank you, Barb." Dr. Pratt finally looked away from her computer and picked up the paper. "Sorry," she said. "Excuse my distraction; I'm dealing with a representative from the school board, and I have to watch for his email."

She looked at Kelli then, her face brightening with a smile. "You grew up on Five Island Cove?"

"Yes, ma'am," Kelli said. "Bell Island. My mother still lives there."

"You've been teaching yoga for nine years."

"Yes," Kelli said. "In New Jersey."

Dr. Pratt didn't ask her what brought her back to Five Island Cove, and a measure of relief tore through Kelli. She did ask about college, and why she wanted to work at the junior high.

Kelli hadn't been to college, and she glossed over that part of her history quickly. "Honestly," she said. "I have a nine-year-old son in fourth grade that I'm bringing to Diamond Island every morning. I'd like to find a job here with similar hours to his school schedule, so I don't have to ask my mother to watch him." Or anyone else. "And you had several jobs open. I can do any of them, Dr. Pratt. I learn fast, and I'm smart, even if I didn't go to college."

She forced herself to stop talking. But she wanted the woman to know she was serious about the job. Her first couple of interviews hadn't gone well, because she'd spent too long talking about her weaknesses and not her strengths. Alice had told her last night to say she was smart and could learn, "because you are, Kelli, and you can. Lead with what's amazing about you."

Dr. Pratt smiled and nodded. "Of that, I have no doubt, Kelli. And you don't have to call me ma'am." She glanced at her computer again, sighed, and stood. "I think you'd be amazing in our CCHE class, if you're game to do something besides English."

"I'm game," Kelli said, standing too. "What's CCHE?"

"Computers, Career, and Home Economics," Dr. Pratt said. "The teacher does four or five units; one on coding, one on cooking and foods, one on personality testing for careers, one on personal finances and family. Things like that."

Kelli could probably learn a lot in a class like that, and she wasn't in junior high. "Sure," she said.

"The teacher is Mrs. Hewes, and she's got a lot going on." Dr. Pratt led Kelli down a hall, made some turns, went up some stairs, and down another hall. Kelli wouldn't be able to get out of the building without a map, despite having attended the school thirty-plus years ago.

"Hyedi," Dr. Pratt said, upon opening the door. An elderly woman set a cookie sheet down on the mock kitchen counter and turned toward the door. All the students did too, and Kelli suddenly felt so out of place in her pencil skirt and blouse—the nicest clothes she owned. She'd bought them with her credit card three days ago, because up until now, her work wardrobe had consisted of tight leggings, sports bras, and tank tops.

She tried to smile, but she wasn't quite sure she pulled it off.

"This is Miss Watkins," Dr. Pratt said. "She's going to shadow you for a class period or two and see if she'd like to be your assistant this year." She beamed from Mrs. Hewes and back to Kelli, nodded, and started to step past Kelli again. "Good luck, Miss Watkins. Come find me before you leave and let me know if you still want the job."

She'd taken one step through the door when Kelli came to her senses. "Wait," she said, interrupting Mrs. Hewes, who'd gone on with her lesson. She held up her hand in apology and ducked out into the hall with Dr. Pratt.

"Come find you?"

"If you want the job, it's yours," Dr. Pratt said. "But

you really should sit through a class period or two to see what you'll be dealing with."

Kelli swallowed and nodded. "Okay." She squared her shoulders as she faced the door again. Dr. Pratt's heels clicked down the hall away from her as Kelli reached for the door handle.

She needed a job. She'd take it without attending a couple of classes, because no one else was calling. How hard could CCHE be?

She opened the door and stepped back inside to find the students had gotten up from the chairs facing the demo kitchen and were now grouped together in their own kitchens.

As Kelli stood there, Mrs. Hewes hobbled over to her and said, "They're making oatmeal chocolate chip cookies today," in a high-pitched, feeble voice. "We just go around and make sure they don't light anything on fire."

Kelli looked at her with alarm pulling through her. The older woman didn't seem to be joking, and a boy called, "Mrs. H, we've got a problem here," and off the lady bustled to see what it was.

Kelli went with her, because she might as well see what she was dealing with before she accepted the job.

————

"It was *insane*," Kelli said later that night. She smiled and shook her head as Alice opened a bagged salad.

Her daughter, Ginny, had put together a pot of pasta with shrimp and crawfish, and a moment later, she said, "Let's eat."

"Baking soda everywhere," Kelli continued. "One girl managed to light paper towels on fire when she tried to use them as oven mitts." Kelli picked up a plate and held it out for Ginny to serve her. She smiled at the girl. "Thanks, Ginny."

"When I took Foods," she said. "There was this boy in my class who literally lit everything on fire."

"You're kidding."

"The teacher put him on making lemonade once, and he managed to char a lemon to—he said—add depth of flavor." She giggled and shook her head. "He was hopeless in the kitchen."

"So a lot like me," Alice said with a smile. She put down the tongs she'd been using to serve herself some salad. "I can open a bag of salad though, so that's something."

"David probably would've left it on the stove and melted the plastic bag," Ginny said, serving her twin brother.

"Some boys do it on purpose," Charlie said. "They're idiots."

"Oh, because you're so mature?" Ginny asked.

"I know enough to do really well in stuff like Foods," he said with a smile.

"Why's that?" Alice asked, a slightly narrowed squint

on her eyes.

"Because," Charlie said, taking a very small tong-full of salad. "That's where the girls decide if you're worth dating or not."

Ginny burst out laughing, and Alice rolled her eyes.

"What?" Charlie asked, smiling too. "I'm not stupid. Girls are *so* judgmental, and they all want a guy who can cook." He shrugged. "I didn't make the rules. I just try to play by them when it comes to the ladies."

"Okay, never say *ladies* again," Ginny said.

"Okay, never hold Robbie's hand again," Charlie shot back, glancing from Ginny to Alice.

Kelli enjoyed the banter as she put some pasta on Parker's plate and helped him get some salad too. She watched Alice shoot Charlie a look that said *stop it*, and she noticed the way Ginny clammed right up.

So there was something going on with a boy named Robbie. Kelli did not envy Alice—or anyone with teenagers. She'd take her quiet eight-year-old any day of the week, that was for sure.

The five of them sat down to dinner, and Kelli looked at Alice and her twins. "Thanks for having us," she said.

"Sure," Alice said.

"The Internet guy is coming tomorrow," Kelli said. "Then we'll be out of your hair." The truth was, she hadn't invaded Alice's family since moving into the beach house last week. But she didn't have the Internet yet, and she needed to do some heavy research that required more than what she could do on her phone.

After dinner, she sent Parker out to the pool with Ginny and Charlie, and Alice said she could go into the office and use the computer for as long as she wanted.

Kelli didn't want Alice to think she wasn't welcome to sit with her, but she didn't invite her in.

"I have a case I need to review," Alice said. "I'll be in my front office." She glided away, turning right and heading toward the foyer, where her giant "front office" stood.

Kelli's whole house—which did not have even one home office, let alone two—could've fit in Alice's kitchen, dining room, and living room.

She hadn't had any of her friends over yet, because she was still treading water and trying to keep her head above the tide. She would eventually, though with just the three of them, plus Kelli and Parker, and the house would be full. If Robin and Alice brought their children, and Eloise brought Aaron and his girls, they wouldn't fit at all.

Kelli supposed that was what the beachfront was for. They could easily set up tables and chairs out there—if she owned any tables and chairs.

She closed the door behind her and woke the computer. If anyone came in, they'd be able to see what she was looking at on the giant screen. She thought Alice had done that on purpose, so she could walk in and see what her teenagers were doing at any moment on the computer.

Kelli felt more exposed than she'd like, but she'd taken the ferry here and interrupted Alice's dinner with her twins for a very specific purpose.

She'd done some rudimentary searches on Zach Watkins and as many variations of the name that she could think of. Zachary. Zackary. Zach and Zack. She'd even taken the K off, and then the C out.

On her phone, she hadn't been able to find anything linking any version of his name to her father's name. She'd seen the birth certificate he'd produced a few months ago, but she hadn't kept it. She hadn't even made a copy of it.

Aaron Sherman had seen it too, as had Kelli's friends, but she hadn't asked any of them what they remembered about it.

She knew her father's name had been left off of it, and Zach had claimed that his mother had only told him who his biological father was, because she was now in a nursing home in Maine.

Kelli pulled a small notebook out of her purse and got to work. She needed to figure out who Zach really was, where he'd really come from, and what to do about him.

She hadn't pressed charges or filed a complaint against him, so Aaron had kept him until he was sober, and then he'd released him. As far as she knew, he was right back in that apartment above the Chinese restaurant.

Kelli hadn't tried to contact him again; he hadn't tried to call or text her. He'd stayed away from her mother.

"You should let this go," she told herself. Something nagged in the back of her mind, and she needed to know what his end game was. She needed to protect her mother, herself, and her son.

She put in the search terms to find the art curators at galleries in Maine and started combing through them. A lot of the nicer places had full-color photographs, and several listed their previous curators of larger collections.

She got lost in the art for several minutes, finally pulling herself away from the Dead Sea Scrolls at a coastal museum, and the watercolor butterfly collection at a gallery on the border of Maine and Canada. She reminded herself what she was doing—and that she was almost out of time.

Zach had found out about the Glassworks somehow. She leaned back and closed her eyes, trying to remember everything about him, as well as everything they'd ever talked about.

His mother was getting older. She was in a nursing home. His aunt had given him the letters from their father from the house. He'd been an art curator and loved to sculpt.

She switched gears and put in her father's name along with the word *Zach*.

Pictures always came up at the top of the search, and for the most part, Kelli had ignored those whenever she did Internet searches. She wasn't interested in images or videos—until she saw her father's smiling face.

She froze, her heart pounding like a tribal drum. It boomed in her ears, and she physically felt it vibrating through her body.

Her father had left Five Island Cove before his death, and he'd done a lot of things off-island before that. He'd been commissioned for big glass pieces in New York City and the White House.

She'd seen a couple of the photos before, because her father had been so proud of his appearance at the White House, and when she clicked on the one of Guy Watkins and the President of the United States, she could feel her father's pride coming right through the screen.

He'd told her that story so many times, and she wondered what he'd seen in these pictures after he'd lost everything in the cove.

"After Joel Shields ruined him," Kelli said, her voice full of bitterness. As quickly as it had come, it fled, and Kelli clicked away from the picture she'd seen many times.

She clicked on the word *images* and let them load. There were plenty she hadn't seen, including several of her father hiding his face as he got into cars or holding a newspaper over his head to shield himself from the cameras as he went through a doorway and into a brick building somewhere, in some city.

The headlines hadn't been kind to him, that was for sure, and now that Kelli knew more about what had really happened with his business and the Glassworks, she wondered what he'd felt during those last years of his life.

If it had happened to her, she'd want the world to know that nothing they'd thought was really true. Yet she saw no attempts by her father to set the record straight. None whatsoever.

She scrolled down, scanning the pictures. They started to be about other Guy's and other Watkins's and maybe even other Zach's.

Then her eye caught on a photograph with three people she recognized.

A younger version of her father.

Zach Watkins—almost exactly as Kelli could picture him in her mind.

Rueben Shields—Kristen's son, who now lived in the cove with his wife and ran the lighthouse.

Kelli sucked in a breath, but other than that, she couldn't move. Her mind raced.

She needed to print this picture, and she managed to right-click on it and send it to Alice's printer.

Then she clicked on the picture to get the article open. The headline read *Local architect partners with renowned artist and art student.*

It wasn't hard to assign roles to the three men in the picture. Rueben had been an architect in Charleston for a few years. Zach was obviously the art student. Her father, the renowned artist.

She scanned the article, learning that the three of

them had worked on a new children's wing in the public library, and she sent that article to print too.

Zach's name had been listed as Zach Oakwood, not Zach Watkins.

He'd lied.

She had no idea why he'd had to follow her from New Jersey in June, spewing some story about being her half-brother. Her father was dead; she couldn't ask him. Zach had attacked her in the street; she'd promised Aaron she'd stay away from him.

As she gathered the papers from the printer, she knew she had to get to the lighthouse as soon as she could.

CHAPTER TWELVE

A lice took pictures of the three checks she'd been given for her last three cases that had all wrapped up within days of each other.

She sat at her oversized desk in her law office, the air conditioner humming as she tapped through the app to deposit her money.

She'd promised Eloise she'd come help at the Cliffside Inn that morning, and she'd just finished up Louise's power of attorney and her will, adding them both to the woman's portal.

If she left in the next five minutes, she'd make the ten-oh-five ferry, and she'd be right on time to meet Robin at the ferry station. They could share a ride up to the inn, and that would save Alice some money.

She hated that she had to think about saving money at all, and a breath of relief moved through her as the deposits finished loading and she got a confirmation message on her screen.

It had been so long since she'd worried about money that she'd forgotten what the constant stress of that looked and felt like. The past few months had definitely re-introduced that back into her life, and while Alice didn't like it, she was willing to deal with it over being married to Frank.

As it was, she couldn't believe she'd stayed with him as long as she had. She was rebuilding her pride one day at a time, but the truth was, that was taking longer than she'd like.

She had supreme confidence in her ability to argue for her clients' rights. She couldn't believe she'd turned such a blind eye to Frank's infidelity for so long, or how much it was affecting her now.

How little did she think of herself to put up with that? What had been so amazing about Frank? Had the money, the big house, the prestige of being PTA President, been worth it?

Alice shook her head to get the thoughts to go. She needed to see a counselor, but they cost money, and while Frank had upheld his end of the divorce decrees, she didn't quite have the money to pay for therapy. Not yet.

She needed to get going, and she stood as she tapped to exit the deposit portion of the banking app. She hadn't been removed from the joint account yet, and she hadn't expected to be—Frank transferred his alimony and child support through their bank accounts.

She had a personal savings account, her personal checking account, where she'd just deposited her checks, and the joint checking Frank had left in her name.

He had access to her personal savings and the joint checking, but not her personal checking.

"These aren't right," she said, sitting back down as she stared at the numbers on the screen.

She'd gotten a notification last night about the large deposit in her personal savings. Frank had transferred that month's money. She'd left it, because she could move it later, when she needed to pay the bills.

It was all gone.

"*More* is gone," she said, tapping to open the account. She tried to keep a few hundred dollars in there as a small cushion, but the account balance was below one hundred dollars.

The last two transactions were telling. The second-to-last had been Frank depositing the monthly amount to pay for the house on Rocky Ridge, the cars, her alimony, and the child support, as agreed.

The last transaction was a transfer of that amount, plus an additional three hundred dollars that did not belong to Frank.

Alice peered at the transaction numbers, trying to make sense of them. It looked like the money had gone right back to the checking account it had originated from, and Alice tapped back to her main screen, her throat so narrow she couldn't swallow.

What had Frank done? Without that money, she couldn't pay for anything this month.

She tried to breathe in slowly as she waited for the absurdly slow Internet to work on her complex app. It finally loaded, and she tapped on their joint checking account.

Sure enough, the last two transactions were the same she'd seen in her account, simply reversed. Frank had paid the monthly amount, and then taken it back, plus three hundred dollars.

He had not texted. He hadn't called. There had been no explanation at all.

Acting quickly, before she could second-guess anything, Alice transferred the money back to her account and then called the bank.

"Yes," she said. "I need to make sure my ex-husband can't remove money from my personal savings account. How can I do that?"

Twenty minutes later, Alice had severed the connection between her personal savings and the joint account she shared with Frank.

She was late getting to Sanctuary Island now, and as she left the house, she called Frank. He didn't answer, of course, not that Alice had expected him to.

"Frank," she said crisply. "It's Alice, and I need to talk to you about the finances. Call me back as your earliest convenience."

She hung up, wishing she'd told him to call her back as

soon as possible. She didn't care if it was convenient for him. Nothing about their arrangement was all that convenient for her, and he didn't care. She'd left plenty of money in the joint checking account. So much that she should seriously file a petition with the judge in New York to get more of it. Frank was obviously still doing very well with his firm, and there was no reason for him to take any of her money.

She stewed on the situation the whole way to Sanctuary Island, but by the time the RideShare driver pulled up to the Cliffside Inn, Alice had buried the troubling transactions as deeply as they would go.

"There you are," Robin said when Alice walked through the front doors. She pushed her sweaty bangs back off her forehead. "I just got your texts a couple of minutes ago, though I assume you sent them a while ago."

"Yeah," Alice said, stepping in and giving Robin a quick hug. "Sorry, I had a couple of extra things to do this morning, and I didn't get out of the house on time."

"I wish I had a couple of extra things to do," Robin said, glancing over her shoulder. "Eloise isn't getting the air conditioning fixed until next week."

"That's the soonest they could come," Eloise said as she came out of the room just inside the front door. "I have fans."

Alice beamed at her friend and hugged Eloise too. "Things are looking better and better every time I come," she said as she stepped back and looked around at the little of the inn she could see.

Eloise blinked and then burst out laughing. "You're so full of it," she said amidst her giggles. "It just gets worse and worse as the days go by. Aaron came over the weekend, and he looked like I'd hit him with one of the pipes I pulled out of the bathroom."

"She's right," Robin said. "It's a huge mess."

"We have to demo it all to get it ready to fix up," Eloise said. "Today, we're finishing this front room, which I'm going to convert to an upscale lobby and breakfast nook." She turned back to the room, and Alice followed her.

"What used to be in here?" she asked, taking in the piles of stuff in the middle of the room. The wallpaper had been stripped from the walls, and the carpet in half the room had been ripped up to reveal some wood floors underneath.

"It was part of a family suite," Eloise said. "There were three beds in here." She put her hands on her hips and sighed. "So I'll have one less room, but no one rented this suite very often. I think a lobby and breakfast bar will be better. In the hours during check-in, I'm going to have hot teas, coffees, and chocolates. Freshly baked cookies. Local artisans who can come give samples. I've already talked to Jane Byrd, and she's going to bring her salted caramels. She can give out samples and have gift boxes and bags to sell. She's excited." Eloise looked at Alice and Robin, and Alice could see the excitement on Eloise's face too.

How she had the vision for the rooms in the inn, Alice didn't know. When she looked in the room, she just saw ruin and junk. She had no idea how to transform it from what it was into something else.

Eloise did, though, and Alice could pick up whatever she was told and haul it outside. She could help pull a carpet roll all the way back. She could make trip after trip to a Dumpster with armfuls of ancient wallpaper.

"Are you moved in to the caretaker's suite?" Robin asked.

"Yes," Eloise said, glancing at them. She looked away again, and Robin swung her gaze to Alice. Her eyebrows went up as if to say, *Did you see that?*

Yes, Alice had seen it. "How did shopping go with Aaron and the girls last week?" Alice asked. "We haven't had lunch yet to get all the news."

"No news," Eloise said. "It went really great. Billie asked me to come into the dressing room with her, and I didn't undermine Aaron by siding with her instead of him."

"That's all news," Robin said, plenty of encouragement in her voice. "That's great, Eloise."

"Did you ask him about you know," Alice said. "Your future?"

Eloise stepped away from the group and bent to pick up a fake plant. A groan came out of her mouth, and Alice barely had time to exchange another look with Robin before Eloise turned to face them. "Yes," she said. "It was okay." She took the plant past them as if she'd take it outside and leave them there.

Robin nudged Alice, who glared back at her. "Your turn," she hissed.

"No," Alice whispered back. "Let her have a minute. She'll tell us when she's ready."

"Have you met Eloise?" Robin asked.

"If it was bad, she'd have texted us," Alice argued. She hadn't heard from Eloise—other than to set the time and date to come help with the inn this week—since last week.

Robin sighed and went to pick up the ugliest lamp Alice had ever seen. "Fine. Pick something up and lets go."

Alice grabbed a box of old light bulbs, a statue of Poseidon, and a box full of pamphlets that were probably from 1982. She went outside with the other two women to find Eloise on her way back in.

"You don't have first rights of refusal," Alice said, almost out of the corner of her mouth. "Robin wants the news."

"Okay," Eloise said, but she didn't slow down or stop.

They hauled out the entire pile of junk in the main room before Eloise even slowed down. "Come get something to drink," she said. "I have shrimp salad from Mort's too."

"Mort's?" Robin asked. "When did you get that?"

"This morning," Eloise said. She led them through the inn to the back door, down the steps, and over to the entrance to the caretaker's suite. She could get to it from the kitchen in the inn too, but Eloise claimed she didn't like going that way. Apparently, the floor was covered in an unknown substance, and she didn't want to track that into her house.

Alice, the last one through the door, paused and looked around. "Wow, Eloise. This is amazing."

"Isn't it?" Eloise beamed around at the small space. She'd pulled up the carpet here too. All of the mold had been removed. A fresh coat of bright white paint shone down from the walls and ceiling.

To Alice's left sat a built-in counter that ran the length of the wall. A new dishwasher, stove, sink, and fridge punctuated the countertop, and Eloise had put in a temporary breakfast bar with two barstools to separate the kitchen area from the living area.

A couch sat in front of the windows, with an armchair facing the wall, which had built-in bookcases. A TV sat on the shelf there, along with several of Eloise's trinkets and pictures.

"Kelli came and helped with the curtains," Eloise said. "Aren't they cute?"

"They sure are," Robin said.

Alice admired the red-and-white striped curtains too. "They remind me of a lighthouse."

"Exactly," Eloise said, smiling. "Come eat."

They followed her into the kitchen nook while she told them about the single bedroom and bathroom, which were down a short hall and also remodeled.

"Do you like living here?" Alice asked. "It's pretty far from anyone else."

"Sure," Eloise said, that false note in her voice another giveaway that she was hiding something. She served the shrimp salad and got out cans of diet cola and bottled lemonade.

Alice loved everything about the caretaker's suite. It screamed Eloise—the whole inn did—and she experienced a moment of joy for her friend.

"How's Aaron?" she asked, and Robin nodded as she took a bite of her salad.

"He's good," Eloise said. "He admitted that he wasn't too keen to rush into another marriage."

"Rush?" Robin asked. "Come on, Aaron."

Eloise smiled at her. "I was a little annoyed with him, I'll admit." She took a bite of her shrimp salad too. "I understand where he's coming from, but I'm not his ex-wife."

"Exactly," Robin said. She looked at Alice, but Alice didn't have anything to say. Robin had never been divorced. She didn't know how she'd feel. Eloise had been divorced, but it had been twenty years ago. She'd had plenty of time to heal and move on.

"Perhaps he's not ready," Alice said quietly.

"It's on his mind now," Eloise said. "Which is good. I don't need to push him. I just needed to know where he was."

"And you're happy with where he is?" Alice asked, scooping up another forkful of her salad.

Eloise nodded, her face taking on a pink hue and a glow. "I've actually been staying with him for a couple of nights now."

Robin choked and coughed, her face turning red too. "Eloise," she gasped, reaching for a can of soda. She popped the top and drank, putting on quite the show.

Eloise actually rolled her eyes, but Alice just watched them both.

Robin lowered her can. "You're staying the night?" She looked from Eloise to Alice and back. "All night? Like, you have a toothbrush and stuff in his house?"

"Yes," Eloise said.

"What do the girls say?" Robin asked, her lunch completely forgotten, though Mort's made some of the best shrimp salad on the planet.

"Aaron takes Billie to school in the morning," Eloise said. "She hasn't said anything about it to me. He's spoken to them. I take Grace to the elementary school, and then I come here to work." She forked another bite of seafood into her mouth. "If we've agreed to get together, I go back there in the evening."

"Are you—?" Robin cut off, and Alice hoped it was because her question was far too personal.

"He's amazing," Eloise said with a sigh. "I told him I loved him last week." She looked down at the counter, pure happiness streaming from her. "He said it back."

"Oh, my goodness," Robin said, pressing one hand to her heartbeat. "Eloise!" She squealed and went around the breakfast bar to embrace Eloise. "I'm so happy for you. You deserve the very best, and Aaron is perfect for you." They hopped a little, and Alice's guilt and jealousy started to tornado together inside her.

She hadn't been planning to tell them about Frank's antics with the money, but this only solidified that decision. Of course she was happy for Eloise. *Of course* she was.

When Robin started around the breakfast bar again, Alice stepped over to Eloise. "Congratulations, El," she said, much quieter than Robin. "I agree with Robin. He is perfect for you, and you've waited a long time for someone like him." She pulled away and looked into Eloise's eyes. Thankfully, she was well-versed enough to bury anything she didn't want anyone to see, and Alice felt certain Eloise didn't detect any of her jealousy, resentment, or guilt.

"Okay," Eloise said. She inhaled deeply. "Has anyone heard what Kelli is doing? We're still doing our Wednesday lunches, right?"

Kristen.

Alice seized onto the name, because she needed someone she could confide in. Eloise and Robin would happily take whatever Alice had to tell them about Frank. Anything she wanted to unload about Ginny's new *senior* boyfriend, or life, or her law practice. She knew that.

For some reason, Alice didn't want to give them one

more thing to feel bad for her about. The last time all of the Seafaring Girls had gotten together, she'd been a complete wreck. She'd lost a ton of weight, and she'd disappeared after returning from New York to find her friends had forgotten about her.

That hadn't been true, and Alice still felt silly about it. Robin and Eloise didn't need to know about the money issues. Not yet.

Alice didn't even know if there *were* any money issues to tell them about.

She could talk to Kristen though, and she determined to call the woman who had been like a mother to her the moment she left the inn.

CHAPTER THIRTEEN

"I'm taking the weekend off," Eloise grumbled to herself as she stretched up to peel off another piece of disgusting, dated wallpaper.

Thankfully, the old stuff had given up the fight pretty easily, and it was really just a matter of her going through the motions of pulling it all down.

At only five-foot-three, she wasn't tall enough to reach the ceilings, and she hated climbing up and down on the step stools and chairs she'd been using. She had lost ten pounds in the past two weeks since starting work on the inn, so she supposed that was a positive.

She certainly felt sexier as she dressed to go out with Aaron, and when he undressed her...Eloise was very happy for the reduced waistline and a bit more muscle in her core and arms.

Her mind wandered along the path where Aaron was,

and bit by bit, the room lost the flowers and stripes her father had once loved. She normally tossed everything in a huge garbage bin in the middle of the room, but she didn't stress out if she missed. There was always stuff to pick up and place in the bin, and she sometimes had to empty it in order to be able to lift it and take it out to the main Dumpster.

She'd upgraded that to getting emptied three times a week since her progress on the inn was moving faster than she'd anticipated. With Robin, Alice, and Kelli coming to help, they'd been able to clean out almost all of the rooms now.

Eloise had two left on the second floor, and after she took all the trash out of the room where she'd spent the morning, she set up her trash can, her Bluetooth speaker, and a fresh bottle of ice-cold water in the second-to-last guest room that needed to be demolished.

She'd had a plumbing expert out to the inn yesterday, and he was supposed to be texting her a bid to upgrade all the pipes, put in another water heater, and make sure the pool lines were up to code. She hadn't gotten it yet, and she hope it wouldn't put a massive dent in her remodeling budget.

On Monday, she had a meeting with a master electrician, as the inn had been built eighty years ago, added to, and then taken care of by her father, who read manuals to know how to wire things.

Eloise didn't want to go to bed at night with the worry

of something sparking behind the walls and lighting the whole inn on fire. Everything she'd been paying for over the past sixteen years would go up in flames, and Eloise reminded herself that she needed to call for commercial insurance too.

"Monday," she told herself as she went downstairs again. She hadn't tackled the kitchen yet, as it needed the most work, and she figured she could get the rooms cleaned out and repairmen in to work on those while she then turned her attention to things like the kitchen, the outdoor grills, the swimming pool, and the outdoor volley-ball court.

She'd completely forgotten about that gem, and it sat down a set of steps on another terraced level that over-looked the ocean below. She needed to put up nets, because she could see many volleyballs going over the edge of the cliffs and being lost forever.

If that area could be used, she'd also need to put up a ten-foot wall, so people couldn't go over the side too. The last thing she needed was to be responsible for the death of a teenager trying to get a ball to win the point.

Eloise pushed those thoughts out of her head. It was much too hard to keep everything she needed to do on a list in her mind. She had physical checklists for that, and she looked at them each day, made adjustments, and focused on what she could do in eight or nine hours.

The end.

Anything else would drive her past the brink of madness, and Eloise didn't want that.

She hadn't stayed with Aaron since Tuesday, when she'd had Robin and Alice to the inn to help. She'd gone to lunch with them on Wednesday, but Kelli couldn't come, because she'd taken a job at the junior high.

Alice had come yesterday morning to help at the inn, and Robin had come in the afternoon. Both of them seemed distracted, but Eloise didn't mind.

They worked hard, and it was nice to have a companion there with her. Plus, they didn't ask about Aaron when they were distracted with the details of their own lives.

Eloise didn't have any more answers when it came to Aaron. She'd called him Tuesday night after her friends had left and said she was going to stay at her inn. He hadn't acted strange about it at all.

He'd just said, "Okay, El. When will I see you again?"

She liked that he'd asked that. She also knew he was terribly busy with back-to-school, because there was always something they'd forgotten to buy. Notebooks, pens, socks. He had all of his men and women out to make sure school zones were safe and ferry stations were manned for those kids who had to travel in from the outer islands alone.

Billie had been texting Eloise that week to say how things had gone at junior high. Eloise smiled just thinking about the thirteen-year-old. She'd asked for a first-day-of-school picture, and Billie had sent her a selfie in the bathroom mirror. She'd worn the pink pair of shorts with a cap-sleeve, tie-dyed T-shirt. Eloise couldn't believe tie-dye was back in fashion, but it sure seemed to be.

She'd asked Billie about her classes, and she got long texts about who was in them with her, what the teachers were like, and what she thought would be hard or easy.

Eloise loved the girl a little bit more every day, and her heart squeezed with impatience.

She compartmentalized those feelings as she pulled out a salad she hadn't eaten with her pizza last night. She'd learned to order more than she could eat, because then she had lunch the next day.

Thirty minutes later, Eloise returned to the second floor and started pulling down more wallpaper. The fan in the room barely put a dent in the heat, but she'd learned to simply sweat all day and shower away the stickiness at night.

She pulled off one piece and found a huge depression in the wall. "Great," she muttered to herself. That was one risk she took by demo-ing everything to replace it. Unknown damage could be found.

She bent down to examine the wall, and it crumbled beneath her touch. She started ripping it away, tossing the soft drywall over her shoulder. She'd have to pick it up piece by piece later, so she got up and dragged the garbage can closer.

She yanked on one portion of the wall, and a big

chunk came off, revealing a clean edge. "Someone's cut into this wall," she said to herself, examining the edge.

Her eyes followed it up and easily found the top of it. Beneath a fold in the sheetrock, she found a hinge.

This was a hidden a compartment in the wall.

Eloise stood, her heart pounding. Her mind raced as she tried to recall what had been in this room.

As far as she knew, it was just a guest room. Her father had kept safes in the main office for valuables, so there was no reason for a hidden compartment in the wall—behind the wallpaper—in a guest room.

Eloise's pulse calmed as she asked herself what she expected to find. "A dead body?"

She took a deep breath, trying to imagine the worst thing she could find hidden in the wall.

"Definitely a dead body," she said again, and she got down on her knees and switched on the flashlight on her phone.

With that, she peered inside and found the outline of a wooden box. Gingerly, as if the box would come alive and bite her, she reached inside and pulled it out.

In the brighter sunlight, she examined it. The box was about the size of a large jewelry box, but somehow, Eloise was sure she wouldn't find anything like bracelets or diamonds inside.

The lid creaked as she opened it, and she noticed there was no lock or clasp on the box at all.

Eloise peered inside the box, her heart still pounding

at a rapid pace. Old, yellowed envelopes sat in the box, and she saw the tremble in her fingers as she reached into the box and pulled them out.

A yelp came out of her mouth as a spider scuttled across the top envelope, and she threw the whole stack away from her.

She fell backward onto her tailbone, and pain shot up her spine. She braced herself with her hands and paused, taking in lungful after lungful of air.

"It's fine, Eloise," she told herself. "It was a spider."

She got up and gathered the envelopes, reading the names on them as she did.

Stevenson Ranch.

Galveston Distillery.

Proffit Beach Property.

Coilstone Cabin.

In all, there were seven envelopes, and each bore a name. She opened the first one and pulled out several pieces of stapled paperwork. She wasn't a lawyer or real estate agent by any means, but she knew enough to read and understand a contract when she saw one.

"This is a property," she said, her voice so loud despite the music still playing from the windowsill. Gary Stevenson owned a ranch in Montana—or he had until he'd signed it over to Eloise's father.

The transfer of ownership paperwork was pinched right there in her hands.

The date was 1997.

Her father's name was listed as the beneficiary.

"This makes no sense," she said, flipping the pages. Gary Stevenson had signed the last page, with her father's handwriting below it.

She stared at his signature, because she hadn't seen anything of his like this in a long time.

She couldn't identify the feelings moving through her. Shock, disbelief, anger.

Her father had acquired all of these properties, and she needed to go through the guest register and see if these people had stayed at the inn.

Her memory fired, and Eloise looked up from the sheaf of paperwork that had made a ranch in Montana— somewhere Eloise had never been, and she was sure her father had never been—his.

A line from his will ran through her mind.

Except the Cliffside Inn, all properties, accounts, and investments, I leave to my daughter, Eloise Hall.

She'd gotten his bank account, which at the time, had thirteen hundred dollars in it. With the inn specifically being left out, Eloise had simply gifted the house to her mother and moved on with her college career. She'd bought the inn a year later, and she could admit it was mostly out of spite. Her father hadn't seemed to want her to have it, but she'd gotten it anyway.

But if these were his properties too...

She refolded the papers and put them back in the

envelope. Every one she opened had the same contract, but a different name and a different property.

He owned a cabin in Utah, a beachfront property in South Carolina, a whiskey distillery in Kentucky, a horse farm in Texas, a vacation rental in the San Juan Islands, and what looked like a large parcel of undeveloped land on Rocky Ridge.

Eloise looked up. She needed to talk to Alice. She'd be able to help her make sense of all of this.

"Alice."

Eloise returned her attention to the undeveloped land on Rocky Ridge. With horror, she realized it was no longer undeveloped.

Alice's house was within that parcel of land, as were several other houses.

Confusion filled her mind. What had the ranch, the distillery, the vacation property, and all the other things in these envelopes been doing for over two decades?

If her father owned them, wouldn't they be vacant? Abandoned? Deteriorated?

She shook her head and slipped the Rocky Ridge paperwork back into its envelope. The last one said Oakwood IOU, and Eloise's chest pinched.

She reached into the envelope, noting that it was much thinner than the others. Only two pages came out, and Eloise read that a man named Karl Oakwood owed her father a 1992 sum of half a million dollars.

She sucked in a breath. Had that been paid? If so,

where was that money? If not, was this a binding contract that she could collect on?

Horror filled her. She didn't want to collect on this debt. She had no idea who Karl Oakwood was, but she'd known what kind of man her father was. Whoever he'd gotten involved with would not welcome her back into their lives.

She needed to talk to someone about all of this. Lay it all out for them to look at and make sense of. Then maybe then they could explain it to her.

Aaron was the first name that popped into her mind, but Eloise bit her lower lip in indecision. He was so busy with work, and he'd take the completely legal stance on anything he saw.

She wanted to do that too, but she could hear Aaron telling her to put everything back in the box and forget about it.

She couldn't go to Alice, as it now seemed that her house sat on land that Eloise actually owned.

Eloise dismissed all of her friends. She needed more information before she went to any of them. She didn't want to explain that her father had been a horrible drunk that cheated people out of their properties at the inn she'd loved so much.

"Oh, no," she moaned. Her father had loved to gamble —how had she forgotten that? He'd obviously gotten these people drunk and then raised the stakes on them, stealing things from them.

"Then why put them in this box in the wall?" she asked. "Why not tell someone about them?"

She thought of her mother, and how cheaply she and Eloise had lived after her father had left. How dare he have all of this opulence and wealth and not say one thing?

Her anger rose within her, and whenever Eloise had felt this angry and this helpless, she'd gone to one place—the lighthouse.

She looked into the wall one more time, almost as if she had a sixth sense there'd be more there. She didn't immediately see anything, but she reached in and ignored the cobwebs and grime.

Her hand met the distinct feel of paper, and she got her fingers around the large, legal-sized envelope. She took it out, and the word on the front stole her breath for at least the third time in the past fifteen minutes.

Bank accounts.

She didn't waste time sifting through the paperwork, though there was probably half an inch of it in the envelope. She got to her feet, left everything in the room just how it was, and headed downstairs to her car.

The ferry ride to Diamond Island seemed to take an hour instead of only twenty minutes. The ride to the lighthouse drained the rest of her patience.

A few cars sat in the parking lot, but Eloise was past seeing at that point. She paid the RideShare driver and leapt from the car, the dirty box and grimy envelope tucked into her purse.

She strode up the sidewalk that led to Kristen's cottage, calling the woman's name as she twisted the doorknob.

She'd burst into the house and taken two steps when she realized Kristen wasn't in the living room, where Eloise had expected her to be.

Instead, she stood in the kitchen with Kelli. Alice sat at the bar, a drink in her hand.

All three of them looked at Eloise with wide eyes and surprise on their faces.

Kristen recovered first. "Eloise, dear," she said, glancing to Alice and then Kelli as she stepped past her. "What are you doing here?"

CHAPTER FOURTEEN

K risten felt Alice's displeasure on her back as she walked toward Eloise. A slight pinch of guilt accompanied the hug she gave the brunette, but Kristen refused to let the emotion take root and influence her decisions.

Kelli had called before she'd come over. So had Alice. Kristen had told them to come at the same time, and she'd barely gotten off the phone with Robin before Kelli had arrived, twenty minutes early.

Alice had also come early, and Eloise had shown up out of nowhere. Kristen certainly couldn't help that.

"Hello, dear," she said to Eloise as she stepped back. "How are you?"

Eloise pushed her purse back behind her elbow as she adjusted the strap. "Fine."

Kristen didn't think so, and she didn't like beating

around the bush. "Come in. We're just sitting down to lunch."

Kelli rounded the kitchen counter as Kristen turned back to them. Neither she nor Alice looked pleased to see Eloise, but Kristen painted on a smile. "Eloise is here, girls."

"Hey, El," Kelli said.

"Eloise," Alice said, her voice so formal that Kristen threw her a pointed look. Alice used to wither under such looks from Kristen, but she had more backbone now. She had more confidence.

They'd both called claiming to need her advice and help, and Kristen welcomed them with open arms. There was nothing she wanted more than to feel useful and needed, and she'd put together a simple lunch of cheese and fruit, chilled shrimp and cocktail sauce, and a vegetable platter. According to Robin, Alice had been eating better, but both of them had picked very little from the trays of food.

"Help yourself," Kristen said, picking up a paper plate. "Kelli was just going to tell us something."

"No," Kelli said. "Alice was going to go first."

"I have something too," Eloise said, joining Kristen in the kitchen where Kelli had been. She glanced at the other two nervously, and Kristen's heart flipped over, beat, and then returned to a normal position in her chest.

"Okay, girls," Kristen said, not used to addressing them this way. She loved them each so dearly, and she didn't want them to have anxiety here. They'd always—*always*—been able to come to her and the lighthouse for comfort.

She didn't want to lose that. Just the fact that all three of them were there, in her small cottage, meant the world to her.

"You need each other. I don't know why you don't know that, after all you've been through in the past four months together. Heck, the past thirty years." She glared at Alice first, because she could take the brunt of it. Then Eloise, who had the good sense to drop her head, and then Kelli, who nodded with a brave look in her eyes.

"You've all come here today for something, and I'm pretty sure you're not going to get it from me. But from each other." She surveyed them again, and finally Eloise nodded.

"I'll call Robin," Alice said. "See if she can come." She slipped off the barstool and stepped a few feet away into the living room, her fingers moving over her phone.

"I can video conference in AJ," Eloise said. "If she's available. I did it last week." She started texting too, and Kristen picked up a few shrimp and put them on her plate, as if this Friday afternoon luncheon was the most pressing thing on her schedule.

Secretly, a vein of excitement wound through her. She'd been so lonely in the past few weeks, and she'd been looking forward to Eloise's return to the cove.

Yes, she had her Wednesday lunches to look forward to, but she needed more than one event each week.

Alice returned, her phone tucked under her arm as she hugged herself. "Robin said she'd try to come."

"Try to come?" Kristen asked.

"She's talking to Duke," Alice said. "She sounded frustrated."

"Oh, dear." Kristen looked at the food on her plate, and she didn't want to eat any of it. She suddenly understood Alice on a whole new level, and when the woman picked up a baby carrot and put it in her mouth, Kristen admired her.

"AJ is in a meeting," Eloise said. "She said she'd be done in twenty minutes."

"I can wait twenty minutes," Kelli said. "Parker won't be done with school until three-thirty."

"The twins can go home alone," Alice said quietly.

Eloise didn't have children she needed to be anywhere for, and Kristen nodded with the others. "I'm happy to have you here as long as you want to stay." She moved toward the small table in the corner. "If we pull this out, we can all sit around it."

Kelli got up and got the job done. Kristen told Eloise to get a couple more folding chairs from the bedroom, and a few minutes later, they all had a spot around the table.

The silence pressed down on them, and Kristen squared her shoulders and looked around at her girls.

"I'm so glad you're all here," she said, the emotion gathering in the back of her throat.

Alice reached over and took Kristen's hand, giving it a

squeeze. Gratitude for her girls filled her, and Kristen shook her head.

"I'm getting old, ladies." She gave a light laugh. "How's the shrimp?"

Before anyone could answer, Alice blurted out, "Frank is having money problems."

Kristen calmly put her shrimp in her mouth while Kelli demanded, "What?" and Eloise said, "How is that possible?"

Alice looked at Kristen, her eyes wide and afraid. "I don't really know if he is or not, but he put my monthly deposit in my account earlier this week. Then, the next morning, he took it all back out, *plus* some of my money."

"He can't do that," Eloise said.

"I got it all back," Alice said, her hands pressed flat to the table in front of her. Kristen had seen her do this before when she was trying to control something she absolutely couldn't.

"I called the bank and removed his access to transfer into or out of my account. But that means we have to work out how he's going to pay his child support and other things in the future. I've called him six times, and he hasn't called me back."

Eloise looked from Alice to Kristen, the message clear.

The question screamed through the cottage. *What should she do?*

Kristen didn't know. She'd never been divorced. She

picked up another shrimp and swiped it through her pool of cocktail sauce.

"Have you done any digging?" Kristen asked calmly. Alice was exceptionally good at digging for information. "You have contacts in New York City, don't you?"

"I called Susan," Alice said. "She said she'd look into things, but she'd extraordinarily busy, and I haven't heard back from her."

"This could be nothing," Kristen said. "When did this happen?"

"Tuesday night to Wednesday morning."

She'd said nothing at their luncheon on Wednesday, and when Kristen met Eloise's gaze, that was the conversation they had.

"So it's only been a few days," Kristen said. "He could be busy in court."

"I'm almost to the point where I'll have Ginny text him and see if he responds." Alice shook her head, her eyes falling to the vegetables she'd put on her plate. She hadn't touched them. "I don't want them to worry, though. If he can't pay the alimony and the child support, I can't—I won't be able to stay in that house. I can't pay my car payments. Everything would change."

"Kristen's right. You don't know any of that yet," Kelli said.

"I have less than a month to figure it out," Alice said, and her voice pitched up on the last few words. She took a deep breath, and Kristen watched her compose herself in two seconds. Maybe less.

The woman was tough as nails. She'd get through this, even if Frank never paid her another dime.

"How is your practice going?" Kristen asked.

"Decently," Alice said. "For how long I've been out of things, and for the size of Five Island Cove."

"Perhaps you won't need Frank."

"I would have to move," Alice said. "That house is enormous, and so is the mortgage."

Eloise shifted in her seat, but she said nothing.

"Moving isn't the worst thing ever," Kelli said quietly. Alice's attention shifted to her, and her expression softened.

"Of course it isn't, Kel. I'm sorry. I didn't mean to imply it was."

Kelli lifted her chin to face Alice, and she smiled. It was wobbly, and a bit off-center, but it was there nonetheless.

The conversation stalled, and Kristen actually twisted to look over her shoulder. Robin should be here. Missing out on something like this would cause her great distress, and Kristen couldn't help thinking that something must be terribly wrong at her house for her *not* to be here.

Kristen finished eating and so did Eloise. She got up and picked up their plates, took them into the kitchen, and started cleaning up. Once that was done, she looked back at the other three women still sitting at the table.

"Who's going next?" Kristen asked.

"Not me," Kelli said instantly.

"Kelli, dear," Kristen said. "You called first. You clearly have something we need to know about."

She shook her head, and Kristen sighed. Kelli had never liked leading, and Kristen had forgotten how hard it had been to get her to share first, get on the boat first, or even lead the way to the deck on the lighthouse, which overlooked the ocean to the east.

Alice had already shared her concern, and while there'd been no solution, the woman had eaten a little bit afterward, so she must've felt better.

"I'd like to wait until everyone is here too," Eloise said. "I was only planning to tell you, Kristen."

"Same," Kelli said. "I didn't know I'd need to be ready to share with everyone."

"Sorry," Kristen said, not sorry at all. "You five need each other, even if you still don't see it."

"I see it," Eloise said, plenty of defensiveness in her voice. "I just wanted to get your opinion first, before I went to the others."

"My...stuff involves you," Kelli said.

Kristen met her eyes, alarm pulling through her. "Me?"

Kelli pressed her lips into a thin line. "Yes."

"Well, let's hear it."

"Not until Robin gets here," Kelli said, leaning away from her nearly empty plate and folding her arms. She had regained some of her confidence in the past couple of months, and even if Kristen had had to hear through the grapevine about her marital problems, she still wanted the very best for Kelli. For all of her girls.

The things she'd learned about Joel had severely shaken her, and she'd done a good job of hiding it from everyone. Sometimes she thought she might be deluding herself, but just the face that all of these women had come to her proved her point. They still trusted her. They didn't blame her for the dastardly things her late husband had done to them, to their mothers, or to their families.

Kristen still carried some guilt from that, and when it got really bad, she went up the path and past the picnic table. She went as far as she could get and still be on stable ground, and she shouted her frustrations and anger at her husband and the secrets he'd kept into the sky.

The wind carried them over the ocean and far from her, and Kristen didn't have to deal with those feelings, that betrayal, or the consequences of Joel's actions for a while.

She could chase them away, but she hadn't been able to rid herself of them completely. Not yet, anyway.

Thankfully, the water, wind, and sky never went anywhere, and they were excellent at keeping secrets.

"I'll tell AJ we're waiting for Robin," Eloise said. "It's been longer than twenty minutes."

"I'll call her again," Alice said. "Just so she knows we're waiting."

"Maybe she can't come," Kristen said, worry filling her now.

"I'll find out," Alice said. "Because if she can't, she should just say so. Then we'll be able to get going."

Alice had never liked wasting time. Kristen watched her walk out the front door this time, and a part of her heart actually hoped she could keep her girls with her all afternoon. Once they left, she'd be alone again, and Kristen bore that burden more than she'd like.

"AJ says to call whenever," Eloise said. "She's headed home for the weekend, because of a burst pipe. They evacuated her building." She turned to Kelli. "How's your job at the junior high? Do you ever see Billie?"

The two of them started talking, and Kristen's heart swelled. None of her other groups of girls had bonded the way Robin, Alice, Eloise, Kelli, and AJ had. Kristen often wondered what the difference was, and she always came back to circumstances.

They'd simply needed each other at that specific time in their lives. She'd needed them. They'd shared things and gone through things together that couldn't be replicated, though Kristen had tried with other groups.

Alice slipped back into the house and said, "She wants us to wait, if we can. She's hoping to be here in fifteen minutes."

Kristen nodded and pointed to the couch. She and Alice sat side-by-side, and Alice leaned her head against Kristen's shoulder the way she had as a sixteen-year-old.

Kristen patted her leg and said in a voice no one else could hear, "Alice, you're a strong, capable woman and an excellent mother. Whatever is happening with Frank, you'll be able to weather it."

"Thank you, Kristen," Alice whispered. "Thank you."

CHAPTER FIFTEEN

R obin worked not to slam the coffee pot down onto the burner. She needed a minute to cool off, but Alice had called twice now, and she just wanted to *go*.

"I'm just saying that you're always headed off somewhere," Duke said.

"Always?" Robin asked, trying to keep the sarcastic bite out of her voice. Trying, and failing. "That's not true." She turned around and faced him. "Number one, I have clients I have to meet with. Number two, I like to work out with weights, and that requires that I go to the gym. Number three, Alice, Kristen, and I have been getting together for weeks for lunch. It's one day a week, not every day, and that never bothered you before you went to Alaska."

Nothing she'd done had bothered him before Alaska. The things she'd been worried about when Duke had left

Five Island Cove seemed to be coming to fruition right before her eyes. He was short with the girls in the morning before school. They'd only been going for five days, and while Duke had driven them almost every day last year, Robin had taken them all five days this week.

Praise the Lord that his boat would be back on Sunday evening. If it wasn't, he might be out on the street until it arrived, and then he'd be living on it.

He'd been home for two weeks, and while Robin sure did like having him in bed with her—and showering with her and making love to her whenever their eyes happened to meet—she needed space too.

"I'm going to the lighthouse," she said. "Alice has called twice, and they're all there, and there's something going on."

"It's Friday," he said. "I thought we'd get the girls and go get fish and chips."

"Mandie has a drama meeting after school," Robin said, something she'd told Duke at least four times that week. "After that, she'll probably go out to Rocky Ridge to see Charlie. That's what she's been doing on weekends."

Duke frowned and rubbed one hand down his beard. "I don't like this Charlie boy."

"Yes, you do," Robin said. "You just don't like Mandie dating any boy."

"Do you?"

"No, I do not," Robin said. "But I dealt with it all summer while you were gone, and you'll just have to get used to it." She turned to get her keys out of the drawer. "Jamie is done at two-forty."

"I know."

"Okay," Robin said, infusing some semblance of brightness into her voice. "Great. I'll call you and let you know when I'm done. We might still be able to get fish and chips."

She was sure they would, because Kelli had an eight-year-old she wasn't going to abandon that day. Alice had kids too, and Eloise would want to spend her Friday night with Aaron.

There would be plenty of time for fish and chips, as Robin had told Duke twenty minutes ago.

He jumped up and intercepted her as she started for the door that led to the garage and the minivan that was only a few miles away from a complete break-down.

"Robin," Duke said in that smooth, sexy tone that would allow him to get his way. "I just miss you. I want us to have date nights."

"Then you should *ask*," Robin said. "I go over all of our schedules with you constantly." She put her hands on his chest and fiddled with the collar of his shirt. That usually helped her get her way. "You knew about Mandie's meeting after school, or you should've. I've told you multiple times this week. I tell you everything. If you want to go out with me—and baby, I want that too—then you should *ask* me. I want to be asked. I want you to at least *pretend* like you're courting me."

Duke ducked his head, and Robin wrapped her fingers around the back of his neck. She pressed her forehead to his and swayed with him. "I love you, Duke," she said. "If you want a romantic date night with me, let's put it on the schedule."

"Tomorrow?" Duke asked, planting his hands on her waist and pulling her closer.

"Tomorrow night is fine," Robin said. "Now kiss me and don't sit around here and brood."

Duke kissed her, and he sure did try to persuade her to stay home with him. Robin broke the kiss despite the tingling in her bones. "I'll call you later."

"Okay," he said, and he released her. Robin stepped out into the garage and hurried around to the driver's seat of the van. Thankfully, it started, and she got on her way to the lighthouse.

Her shoulders held tightness in them she couldn't roll out, and she wished she could've left the moment Alice had called. She hated missing out on conversations, and Alice had said there was something happening at Kristen's cottage, and they all wanted her there.

She'd been in the middle of the argument with Duke, and she hadn't been able to simply run out.

She exhaled as she pulled into the parking lot, and she hurried up the sidewalk to Kristen's cottage. She knocked as she opened the door, and she said, "I'm here."

Alice sat with Kristen on the couch, and Eloise sat with Kelli at the dining room table.

Alice got up quickly, and she gave Robin a hug. "You're here."

"I'll call AJ," Eloise said.

Kristen got up too, and Robin embraced her too. She smiled at Kristen and turned to hug Kelli. "What did I miss?"

"I'm the only one who's said anything," Alice said. "It's nothing yet, but Frank put my monthly money in my account this week, and then immediately took it back the next morning. I've called him a bunch of times, but he hasn't returned any of my calls."

Robin listened while Alice spoke, and Kelli interjected several times about how Alice had cut off Frank's access, and that they didn't really know anything yet.

"I'm so sorry," Robin said.

"What kept you, dear?" Kristen asked.

"Ohhh," Robin said, her breath elongating the word. She could barely put into words her frustration. "Duke's home, and his boat isn't. That should sum it up."

"He's driving you crazy, isn't he?" Kristen asked with a knowing smile.

"He thinks I'm spending too much time at the inn, or at lunch with my friends, or heaven forbid, with my clients." Robin rolled her eyes, and she really got going.

"I tell him about our schedule about ten times a day, and he still acts like he doesn't know. He doesn't listen to me, not even a little bit." She drew in a deep breath as if she'd start again.

She met Alice's eyes, and all of Robin's complaints dried up. Pure horror and guilt hit her like a load of bricks right in the chest.

"It's fine," she said. "We're just adjusting to him being home with nothing to do."

"You got used to running the roost," Kristen said.

"Yes." Robin cleared her throat and looked at Eloise.

Eloise, who was in love with Aaron Sherman, a man who would treat her right and take good care of her, but was a little gun shy to pull the marriage trigger again.

Kelli, who'd recently separated from her husband, because he wanted a polyamorous relationship. Talk about a man who didn't listen to the needs of his wife.

Robin recalled the thought, because she didn't know Julian at all. She only knew Kelli's version of Julian. But Robin knew that Kelli had told Julian she didn't want that type of relationship, and he hadn't yielded what *he* wanted for her.

Alice, whose husband had been cheating on her for years, and had tried to reduce what he had to pay for in the divorce, and who had now started some financial trouble.

Kristen, whose husband had died four months ago. Robin knew she was lonely. She knew she missed Joel, despite the secrets that had come out and caused ripples in all of their normal lives.

Foolishness wove through her, increasing with every

moment that passed. "Anyway," she said. "What else do we need to talk about?"

"I have AJ on the line," Eloise said, turning the phone around so everyone could see AJ.

Robin faded into the background, her throat still too narrow to swallow properly.

AJ, who'd been dating for three decades and just wanted to find someone to love and someone to love her.

Robin had never felt like such an idiot. Nothing seemed to be going right today, and she took a moment while everyone said hello to AJ to press her eyes closed and take a deep breath.

Be present, she thought. *Be supportive. Listen. Be ready to help.*

Nothing that was happening at the lighthouse today had anything to do with her. She hadn't shown up with a problem she needed help with.

"I'll go next," Kelli said. She drew a deep breath. "I really came to talk to Kristen, because I've been doing a little digging into Zach." She paused, specifically looking at Alice, who'd given her a lot of flak about her half-brother.

Alice said nothing, and Kelli reached into her purse and pulled out a folder.

"I printed these at Alice's the other night." She handed Kristen a piece of paper. "That has my dad's name on it. Rueben is mentioned as the architect. And Zach Oakwood as the art student."

"His name isn't Watkins?" Eloise asked, peering over Kristen's arm.

"Not in that article," Kelli said. "He knew my father though, obviously." She took out the other paper. "This article says they worked on the children's wing of the library in Savannah together."

"That was years ago," Kristen said, looking over the top of the paper. "Probably twenty years."

"Eighteen," Kelli said.

"That means Zach isn't in his thirties," Robin said. She scanned the paper with the article on it. "This says he was a senior. Plus eighteen years...he's probably almost forty."

"Everything he said isn't true," Alice said.

Eloise took the article and read it, and her frown only deepened with every passing second.

"Kelli?"

"I was wondering if you knew anything about it," Kelli said to Kristen. "I wondered if I should go talk to Rueben about it."

"He's out on the claw today," Kristen said. "He'll be back late tonight after he checks the lantern."

Robin remembered how rough the waters could be in the rowboat out to the claw, which was just a patch of stand shaped like a rooster's foot where a light tower had been erected. It was part of the lightkeeper's job to make sure that lantern stayed lit too, and Kristen had worried over Joel rowing out to the claw several times.

"But we can talk to him as soon as he gets back."

"Do we really need to?" Alice asked. "This is obvious, Kel. He's not who he says he is. He's not your half-brother."

"Alice," Robin said softly. Alice turned toward her, and the fire in her eyes went out.

"Okay," Alice said, holding up her hand. "Okay, I'll stop."

"She just doesn't need to hear it."

"I haven't been able to find a birth certificate in Maine for him," Kelli said. "But I've just been using my phone." She looked around nervously. "He knows about the Glass-works." Kelli zipped her purse and looked around, vulnerability in her expression.

"I need help to figure out who he is and what he wants."

"Of course we'll help you," Eloise said.

"I think we know what he wants," Alice said. "Money. He thinks you have some money, because your father was a famous artist."

"He should've seen us after my dad lost everything." Kelli accepted Robin's hug, and something suddenly occurred to her.

Robin pulled away and studied Kelli's face. "Do you think he even knows your family lost everything?"

"I don't know."

"Maybe you should show him some pictures," AJ said, and Robin turned toward the phone. She'd forgotten AJ was even there.

"I've burned them all," Kelli said. AJ burst out laughing, and that broke the tension in the cottage.

"We'll make a plan of attack," Eloise said. "Maybe I can ask Aaron if he can find anything with some of his resources."

"No," Kelli said quickly. "I don't want the police involved. It has nothing to do with anything legal."

"Are you kidding?" Eloise asked at the same time Alice said, "Sure it does, Kelli."

Kelli looked at Alice. "It has legal ramifications?"

"If he forged a birth certificate in order to claim some inheritance he thinks he has? Absolutely," Alice said. "I'd have to do some research, and this isn't legal advice at all, but yes. I think we need to find out about this birth certificate—and anything else we can."

"Okay." Kelli took the printouts from Kristen and Eloise and tucked them back into her purse. "That's my problem."

"Come tomorrow afternoon," Kristen said. "We'll go talk to Rueben together."

Kelli nodded, and all eyes turned to Eloise.

"I need legal advice for sure," she said. "I'll hire you, Alice." She crossed the room to her purse and pulled an envelope and a wooden box from it. "I found these hidden in the wall at the Cliffside Inn..."

No one moved, not even Alice.

Robin took the first step forward, and she looked at the envelope. "Bank accounts?" she read.

"My father was a gambler," Eloise said, her voice barely loud enough to be heard. "I think these are things he swindled from other people, but I need to know if they're legal contracts or not."

She opened the box and took out several more envelopes, most of them quite bulky with folded papers.

"Galveston Distillery?" Kelli read.

"Proffit Beach Property," Alice said. "Stevenson Ranch." She held up the two she'd picked up. "What are these?" She started to open them, so Eloise didn't answer.

Alice read the papers, her eyes alive and bright as they moved from left to right.

She looked up, her gaze meeting Eloise's. "I think these are legit," she said. "They're dated and signed. They have property addresses on them. They say the properties are being transferred to pay a debt, and that that debt will be forgiven with the transaction."

"It makes no sense," Eloise said. "Who's been managing these properties for the past twenty-five-plus years?"

Alice flipped a page and then another. She folded them and put them back in the envelope before opening the next one. "Someone is," she said. "Or whoever these people are could still be there." She looked up. "Have you looked any of these up?"

"No," Eloise said. "I found them an hour ago and came straight here." She met Kristen's eyes. "I wanted to get some insight from Kristen on them."

Kristen smiled at Eloise, and they stepped toward each other and embraced.

"We'll get to the bottom of this," Alice said.

"What are the properties?" AJ asked. "I'll look them up right now."

CHAPTER SIXTEEN

A J typed and clicked, her eyes scanning for anything that would stand out. Her mind raced, and more than just with the items Eloise had read to her over the phone.

So much in her life had changed in the past four months, and she hated that she was the only one not in Kristen's cottage right now. That alone was a huge marker for where she'd been in April and where she was now, this first week of September.

She would've never answered a video chat in April. She would've still been with Nathan, and still chasing that elusive career high she still hadn't found, even now.

She'd returned from Denver, hopeful she'd get on the air from her performance there. She'd landed two exclusive interviews for the on-air talent, and her contact base had both expanded and come through for her.

She'd met with her boss, but he'd said he wanted her to "keep up the good work," and that "there might be a spot opening up in a month or two."

AJ had heard language like that before. It meant they were happy with her on their team, but she wasn't at the top of the list to move into an anchor spot, if one even became available.

A month or two could mean tomorrow or in a year, and AJ wondered if she even wanted to wait that long. She wondered if she even wanted to have this job when everyone else was in Five Island Cove.

After all, she had no one here in New York, and her four best friends were together. Even though she'd abandoned them years ago, without hardly a look back, they'd all been there to greet her with open arms. Where else could she find people like that?

Nowhere, she thought, finally seeing two words that belonged together. "I see a Stevenson Ranch just outside of Billings," AJ said, clicking and leaning closer to her laptop screen.

"Does it have a website?" Alice asked, coming into the picture on AJ's phone.

"Loading now," AJ said.

"See if there's an About section," Alice said. "And see if you can right-click to bring up the source material. We can usually see something from that."

AJ had no idea about things like that, and she was honestly surprised Alice did. The woman was a brilliant lawyer, though, so she probably knew all kinds of things AJ didn't even know existed.

The site loaded, and she clicked. "They're a six-hundred-and-twelve-acre cattle ranch," she said, skimming the text on the About page. "Owned and operated independently, with a caretaker and general manager who lives on the property."

"Who's that?" Eloise asked, crowding into the frame with Alice. The anxiety in Eloise's voice unsettled AJ. Eloise was always so calm and so rational. She didn't let emotions rattle her, and AJ had never known her to operate from a place of panic. She could practically feel Eloise's anxiety pouring over the video though.

"Uh, let's see," AJ said, finishing the About page. She looked back up to the menu, and underneath Contact Us, she found a sub-tab for Employment. She clicked there, and a picture of cowboys and cowgirls came up. The all looked unreasonably happy given what AJ knew about working a ranch, which admittedly wasn't much.

She did know how cold it got in Montana, and there was no way these people grinned through those temperatures.

"You can only apply for a job every other month," she said, scanning the words again. She wished she could speed-read, because it felt like she was right on the cusp of getting the information she needed and she simply couldn't read fast enough.

"When the general manager isn't there, his foreman conducts interviews."

"Who is it?" Eloise asked again.

"Maybe we should just call," Robin said. "Pretend like we want a job and ask."

"How do you do that?" Alice asked. "Hey, I need a job right now, and I see your general manager isn't there. What's his name, by the way?"

"I don't know," Robin snipped back. "I'm just saying that AJ obviously can't find it online, and it feels like we're wasting time." Her face came into the screen too, replacing Eloise's. "Is there a phone number, AJ? I'll just call." She glared at Alice, and AJ loved it when the two of them went at it. They were very clearly best friends who knew each other a little too well, because they did not hold back with one another.

AJ wished Kelli was on-screen, because she missed her best friend. She wished she was there to hug her and tell her she'd find out everything she could about Zach. The traitor. Didn't he know she and her family had been through enough? How dare he try to steal something from her that wasn't his?

Even taking her peace of mind made him a complete villain in AJ's eyes.

She clicked on a link at the bottom of the page that led to available jobs while Eloise joined the argument about calling the Stevenson Ranch. Another picture loaded, and AJ sucked in a tight breath.

It must have been loud enough for everyone to hear, because they all stopped talking, and Eloise nudged Robin out of the picture and asked, "What is it, AJ?"

Her insides quaked, and her mind automatically rejected the things she was seeing. They couldn't be true.

"AJ," Eloise barked, and AJ flinched away from the two men on the screen. It had been a very long time since she'd seen either of them, but she had a memory for faces and names. It was what allowed her to be so good at her job. When she remembered an agent's name or a B-level athlete, they felt important.

"I'm going to share my screen with you," AJ said. "I could be wrong, Eloise. I haven't seen—" She couldn't say it.

"Seen what?" Alice demanded.

AJ just shook her head, making it match with the air as it entered her lungs. She just had to be wrong. She clicked the button to share her screen, and her picture flew up to the top right corner.

"Can you see it?" she asked.

Alice swore, and Robin yelped. Eloise said, "That's my brother," in a voice that hardly belonged to her.

AJ pressed her eyes closed. She hadn't seen Garrett Hall in a very long time, but he'd been tall, dark, and handsome, and no one had been off-limits for AJ in high school. Of course, with the age difference, AJ had been in junior high when she'd first kissed Garrett. She'd been willing to go all the way, but he'd stopped way before that.

"I can't," he'd whispered into her neck. "You're my little sister's best friend." He'd backed up really fast after that. "I can't."

AJ had never told Eloise; she'd never told *anyone* about that particular incident. A keen sense of self-loathing came over her, and she hung her head.

Why had she done all of those things in her youth? She'd hated herself so much that anyone who could make her forget that for even five minutes was welcomed into her life.

"And my uncle," Eloise said, confirming what AJ had first thought.

Chaos erupted on the other end of the line, and AJ just listened while tears gathered in her eyes. She didn't dare navigate away from the ranch website, but she really wanted to book the first flight to Five Island Cove so she could hug Eloise and the others.

As they started to calm, AJ said, "I'm going to take off the screen share." She did, and she got part of the ceiling and part of the living room in Kristen's cottage. Eloise had obviously set the phone down.

Someone cried, and AJ suspected it was Eloise. Robin said, "Shh, El, it's going to be okay."

"We'll make it okay," Alice said.

"I'm going to be on the flight there in the morning," AJ said. "Robin, can I stay with you?"

Robin grabbed the phone, and AJ got a little dizzy

from the movement and shuffling until she filled the video frame. "Of course," she said.

"Take me off speaker," AJ said, and confusion crossed Robin's face.

"I don't know how to do that."

"Then go outside for a second."

Robin nodded and AJ had to look away from the screen as Robin lowered the phone to her side and started walking.

"Okay, I'm outside," she said as if AJ wouldn't know from the new silence that came through the line.

"I need the honest truth," AJ said. "How's Kelli?"

"She's hanging in there," Robin said. "She's afraid, but in the past, she wouldn't have told any of us. She'd have let this thing with Zach go, because she didn't want the confrontation. But...now...she's changed. She's going to see this through."

AJ nodded. "And Alice?"

"Alice will always prevail," Robin said. "She'll get through it, and she has clients now, so even if Frank does skip some months, she'll be okay."

"Eloise?"

"She just broke down. Those documents have been sitting in the walls at the Cliffside Inn for over twenty years. Her father willed her all of his properties and bank accounts, and that includes those properties, if he did in fact, own them."

"And she just found out her brother obviously knew

about the properties and has been benefitting from them since her father's death."

"And her uncle," Robin said.

All the pieces fell into place. "Didn't they know about the paperwork?"

"Obviously not," Robin said "Eloise just said before she dissolved into tears that her dad kept the inn, and the bank repossessed it and sold it at auction. If Garrett had known about the paperwork in the walls, he could've bought it." Robin shook her head, pure concern and displeasure mixing in her expression. "They'll appreciate you coming." Her voice tightened. "*I* appreciate it."

AJ started clicking to get to the airline. "I'll be there as soon as I can."

"You should bring Peterson," Robin said. "Stay for a week and help Eloise at the inn. Alice and I have been going almost every day."

"Sure," AJ said just to placate her. "I'll ask him."

Robin turned back to the cottage door, her eyebrows raised. "Do you want to go back in, AJ?" she asked, already moving.

"No," AJ said. "I have lots to do if I'm going to take a week off. Tell everyone goodbye and that I love them."

"Will do." Robin opened the door to more noise, and AJ quickly clicked on the red hang-up button.

She twisted slightly toward her fish bowl and Peterson. "You can't come, Petey," she said. "I'll text Claire next door to come feed you."

She got busy booking a flight and emailing in her request for leave paperwork. She texted her boss and Claire and while she waited for confirmations on everything, she pulled out her suitcase and started packing.

In times like these, she really wished she could drink, because it would take the edge off. The last time she'd been in Five Island Cove, though, her friends had staged an intervention and thrown away the full suitcase of alcohol she'd brought with her.

She wasn't going to put them in that situation again, nor would she go through that humiliation again.

"Only the one suitcase," she muttered to herself, putting in two swimming suits just in case. It was still warm in Five Island Cove, and maybe they could discuss everything on the beach.

AJ's phone buzzed, and she returned to her desk to check it. Her boss had texted that if she could call in on Tuesday morning for their roundtable, that would be great, and to otherwise enjoy the cove.

Thanks, AJ sent back. With her bag packed, her ticket printed, her leave approved, and her phone charging, all AJ needed to do now was come up with a reason why Peterson hadn't come with her.

And maybe that Peterson was a goldfish and not her boyfriend.

CHAPTER SEVENTEEN

Laurel Baker took Paul's hand as they strolled along the boardwalk that bordered this part of the beach. She could feel him scanning the area too, and she wondered if they'd ever be able to simply go out without acting like cops.

She surveyed the landscape ahead too, but she was actually doing it for a dual purpose. One, to make sure there wasn't any danger ahead, that the teens on the beach around their bonfires were being smart, and that the rules were being followed.

Two, she wanted to find a nice, secluded place where she could share her first kiss with Paul. They'd been out twice before tonight, and Laurel thought a third, amazing date was the perfect time for their first kiss.

He'd been holding her hand since the first date. On

the second, he'd walked her right to her door, kissed her cheek and hugged her goodnight.

He planned dates too, which was something new for Laurel, as most of the men she dated wanted her to suggest things for them to do. Not Paul. Their first date had been a scooter tour of the island, with a miniature concert at three venues along the way. She'd really enjoyed a different way to experience Diamond Island, and she'd still been able to talk to Paul on the ride.

Their second date had been more traditional—dinner and a movie, but he'd taken her to the local drive-in, which was more of a dive-in, where they only showed old movies. They'd watched Jaws, shared popcorn, laughed, talked, and snuggled in the back of Paul's pick-up truck. Laurel had enjoyed herself immensely, as Paul was articulate and kind, broad-shouldered and bearded, and just about everything that attracted Laurel to a man.

Tonight, he'd taken her to a couples cooking class, and they'd made their own stuffed pork chops, garlic mashed potatoes, and basted asparagus. The whole night had been an experience, and Laurel liked watching Paul work with a knife in his hand, his movements slow but sure.

She'd learned that he was a decent cook; it was just a matter of having recipes to make that he knew he'd like. She'd told him about her family and her road to becoming a detective in Five Island Cove.

She hadn't been born on the islands, but her father

was a native. Her parents still lived in Nantucket, where her dad lived, breathed, and sold real estate. Laurel had come to the cove to visit her aunt one summer just out of college, and she'd fallen in love with the islands, the people, the food, and the traditions.

She loved the classic car parade, and the saltwater volleyball tournament. She loved the sailboats that dotted the waters, the many ways to eat seafood, and the hot air balloon festival.

"You said your sister is here?" Laurel asked as she spotted a set of stairs they could take down to the sand. The last bonfire sat twenty feet behind them, and perhaps she could persuade Paul to go out to the water's edge to dip in their toes. Then they'd be more secluded, and maybe she could get her kiss.

"Yeah," Paul said. "For the weekend is all." He smiled down at her. "What do you think about meeting her?"

Surprise moved through Laurel. "Meeting your sister? Wow."

He chuckled and swung their hands a little harder than he had been. "It would be like meeting my mother," he said. "Since she's gone now, the only female I have in my family to constantly nag me about my bachelor status is Julie."

Laurel laughed with him, her whole body warming in the cooling night. "Maybe we can get together for brunch on Sunday."

Paul sobered and looked at her. "If you mean that, I'll text her right now."

Laurel beamed up at him. "I mean it."

He dropped her hand and got out his phone. While his fingers flew across the screen, Laurel checked her phone too. Chief Sherman had messaged her through a private app where she'd turned notifications off. "Erin" had said, *We need pickles tonight at ten.*

Her heartbeat leapt into the back of her throat, and she glanced at the clock. Just after nine. She really needed to wrap this date up if she was going to make that appointment.

A touch of annoyance ran through her. Didn't he spend Friday nights with Eloise? How was he going to get out of the house?

You just assume I'm free on a Friday night, she sent. *I'll do my best.*

On a date? came right back.

Yes.

Name the time. I can get away almost any time after ten.

Let's do eleven, she sent.

Later is better, he said. *Midnight?*

Laurel saw her beauty rest disappearing right before her eyes. *Midnight it is.* She'd barely sent the message before Paul looked up from his phone.

"She's thrilled," he said.

Laurel shoved her phone in her back pocket without looking at Aaron's last message. "What did you tell her?"

Paul turned his phone toward her, and Laurel scanned the few messages. "Oh, I see an interesting word," she teased.

"Yeah?" Paul looked at his phone too, his eyebrows drawing down in the most adorable way. "Which one?"

"Girlfriend," she said, re-taking his hand and tugging on it to get him to walk with her.

"Is that interesting?" he asked.

Laurel giggled and led him down the steps to the sand. "It is to me."

"Why's that?" Paul let go of her hand and slipped his fingers along her waist. "We've been out a few times now. I'm thinking of you like that."

Laurel paused and faced him. "Do you usually kiss your girlfriends?"

He swallowed as his eyes dropped to her mouth. "Yeah, usually."

"I don't really count a man as my boyfriend until that first kiss," she whispered, tiptoeing her fingers up the front of his shirt.

"Let's take care of that then," he said, putting his other hand on her lower back and bringing her close. He hesitated, and Laurel kept her eyes closed, all of her other senses on high alert.

Paul's lips finally touched hers, and Laurel sucked in a

breath through her nose. Fire licked down her throat and through her stomach, and then Paul *really* kissed her.

Hours later, Laurel crossed the dark bit of asphalt from where she'd parked her car behind the short trees to where Aaron had pulled up in his cruiser. The doors unlocked a moment before she reached for the handle, and she slid into the car in the next moment.

The overhead light had not come on, and anyone who happened to drive behind the grocery store wouldn't be able to see her car or her in the passenger seat.

"Evening," Aaron said.

"It's the middle of the night," Laurel said in a disgusted tone.

"Did you find anything?" he asked, ignoring her attitude. They'd met a couple of times in his office, which no one had questioned. But the last two times had been right here, later at night, as they passed documents and information back and forth in person to avoid leaving a paper or email trail.

"The birth certificate is from Maine," Laurel said, handing him a sheet of paper. "It's got his mother's name on it, as well as a man named Hugo Oakwood."

"So he's not Kelli's half-brother."

"I'm almost one hundred percent sure of that," Laurel said. "His mother died last year; she's not in a nursing home. The birth certificate was changed three days later, and only ten months ago. Here's a record of that."

Aaron took the second paper from her and studied it. "Good work, Laurel."

She couldn't help swelling under his compliment. They were hard to earn from Aaron Sherman, and while she didn't crave them now as much as she once had, it was still nice to hear him praise her.

He drew in a long breath and pushed it out. "What am I going to do about this guy?"

"He hasn't done anything illegal," Laurel said.

"Yet," Aaron said. "He has harassed the mother outside her home. He has asked Kelli for the Glassworks. If he tries to use his fake identity to get it..."

"Then we'll close in on him," Laurel said.

"I don't have the manpower to tail him all the time," Aaron said, looking out his window. His unrest carried like a scent on the air, but Laurel didn't know what to do about it.

"Maybe," she said carefully. "It's time you looped Eloise and Kelli in on this."

"No," Aaron said instantly. "El is swamped at the inn, and she's not in a good place to hear this too."

"What about Kelli?"

"Yeah," he said slowly. "I could talk to her. Eloise told me she's found the stuff about the children's wing in Savannah."

Laurel had found that the very next day after Aaron

had asked her to start digging into Zach Watkins. But she hadn't had to find a place to live, register her son for school, or find a job.

"Let's talk to Kelli on Monday," Laurel said. "Then maybe we can sleep at this time of night."

"I wasn't asleep yet," Aaron said.

"I'm sure you weren't," Laurel said, smiling at him.

He grinned back at her, and he was so boyishly handsome when he did. Laurel still felt a tiny spark of attraction for the man, but she told herself any woman would. He was gorgeous, strong, and hardworking. What wasn't to like?

"Who are you seeing?" he asked.

"Oh, uh." Laurel quickly moved her gaze out the window. "We just made it official tonight." She worked hard not to lift her fingertips to her lips, which still tingled with Paul's touch. "We were going to come talk to you on Monday."

"Oh? One of my guys, then?"

"Yes," Laurel said. "Paul Lehey."

Aaron's chuckle filled the cruiser. "I can see you two together. He's a great guy."

"Yeah, I kind of think so too," Laurel said, finally looking at her boss. "We'll fill out the paperwork on Monday."

"Be sure you do," he said. "I can't have you two working together on anything, or we'll find ourselves in a heap of trouble."

"I know, boss," she said, smiling. "We hardly ever work together anyway. He's narcotics."

"Yeah, well, I was thinking of a change for you," he said. "But maybe now I'm not."

Laurel gaped at him. "I don't want narcotics—or a change. I like what I'm doing."

"I'll leave you alone, then," Aaron said. He nodded to the folder. "Anything else in there?"

"No, sir." She handed him the folder anyway, and he replaced the documents she'd found in it.

"Thanks again, Laurel. I better get back to Eloise."

"Oh, she's living with you now?"

He shook his head, his jaw tightening. "No, she just stays over some nights."

Laurel's imagination went into overdrive, and she wondered what it would be like to even kiss Aaron Sherman.

Her whole body flushed. Eloise was a very lucky woman, and Laurel really needed to get out of this cruiser.

"Goodnight, sir," she said, slipping away as quickly and as quietly as she'd arrived.

On the way home, she thought about calling Paul and asking him to come spend the night with her. She couldn't get the images of being intimate with Aaron out of her mind, and that bothered her. She'd been steadily getting past her crush on him, and tonight felt like a complete setback.

She didn't call Paul; she just drove home and went to

bed. She wasn't ready to be intimate with anyone, not after her last relationship. Just kissing Paul had been a big step, and as she relived that, her finally found her focus.

Hopefully this thing with Kelli and Zach Watkins would be over soon, and Laurel wouldn't have any reason to be in a car alone with Aaron, and she wouldn't have to hear about his love life with Eloise Hall.

CHAPTER EIGHTEEN

K elli gripped her son's hand as they approached the lighthouse. "You can go down that path to the beach," she said, indicating the smudge of dirt that led to the left of the lighthouse. "I used to go down there all the time when I was a little girl."

She smiled at her son as he looked up at her. "Really, Mom?"

"Really," she said. "Well, I was a little older." She'd been almost thirteen when she started coming to the lighthouse for the Seafaring Girls classes her mother had insisted she take. Kelli hadn't wanted to go, because the ocean scared her—and that was precisely why her parents had signed her up.

She hadn't gotten over her fear instantly, but steadily and slowly over time, Kelli had come to appreciate the beauty of the undulating waves and the way the sky could take on a personality all its own.

Today, it was a happy, bright blue sky, with puffy, popcorn clouds that made Kelli think of simpler times. Like lying on the beach, the khaki sand hot, with a bag of her favorite red licorice nearby. She could turn her face into the salty, sea breeze, and remember what it was like to be a child running along the sand, trying to get up the eight-legged octopus kite her father had given her for her eighth birthday.

Sometimes the sky was like an angry bear, foaming with gray clouds that warned anyone and everyone away from the shore. She sometimes imagined the sky to be weeping and wailing for some great person who'd died that day, and she wondered if it would ever do the same for her one day.

Other times, the sky took on a color that wasn't quite blue, and wasn't quite white, and wasn't quite lavender. It existed in unnamed shades of gray, with low-lying clouds that suggested the world was thinking of something sad.

Or perhaps something good, but with a type of reflection that required silence and serenity.

"Can I go down?" Parker asked, and Kelli nodded to him.

"Sure," she said. "Mom's going to go sit on the second-level deck, okay?" She nodded to the navy blue door on the lighthouse. "You just go through there, and up, up, up. It's five or six flights. The very top door is white and metal. Come through there, and I'll be up there."

"Okay," he said, releasing her hand. She paused and watched him go, a special kind of love filling her. He was such a good boy. Quiet and reserved, but willing to have fun and try new things in a way Kelli didn't understand.

Her mind flowed back to New Jersey, and the new thing Julian wanted to try. Kelli hadn't been able to stop thinking about him and her life there, though she'd started to build a brand-new one here. She'd taken the job at the junior high, and she actually enjoyed working with the students and Mrs. Hewes.

She was definitely ready to retire, but she didn't let the teens she taught railroad her into anything. They treated her kindly too, and though Kelli had only been there for three days, and she still had plenty to learn, she'd felt a special spirit of mutual love and respect in the huge, industrial classroom that Mrs. Hewes manned.

She postponed going into the lighthouse by pulling out her phone and snapping a picture just as Parker took a big step over a break in the path.

Unable to cut Julian out of his son's life, she sent the picture to him, sans caption. He didn't need one. He'd only come to Five Island Cove once, and she didn't need to detail every aspect of the islands for him.

Familiar bitterness crept into her throat, as well as an awakening to her own permissiveness. She should've insisted they come spend time with her mother together.

Instead, she'd always brought Parker alone, and not even that often.

Her mother had been such a blessing to her in the two weeks since she'd been back in Five Island Cove, and Kelli had given her a long hug the last time she'd seen her and said, "Thank you, Mom. I love you."

They'd embraced silently after that, and Kelli caught her mom wiping her eyes when they finally parted.

"Let me know if you even see Zach hanging around," Kelli had told her. "I know the Chief of Police."

She hadn't involved Aaron beyond the incident from over a week ago, and she was glad about that. Even Eloise talked about how busy he was, and she hadn't gone straight to him about all the documents she'd found because of it.

Unable to postpone going into the lighthouse any longer, Kelli finally reached for the doorknob and heaved open the heavy door.

She only went to the first landing before knocking on the door there. It bore a wreath made of seashells, and Kelli thought of a time when she used to decorate her townhome for every occasion she could.

The door opened before she could contemplate too long on it, and Kristen stood there. "Good morning, dear." She moved right in to embrace Kelli, and streams of gratitude moved through her that she didn't have to approach Rueben alone. "Come in."

Kristen stepped back, and Kelli entered the once-familiar space. It was different now that Rueben and his wife, Jean, had taken over the lighthouse, but it still smelled like coffee and chocolate, and Kelli wondered if the smell had ingrained itself in the walls for generations to enjoy.

"I sent Parker down to the beach," she said as she saw Rueben and Jean sitting on the couch together. "We'll have maybe ten or fifteen minutes."

"I'll go down," Jean said, standing.

"Oh, you don't need to do that," Kelli said.

"I want to." Jean smiled at her in such a kind way that Kelli just acquiesced.

"Thank you," she murmured as the woman passed. She was probably ten years older than Kelli, just like Rueben was, and they didn't have any children of their own.

Once the door closed, Rueben stood too. "My mother says you have something you want me to see."

"Yes," Kelli said, pulling the folder from her purse. She set it on the kitchen counter as he approached. "You worked as an architect in Savannah, on the children's wing of the library there."

A smile crossed his face. "That feels like another life."

"I bet." Kelli opened the folder "You knew a man named Zach Oakwood."

"Yeah, sure," Rueben said easily, obviously not concerned about the topic or the conversation. "He was the artist. Brilliant, too, by the way. He did sculptures of children and animals in a unique, whimsical way. He could paint too, and the library board gave him a bonus for the fairy garden mural he did in the rotunda."

He picked up the newspaper clipping and looked at the picture. "What do you want to know?"

"Did he and my father...?" She looked at Kristen, who nodded and smiled. "He showed up a few months ago, claiming to be my half-brother. He had a birth certificate with just his mother's name. He said Guy was his father. I guess I'm wondering if they seemed like they had that kind of relationship, or if you ever heard him talk about his family, or...anything."

Rueben took his time reading the article, and when he raised his eyes to Kelli's, he seemed thoughtful. "He didn't seem to know your father. They talked a lot, obviously, because they were both artists. I remember Guy giving him some advice, and they got together without me several times."

Kelli nodded, almost wanting to record what Rueben said. "Okay."

"I did not get the idea that they were related. Zach said he was from Maine, and he'd come to Savannah to the SCAD—the Savannah College of Arts and Design. He was a great student."

"Anything about his family?" Kristen asked.

"Yeah," Rueben said. "I remember his family came for the unveiling of the new wing. His mother, his aunt, and two sisters." He pressed his eyes closed. "Julia or Julie, I think? She was the younger one. The oldest one was Katherine, and she went by Kate." He smiled, a fond look entering his eyes. "I remember, because I wanted to ask her out." Rueben chuckled and shook his head. "I didn't, obviously, but that was her name."

"Same last name as Zach?" Kelli asked.

"Yes," Rueben said. "There were no grandparents. No father. No one came for Guy, and you and Dad came to support me." Rueben looked at his mom. "I think that's it."

"Thank you," Kelli said. Her nerves had fled, and armed with more information, she couldn't wait to get back to her computer to see what else she could find. She hugged Kristen and thanked her too, declined any cookies or coffee, and went up to the second-floor deck, where she'd told Parker she'd be.

Her phone buzzed as she went through the door, and she pulled it out to see a text from Julian. *Thank you, babe. Tonight? Eleven?*

Fingers flying and with her heart tap dancing in her chest, she messaged him back. *Just me and you?*

Yes.

Okay.

KELLI HAD JUST ARRIVED AT THE CLIFFSIDE INN, HER lecture to Parker about being willing to get dirty and to pitch in and help no matter what over, when her phone rang.

Her heartbeat leapt, because she preferred texting over calling, and everyone in her life knew it. But a local island number sat on the screen, and she decided to open the call though she didn't know who it was.

"Hello?"

"Kelli," a pleasant, familiar voice said. "It's Chief Sherman."

"Oh, hey, Aaron." She got out of the car and nodded for Parker to go inside the inn without her. "I just got to the inn. Are you here?"

"On my way, actually," he said. "Which works out perfectly. I was hoping to stop by your place, but if you're up there, I can talk to you there."

"About what?" Kelli wrapped her free arm around herself.

"Zach Oakwood," Aaron said. "I've been looking into him, and I have some information for you."

Kelli's blood ran ice-cold for the time it took him to speak, and then it returned to normal. "Sure," she said. "So you know his last name isn't Watkins." She wasn't asking, because Aaron had just said Oakwood.

"Yes," Aaron said. "Did you?"

"I've been doing some digging too."

"Kelli." Aaron's voice turned stern and carried a hint of disappointment. "I asked you not to do that."

"No," she said. "You asked me not to go by his place

again. I haven't. I haven't called or texted him. I did exactly what you asked me to do."

He sighed and said, "Okay, I'm about twenty-five minutes out."

"See you soon." She hung up and faced the inn. Eloise's was the only car in the drive, which made sense with the RideShare system on the cove. Robin and Alice had to ferry to Sanctuary Island, and they'd just used the service to get here.

The front door opened, and Kelli's tears began the moment the tall, leggy blonde stepped onto the front porch.

"You gonna stand there or come hug me?" AJ asked, and Kelli flew toward her best friend.

As they hugged, AJ laughed while Kelli wept. "Oh, I missed you," AJ whispered, and Kelli could only agree.

They parted, and AJ held Kelli by her shoulders. "You look *so* good, Kel. Strong. Sure. Sexy."

Kelli laughed then and shook her head. "That's you, AJ."

"Yeah, well, it's a good look on you too." She linked her arm through Kelli's. "Come in. Eloise is having us tackle the kitchen while we're all here, and it's unlike anything I've ever seen."

CHAPTER NINETEEN

Eloise's heart filled when AJ and Kelli came into the kitchen together. They were all back together again, and there was nothing as comforting for Eloise as being with her Seafaring Girls.

"Okay," she said. "I know this is a disaster." She'd taken two steps into the kitchen ten minutes ago, and her shoes had started sticking to the floor. "They emptied the Dumpster this morning, so we have the whole thing to fill. I've got two carts for anything we can't carry very far." She'd stationed them outside the door that led to the back patio, where she envisioned having at least eight tables for guests to dine.

"Aaron will be here soon," she added, looking at Robin.

"Duke just texted to say he's just dropped Mandie and

Jamie at Alice's, and he's on his way to the ferry," Robin said. "So he'll be here in a bit."

"And we have Parker," Kelli said, stepping over to her son, who looked like he'd been hit with a baseball bat. She smiled down at him, and Eloise really wanted to ask how her talk with Rueben Shields had gone that morning. She didn't, because Kelli likely wouldn't want to talk about it in front of her son.

"So I think we take everything out that we can," Eloise said. "I've rented a high-pressure cleaning system that's usually used on outdoor siding, and I'm going to use that to clean the kitchen." She looked at her friends, their faces ranging from determination—Alice—to incredulity—Robin—to resignation—AJ.

Eloise felt all of those same things flowing through her, but she held her head high. All the other rooms in the inn had been completely cleaned out and demo'ed. The walls would be fixed. The plumbing brought into the twenty-first century. The electrical brought up to code.

Then she'd paint, assess the floors, make decisions about carpet and curtains, design and décor, and anything else she needed to.

But this kitchen had to be cleaned. While the contractors she'd hired did their work, she could order appliances, work on the landscaping—about the only thing she hadn't hired someone to do—and start working on the website that would make reserving rooms easy.

She also needed to start thinking about staff and

putting out feelers about hiring people in the next few months.

But all of that was down the road.

"So anything we can carry out, let's carry it out. Anything we can't, let's leave for the men. But I want the whole thing emptied."

Pure gratitude filled her, and she surveyed her friends. "Thank you all for coming," she said, her voice choking. "This means so much to me to have you all here."

Alice stepped up to her and hugged her. "We love you, Eloise."

Eloise had felt loved off and on over the years, but she'd experienced so much of it lately, and she held tightly to Alice as everyone else piled around them, making a giant huddle of hugs.

Eloise let her eyes water, and when they all separated, she was glad she wasn't the only one without dry eyes.

"I just have to say something first," AJ said. "Before Duke and Aaron get here." She drew in a deep breath. "Peterson isn't a man. He's my goldfish."

Several beats of silence passed, and then Robin pealed out a lungful of laughter. "Well, I guess I'll stop asking you if he's a good kisser."

AJ laughed too, and as the others joined in, Eloise's spirits lifted right up to the grease-stained ceiling. She saw Kelli step in front of AJ, turning her back to the others, and say something. But Eloise didn't want to dwell on unhappy things, though her heart bled for AJ.

She knew the woman just wanted to find someone to spend her life with, and Eloise knew *precisely* what that felt like, what a lonely night looked like and smelled like, and how it sometimes felt like life was incredibly unfair sometimes.

She handed out gloves and she and Alice reached for adjacent cupboards. Eloise flinched at the sight of the cobwebbed dishes in hers, and she took a moment to adjust her mask over her nose and mouth.

Then she got to work.

When Aaron arrived, he swept one arm around her waist and pulled her against his side. "Hey, beautiful."

"Hey." She smiled at him, but he couldn't see the gesture. He got the idea though, because he grinned back, his eyes crinkling up in that adorable way he had.

"I want to talk to everyone," he said, his mouth right at her ear. Shivers raced down her spine, and when he kissed her neck right beneath her ear, she could only think about their night together last night. "Is that okay? Can you guys take a break?"

"Sure," she said. She abandoned the silverware drawer she'd been loading into a box and swiped her mask down. "Guys, Aaron wants to talk to us." She looked at him. "Should we go outside?"

"Anywhere is fine." He looked around. "Maybe not here."

Eloise couldn't blame him for not wanting to spend more time than absolutely necessary in the grimy kitchen.

She hated it with everything she had, and she had no idea how it could've gotten like this.

Her father had been a clean freak, especially with the inn. Time and Mother Nature simply had a way of making things that had once been clean and bending them to their will.

"Let's go out by the pool," Eloise said. She'd only been working for a half an hour, but she felt like she could use some fresh air.

It took a few minutes for them all to gather in the shade of the trees that overlooked both the pool deck and the rest of Sanctuary Island. Robin and Alice had just taken loads to the Dumpster, and AJ had wanted to wash her hands.

"Go get a popsicle, baby," Kelli said to Parker. "Take a break. Mom wants to talk to everyone, okay?"

Her son went into Eloise's caretaker's suite, and Eloise smiled at Kelli and moved over to her, taking her right hand in her left. AJ arrived, and she took up a flanking position on Kelli's other side.

"I've been looking into Zach Watkins," Aaron said, causing a shot of surprise to move through Eloise. She hadn't known he was doing that, and her heart warmed toward him all over again. He was so good. He cared about what she cared about, and Eloise had never had someone like that in her life before—besides the women at the inn that day, sacrificing their weekend to clean out a greasy, disgusting kitchen.

"I've found a few things." He proceeded to outline what he knew, and he produced a birth certificate with the name Kelli had discovered too.

She seemed very interested in that, and when Aaron finished, she said, "Kristen and I talked to Rueben this morning. He gave us the name of Zach's two sisters."

"What are they?" Aaron asked.

Kelli told him, and Aaron typed them into his phone. "I think I'm just going to leave it," Kelli said. "He hasn't bothered my mother again, and there's no reason to poke at him."

"I already called him and told him everything we know," Aaron said. "I advised him to stay far from you, your mother, anything to do with your family, your father's art, all of it." Aaron wore a stern look that Eloise adored as much as his happier smile. "In fact, I asked him to leave the island."

"What did he say?" Kelli asked, squeezing Eloise's hand. She tried to watch Aaron and Kelli simultaneously, but she couldn't.

"He said he was actually thinking it was time to move on."

Kelli nodded, but Eloise still had plenty of questions. Where had he gotten those letters he'd shown Kelli? What was his real goal? How long would he stay gone?

Eloise suspected this wouldn't be the last time they saw or talked about Zach Watkins, but Kelli seemed to want to move on, and Eloise would support whatever she wanted to do.

"What about you, Eloise?" AJ asked, leaning around Kelli. "Did you get in touch with your brother?"

Eloise's gaze flew to Aaron, as she hadn't mentioned much to him. She'd told him last night that she was exhausted because she'd found something at the inn that would require a lot of work. He hadn't asked much about it, but he'd offered to come help her today after he finished at the station.

He'd known she was stressed, because he'd called for dinner instead of making it, and he'd rubbed out her feet before he'd taken her to bed. He'd slipped away soon after they'd finished making love, only to return an hour later to hold her while she slept.

She loved him a little bit more every day, and she'd started to see herself in his house and life permanently.

"Uh, no," she said. "He hasn't called back yet." She took a deep breath, because she might as well report right now too. "I called the banks too, but they were all closed last night, and of course, now it's the weekend."

"Banks?" Aaron asked, and the mood in the shade shifted.

"I'll tell you about it in a minute," Eloise said.

"I called my realtor last night," Alice said. "Asked him who developed the land where my house is on Rocky Ridge."

Eloise's pulse started to bump faster and faster.

"He looked into it and got back to me this morning. He said it was Boyd Proffitt, and the housing developer had signatures from a Garrett Hall."

Eloise nodded, acceptance starting to sink in. Her brother had known about the seven properties her father had won in his card games, and though they'd been passed to her legally in the will, he'd been managing them since their father's death.

Eloise had never felt such a strong sting of betrayal. Her father had once hit her, and while that had been a massive blow, both physically and emotionally, Garrett's deception was somehow worse. Far worse.

Tears pricked at her eyes, but Eloise didn't want to cry. Not today. Not over this.

"If the land wasn't his to sell," Alice said. "Everyone in the Salt Pines community can sue him." She looked at Eloise with a light in her eyes Eloise hadn't seen in a while.

"Then what happens?" Eloise asked. "The houses are there. It's not like I can take them back."

"No," Alice said. "But a judge can decree that he has to pay you the money he earned by selling land that wasn't his."

Eloise nodded, but deep down, she didn't want the money. She wanted Garrett to pay for what he'd done in an emotional way; she wanted him to suffer the way she and her mother had those last few years after he'd gone off to college.

For all she knew, Garrett had conspired with her father against both of them, and that only drove the knife of betrayal further into her back.

She hadn't told her mother anything, which was easy as she didn't live with her anymore. At some point, she'd probably have to tell her, especially if there was a lot of money in the accounts her father had scrawled onto a single sheet of paper in that legal-sized envelope.

Three accounts, each at a different bank, the name on the account and the number all penned in her father's hand. Eloise could see the slanted writing in her mind's eye, and her stomach squeezed tightly, the way it had yesterday afternoon when she'd finally looked inside the envelope.

By the time she'd gotten to Aaron's, evening had arrived, and all the banks had been closed. She'd left the items she'd found inside the walls at the inn locked in her trunk, and she'd done her best to be present for Aaron and his girls.

"I'll know more about what I want to do once I talk to the banks," Eloise said. "And Garrett."

"Hello?" a man called, and Robin spun toward the garage.

"That's Duke," she said, and sure enough, her tall, dark-haired husband rounded the corner in the next moment.

He grinned at everyone, broke the tension in their little group, and shook hands with Aaron. That gave Eloise time to inhale again before she had to face him and tell him what she hadn't yet.

"Come see the volleyball court," she said to him, slipping her hand in his and leading him toward the steps that went down to the terrace.

Once at the bottom, she looked out over the island, the ocean, and the sky. She wondered if God had such a good view of the world, and if so, how He could get anything done besides just standing there and looking over the grandness of His creations.

"I love this island," she said.

"What's going on?" Aaron asked.

Eloise looked at him, ready to share everything with him. "Yesterday, while I was cleaning out one of the last rooms, I found some documents hidden in the wall." She told him everything, concluding with, "I'm trying to get a copy of my father's will right now—I've called the lawyer who read it with me and my mother—and I've called Garrett. That's it."

Aaron's frown had not budged during her story, but now he gathered her into his arms. "I don't know what to say, El."

"You don't need to say anything," she said, pressing her cheek against his chest. "And I don't need you to do anything." She pulled away and gave him a frown of her own. "I don't need you to do any digging on your own. I'm working with Alice to find out about the contracts, and I can call banks and deal with my brother on my own."

"Can you?" Aaron asked, but not in an unkind way. "I don't remember Garrett being violent, but with his scams out in the open, anything is possible. People will do crazy things when backed into a corner."

A slithery, tingling feeling spread across Eloise's scalp, and she nodded. "I thought he lived in Portland," she said. "Oregon. As far from here as he could get."

"I'm sure he does," Aaron said. "But it sounds like not for the reasons you thought."

Eloise nodded. "You're right. Probably so I couldn't get to him quickly, or be involved in his life at all."

"Exactly," Aaron said, folding her into his embrace again. "I love you, Eloise, and I need you to be careful with this."

She smiled to herself, those three little words holding more magic than Eloise had ever known. "I will," she said, pulling back. "I love you too, Aaron."

He leaned down and kissed her, and Eloise realized just how many people she had to rely on now—and how wonderful it felt to not be alone anymore.

"Okay," she said a moment later, pulling away. "We have so much to do before dinner arrives, and I didn't lure you out here so you could kiss me. I need your muscles." She grinned at him, took his hand, and started back toward the steps.

"I know what I'm good for," Aaron teased, and Eloise did too—and he was definitely good for a lot more than just his muscles.

CHAPTER TWENTY

R obin's giddiness could hardly be contained. She was so glad Duke had come to the inn to see what she'd been doing with Eloise. She first led him on a tour of the second floor, detailing all the wallpaper and carpet they'd ripped out. She showed him where she'd single-handedly ripped down a curtain rod that had wanted to stay permanently. She laughed at the story now, though she'd been quite annoyed last week.

"Wow, Robin," he said. "You guys have done amazing things here."

"Right?" She squeezed his hand. "Now you know what I've been doing, and trust me, it hasn't been all that fun."

"I feel like a loser for being mad at you," he said, ducking his head.

Robin paused in the hallway, where bare bulbs

shone down on them from above, because Eloise had gone so far as to throw away all the light fixtures. She wanted the inn to have a complete facelift, and she planned to replace everything, right down to the tiniest details.

"It's okay," she said. "I understand."

"I should've been coming here with you," he said. "You ladies shouldn't have to do this all yourselves, especially when I don't even have a boat yet."

"It'll be here soon," Robin said, though the delay had been hard on both of them. She couldn't control the weather in the Pacific, no matter how badly she wanted to. Once Duke had his beloved boat back, everything would return to normal, and Robin couldn't wait. She loved routines and schedules, and Duke wasn't good with nothing to occupy his time. "And you're here today. Aaron doesn't come very often."

"He's a busy man," Duke said. "I've literally been doing nothing." He looked up, his eyes hooking into hers just like they had the very first time they'd met. "Can you forgive me?"

"Of course," Robin said, stretching up and kissing him.

He breathed in through his nose and held onto her waist with an intensity in his grip that Robin had felt before. He kissed her for a good several seconds, finally moving his mouth to her neck.

"Duke," she said with a giggle. "Control yourself."

He chuckled too and stepped back. "Sorry, Robin."

She cupped his face in her palm and gazed at him. "I love you."

"Romantic dinner tonight?"

"Eloise ordered a seafood feast," she said. "She's having picnic tables delivered this afternoon, and we're eating here." She'd told him all of this already.

"Oh, right," he said, leaning closer. He ran the tip of his nose along the rim of her ear. "Let me make you feel good tonight?"

"I like the sound of that," she said with a smile.

"Romantic lunch tomorrow?" he asked.

"Yes," she said. "Lunch tomorrow sounds great too."

"Perfect," Duke said, straightening. "We better get down to the kitchen before someone thinks we've snuck off like high school kids."

Robin smiled and went down the grand staircase with him. "Did you have your talk with Mandie?"

"Yes," Duke said. "She seemed surprised to learn that boys weren't like girls." He chuckled. "I tried to assure her that Charlie wasn't a pervert for thinking about sleeping with her. He was just normal."

"Has she thought of it?"

"Nope," Duke said. "She even said, 'That's weird, Dad. Why are they like that?'"

Robin laughed with him, and they entered the kitchen just as a phone started to ring.

"Not mine," Eloise said, and Robin knew whose it was.

Alice, who had jerked to her full height. She pulled

her mask down and hurried toward the hooks by the back door, where she'd hung her purse.

She got her phone out of the pocket and the call connected, an anxious look on her face. It took all of Robin's willpower not to follow her friend right back outside. The only reason she didn't was because of Eloise.

She hadn't asked everyone to come to the inn so they could have a Tell-All, confessional, or intervention. She needed their help, and Robin wanted to help her.

She pulled her gloves back on, positioned her mask in place so she wouldn't inhale mold, spider webs, or any other unknown particles, and led Duke over to the fifteen-foot island running down the middle of the kitchen. She'd been working to clear out the cupboards and drawers there when Aaron had arrived.

She and Duke worked together, and she knew he was back to normal when he started telling fish jokes. She'd heard them all before, of course, but she laughed at most of them anyway. AJ, who worked on the other side of the island, hadn't heard them, and she seemed entertained by Duke's bad jokes.

Her phone rang, and it was the special ringtone Robin saved for her mother. Her eyes met Duke's, and he said, "Good luck, babe."

She'd need it, because every conversation with her mother ended with hurt feelings or an argument. Robin was tired of all of it, and she wanted to put the past behind her, make amends, and start to build a relationship with her mother she actually wanted to cultivate.

She'd been talking with Duke about it for a couple of months now, and she'd been trying to exit a conversation gracefully before her mother said something snippy. She'd been inviting her mother to lunch once or twice a month, but they were honestly exhausting, and she'd only done it a few times.

"Hey, Mom," she said, opting to go out into the hallway that led under the grand staircase. Turning right, she headed toward the lobby and the front door. "What's up?"

"Where are you guys?" she asked. "I stopped by to bring you that oatmeal you wanted, but no one's home."

"Oh, right." Robin sighed as she wiped her hair off her forehead. "I forgot about that. The girls are at Rocky Ridge, and Duke and I are helping Eloise at the inn on Sanctuary."

"Hmm."

Robin worked hard not to let her mother's humming annoy her, but it always had. "You know the garage code, Mom," she said. "You can leave it on the kitchen counter."

"All right." Her mother sighed too, and Robin got the impression she was putting her mother out greatly by being unavailable to come running out to the street so her mom could simply hand the sack of steel cut oats out the window as she drove by.

"I haven't seen you all since Duke got back," her mom said. "Why don't you come for dinner tomorrow?"

Robin's first inclination was to say no, but she wondered if her mother was trying too. She never seemed to tire of making sure everyone knew her opinion, or that she was right about something, and Robin knew that none of her siblings had a great relationship with their mother.

"Okay," Robin said. "What time?"

"How about six-thirty?"

"We'll be there," Robin said, because if her mother was willing to try, so was Robin. For many years there, Robin had simply decided that her mother would never change, and there was no point in trying to repair something that had broken so long ago.

Joel Shields's death had changed Robin's opinion on that, though. She'd seen the way Clara had been suffering at the funeral, and she'd spoken to Kristen about their daughter several times since then.

Clara couldn't fix the damage that had been done in her youth, because her father was dead. Robin could at least try with her mother.

"Sounds wonderful," her mother said. "Will you bring that compound butter you make to go with lobsters and crabs?"

"The stuff with the garlic and parsley?" Robin asked.

"Yes," her mother said. "I love it with crab legs."

"Sure, Mom," Robin said. "What else should I bring?"

She didn't want to spend tonight or tomorrow morning cooking, but it was polite to offer to bring something.

"Maybe that applesauce cake," her mom said. "It's Eva's birthday, and we can call her and sing to her."

All at once, everything made sense. Her mother didn't want to see her and Duke and the girls because she hadn't in a while. She wanted Robin and Duke to come during the time when she'd video chat with Stu for his daughter's birthday.

And hey, Robin could bring the cake, and Grandma would be a hero.

Robin reached up to rub her forehead, forgetting about the dirty rubber gloves she wore. She flinched away from the smell and grime, disgusted with herself. That feeling only intensified when she said, "Sure, sounds fun."

"Yay," her mom said as if she were sixteen instead of sixty-five. "See you tomorrow, dear."

"Yep, tomorrow." Robin hung up and let her arm fall to her side. "Unbelievable." She shook her head, her reflection faint in the glass in front of her. The sun shone through the front door while Robin quickly went through the ingredients she needed for an applesauce cake and compound butter. She also needed the internal fortitude to tell her family they had to go to her mother's for dinner tomorrow night and sing happy birthday to Eva, a girl who'd once told Robin and Duke they were freeloaders for living in her mother's house.

She sighed and pressed her eyes closed, searching for the strength to go back into the kitchen.

Noise erupted from behind her, and she spun back toward the kitchen, her feet moving quickly. She stepped inside to find everyone except Aaron and Duke crowding around Alice.

Across the expanse, their eyes met, and Robin hurried toward her friends without further encouragement.

Alice didn't speak, and Robin studied her, trying to the news on her face.

"Speak," AJ said. "You can't just walk in and declare how angry you are without an explanation."

Alice lifted her eyes, and while they'd held emotion when she'd lowered her chin, now they were cold and almost dead. "Frank lost his job," she said, the same iciness in her gaze penetrating her voice. "Got a little too friendly with one of his clients." She ground her teeth together and shook her head. "So he hasn't filed for bankruptcy, but Susan said he's considering it."

"Having less money in his account would make sense for that," Robin said. "Not the other way around."

Alice just rolled her eyes. "Susan apparently talked to him today, and she said if he doesn't call me today to explain, she'll file in court to have a formal, mediated meeting so we can work out how I'm going to get paid now that our accounts aren't connected. He said he would." She shoved her phone in her pocket, her jaw still tight.

As quickly as a blink happened, the strength in Alice

went out, and Robin reached for her at the same time AJ did. She slumped against both of them, her voice full of anguish as she said, "What am I supposed to say to him?"

She looked up, pure desperation etched into Alice's features. "I'm not strong enough for all of this," she said, tears appearing in her eyes. Pure shock flowed through Robin, because she hadn't seen Alice break down like this in decades—not since the night her mother had died.

That night, it was if Alice had cried out all of her weakness, all of her imperfections. That night, a new version of Alice had emerged, and this soft, scared, unsure version of the woman hadn't been seen since then.

"Yes, you are," Robin said, and Eloise added, "Of course you are, Alice."

"This is nothing," Kelli said. "You survived years of your husband cheating on you. You can handle whatever comes your way from here on out."

"Alice, you are the strongest, most capable woman I know," AJ said.

Alice looked at her, nodded, and started to straighten. It seemed to take her twice as long as normal, but she finally did it. She pulled her shirt down and dusted it off, as if brushing away a bit of dirt and not the fact that she'd very nearly collapsed.

Aaron stepped over to the group. "I know I'm completely out of place here, but I always give this to Billie and Grace when they're stressed." He held something out, and Alice held his gaze for a long moment before taking it.

She smiled at it, and then him, and then held up the chocolate bar for everyone to see. She started to laugh, and while Robin wanted to cry for her—rage, and shake her fists at the sky, and demand to know why Alice had to continue to go through so many hard things—she ended up laughing too.

CHAPTER TWENTY-ONE

AJ entered the grocery store on Diamond Island, stepping back through time as she did so. She'd insisted Robin let her go to the grocery store to get the few ingredients she needed for the applesauce cake and compound butter she was taking to her mother's the next evening.

It was the least AJ could do. But as she glanced around, it felt like the grocery store had been built for a race of humans that didn't grow as tall as AJ. Everything felt like a miniature of the real thing, and AJ felt like a giant pushing her cart around to find cinnamon, nutmeg, and parsley.

The produce section lifted her opinion of the place, as most of the fruits and vegetables she saw there came from right there in the cove.

AJ adored organic produce, and she loved supporting

local farms and businesses. Though all she needed was parsley, she found herself examining the pink grapefruit in a bin that proudly proclaimed they came from Pearl Island.

AJ knew exactly where they came from—the Schnieder orchard. AJ had been out with Tyson Schnieder once upon a time, and she'd let him do whatever he wanted to her in one of the open-front sheds out in the trees.

AJ hated the memories that assaulted her whenever she came to the cove. She'd been toying with quitting her job and coming back to Five Island Cove, especially now that everyone was here. But she couldn't stand the thought of being reminded of the loose, horrible person she'd been in high school.

She'd hated herself so much back then. She still struggled with the feelings of self-loathing, but at least she'd made it past the point of sleeping with every male who looked her way.

She'd just decided to get the grapefruit when someone said, "AvaJane?"

She froze, both hands full of grapefruit, as her memory fired. Her nerves frayed all the way to the ends, because she knew this voice.

This voice haunted her in her quietest moments, because it belonged to Matt Hymas, maybe the only boy AJ had ever loved as a teenager.

They'd dated a little bit, and Matt was the only boy

who'd *seen* AJ for who she really was. The last time they'd slept together, he'd asked her why she went out with so many boys.

She hadn't been able to answer him; he hadn't needed her to. He already knew, and AJ knew he knew.

She turned slowly, almost afraid she'd find a specter there, speaking with Matt's voice. Instead, she found a strong, tall, broad-shouldered version of Matt Hymas. He'd aged almost thirty years, just as she had, but he wore his age well. Really well.

He had a full beard that he obviously kept trimmed and neat. The dark hair was littered with gray, as were his sideburns and the sides of his head, all the way up toward his crown.

A smile burst onto his face. "It is you." He tapped his chest. "It's Matt Hymas."

"I know who you are," she said, putting a smile on her face too. A moment later, she couldn't contain her excitement at seeing him, and she set down the grapefruit and turned into his embrace.

And, oh, standing in Matt's arms was a special kind of heaven AJ *had* forgotten. He chuckled, the vibrations from his chest flowing into hers. "What are you doing here?" He stepped back and behind his cart again.

"Just visiting," she said. "What about you? You don't live here, do you?"

"Actually," he said, his smile staying exactly in place. Only the joy in his eyes went right out. "I've moved back.

My, uh, wife—" He cleared his throat. "My *ex*-wife and I just finalized our divorce last month. My youngest left for school a week ago, and my dad needed a general manager for the golf course."

AJ absorbed all of the information in the blink of an eye. "I'm sorry about the divorce," she said, though she wasn't at all. Still, if it had only been final for a month, Matt wasn't ready for a new relationship. He was bulkier than the tall, skinny kid who drank protein shakes to bulk up. He had the same great head of hair, made even better with that gray. And he'd be the same sensitive, caring man that he'd been as a teenager, as most people didn't like who they'd been in high school and worked to be better.

"Thanks," he said, glancing away. "It's for the best. She, uh—we decided it was for the best." He pinned his smile back in place, and AJ wanted to tell him he didn't have to pretend with her.

He'd told her that once, and that small bit of permission had meant a lot to her.

"You don't have to pretend with me, Matt," she said, her own smile fading.

He nodded, the light coming back into his eyes. "Thank you, AvaJane."

"You can call me AJ," she said. "Everyone has for years, Matt."

"Yeah, but not me," he said.

"Yes, you too," she said, teasing him now. "I distinctly

remember you calling me AJ before we went to college."
He'd been the last boy she'd been with in the cove, and he'd
said, "I'll miss you, AJ," as they'd laid in his bed together.

Matt tipped his head back and laughed. "All right, AJ.
You win."

She almost said, "I always do," but she pulled the
words back. "So," she said, nodding to his basket.
"Stocking up on spinach and celery? You must be doing
that smoothie diet."

"A little," he said. "I do it about half the time."

"What do you do the other half of the time?"

"Eat steak, lobster, and potato chips." He laughed
again, and the sound of it filled AJ right to the top of her
head. She missed him so much, and she hadn't even
known it until that very moment.

"Are you living with your parents then?" she asked,
reaching for her grapefruit again.

"No, I've got my own place," he said. "Are you at a
hotel?"

"I'm staying with Robin," AJ said, bagging her fruit.
She put it in the cart with the things her friend needed.
"She's waiting for me to make this cake." She didn't want
to just walk away. She wanted his number. She wanted to
go to dinner with him. She wanted to get caught up on his
life and tell him all about hers.

Not that she had anything all that impressive to tell,
but somehow, with Matt, it wouldn't matter. Everything

was an adventure for Matt Hymas, and AJ stepped into him to hug him again.

"Can I have your number?" she asked. "Maybe we could get together while I'm here. Dinner or lunch, and just get caught up." She told herself quite sternly that she would not be sleeping with him. She was worth more than that now, and while she did remember what it was like to be beneath the sheets with him, and she'd like that very much, she didn't need to do it to feel good about herself.

"Yeah, sure," he said, and she plucked her phone from her purse and handed it to him. As he tapped to put in his number, he said. "I'd love to get caught up. What are you doing tomorrow?" He looked up, his eyebrows up, his expression open and vulnerable. Hopeful.

"Nothing," she said. "Robin's going out with her husband for a romantic brunch. Then we were going to her mother's for dinner, and you'll be doing me a *huge* favor if you got me out of going to that." AJ grinned at him, knowing she was flirting. But this was safe flirting. This was normal; what any woman would do for a man like Matt.

"Dinner tomorrow then," he said, chuckling. "You sure Robin won't be upset?"

"I'll talk to her, and text you," she said. "Okay?"

He handed her phone back to her. "Perfect."

She tucked her phone in her purse and grabbed him in another hug. "Sorry," she said as she laughed in his ear. "It's just so good to see you."

"And you." He stepped back, and AJ caught a hint of redness crawling up underneath his beard. She'd always adored his embarrassment, and he seemed not to know how utterly handsome he was. How kind. How just wonderful.

AJ certainly hadn't known all of that about him when they were teens. She'd known he was different, because he'd made her feel differently about herself than the other boys did. He'd treated her with respect, despite her reputation.

"See you tomorrow," she said, and she forced herself to walk away.

"AvaJane?" he called after her.

She turned back to him, wishing she could use his full name the way he used hers. "Yeah?"

"Can I get your number too? That way, I can follow-up with you if you don't text me."

"Hey." She cocked her hip, feeling far too old to be doing such a thing. "I'm going to text you."

"I'd rather be safe than sorry," he said, pushing his cart over to her. He looked down at her, and AJ had a feeling he was sizing her up, evaluating her, and making multiple decisions all in the space of a few seconds. "I let you get away once," he said. "I'd rather not make that mistake again." He held his phone at the ready, looking from it to her, his eyebrows raised.

Let her get away?

AJ didn't know how to respond. She quickly recited

her number, and Matt put it in his phone. "Thanks." He leaned down and swept his lips along her hairline. "I'll talk to you tonight."

With that, he went back to the onions and garlic, leaving AJ to stare after him.

I let you get away once.

She checked out, loaded up her groceries, and drove back to Robin's house, where the woman had bowls filled with wet ingredients, dry ingredients, and one with butter and garlic.

"Sorry," AJ said, lifting the bags to the counter.

"You're fine," Robin said, taking out the parsley first.

AJ unpacked the other ingredients, her mind spinning around one question. "Robin, do you believe in a soulmate?"

"Sure," Robin said without looking up from the cutting board. "I don't think they're exclusive, but I absolutely believe two people can be soulmates."

AJ nodded and folded up the recyclable bags. She turned to tuck them into the cupboard where Robin had gotten them when she asked, "Why?"

"I ran into Matt Hymas at the store." AJ spoke slow enough that she could turn around and face Robin before she finished the sentence.

That got Robin to stop chopping. "You're kidding."

"He said he let me get away once, and he didn't want to let me go without getting my number." AJ smiled just thinking about the man and the way he'd touched his lips to her forehead. "He said he'd rather be safe than sorry."

"Wow."

AJ sat at the bar and looked at Robin as she went back to chopping parsley. "He asked me to dinner tomorrow night. Do you care if I skip eating at your mother's?"

Robin's movement didn't stutter or pause. "Of course not. I'd kill not to go." She wore a disgruntled look on her face. "Go with Matt. You'll have way more fun."

"Okay," AJ said. "If you're sure."

"Absolutely," Robin said, finally glancing up. Her expression changed from displeasure to happiness. "And you know, AJ, maybe he is your soulmate. You've had such a hard time finding someone, and maybe it's him."

"He was the only boy I ever truly liked in high school," AJ admitted.

Robin's eyebrows went up. "Is that right?"

"Yeah." AJ shrugged. "He got me in a way no one else did, except for you guys."

Robin nodded. "I know what you mean."

"I'm not going to sleep with him," AJ said.

Robin scooped up the parsley with the edge of her knife and dumped it all in the bowl with the butter and garlic. "AJ, you can do what you want. You're forty-five years old."

"I'm not the same person I was when I was fifteen," she said. "Or eighteen."

Robin pulled her gaze back to AJ's. "I knew you snuck

off to see him that night." She laughed and shook her head as she started stirring the butter. She really leaned into the movement, and AJ thought she was trying to churn a whole new crock of butter for how hard she mixed it.

"I can admit it now," AJ said. "I just felt so stupid. Did you know he called me in Miami, and I ignored him?"

"No." Robin pushed the bowl of butter and a mold toward AJ. "Put this in there. Really pack it in."

As AJ started on that, she told Robin about the phone calls from Matt that her roommate had screened for her at Miami State. "I just figured I'd never see him again, and there was no point. We'd had our fun; he needed to move on."

"Do you think he did?"

"He just said his youngest started at college last week, and his divorce was final last month."

"And no, he hasn't moved on," Robin said. "Or else he wouldn't have asked you out, only a month after his divorce."

AJ didn't dare hope for such a thing. She'd thought about Matt over the years, of course. She'd simply never acted on any of her thoughts, and he obviously hadn't either.

"I'm going to go call him," AJ said, after she finished molding the butter. She slid the molds into the fridge and turned to hug Robin. "Thank you so much for letting me stay here. Thank Duke for me too."

"Oh, he's going to get his thanks," Robin said with a devious smile.

"Robin." AJ rarely heard Robin say anything about her sex life, but the two of them laughed together, and AJ was so glad she'd come to Five Island Cove, even if it set her back from earning an on-air position.

"Say hi to Matt for me," Robin called after AJ as she headed for the staircase that led up to the guest bedroom.

"I will," AJ said, her heartbeat prancing in a way it hadn't in years. For the first time in at least that long, she had real hope that she wouldn't have to live the rest of her years all alone.

CHAPTER TWENTY-TWO

Eloise turned and put the salad bowl on the dining room table. "Time to eat," she said. "All devices, please." She twisted back to the counter, where she'd put a small basket. She held it out to Grace, who smiled as she put her tablet in the basket. Billie didn't look as excited to give up her phone, and she cocked her head toward Aaron, who hadn't looked up from his device.

"What about him? Does he have to give up his phone too?"

Eloise wanted to warn her to watch her tone, or her father was going to flip out. Instead, Eloise pulled her phone from her pocket and placed it on top of Billie's. "Yep. Everyone. It's family dinner night."

"Are you in our family?" Grace asked, looking at Eloise with wide eyes, filled with something like hope.

"I—"

"Of course she is," Aaron said, standing. He deposited his phone in the basket and put his arm around Eloise's shoulders. "Girls, Eloise and I have started talking about getting married."

Billie squealed and leapt from her chair. She hugged both Eloise and Aaron at the same time, and Eloise put one hand on the girl's back while she looked at Aaron, surprise threading through her.

Aaron beamed back at her, and he held secrets in those dark eyes. A thrill ran down her arms, and Eloise hugged Grace too.

"All right." She stepped over to the fridge and started to raise the basket to the top of it when Aaron's screen brightened with a text.

No notification sounded, and Eloise saw the message appear at the top of the screen.

Tonight. 11:30. I'll be there.

Eloise's lungs froze, with all the air in them. While she still stared at the phone, the text disappeared.

Her brain screamed at her. *That was Laurel.*

One of Aaron's detectives, and the woman who had been on the scene with Kelli and Zach.

Behind her, she heard the angry voices of Aaron and Billie, and she quickly put the basket on top of the fridge and retraced her steps to the table.

"If you'd just listen," Billie said. "I have prepared a really great argument for why I should be able to go to Kara's party."

Aaron rolled his eyes, and Eloise wished he wouldn't do that. Didn't he know that only fueled Billie's attitude?

"I'll listen," Eloise said, never taking her eyes from Aaron. He looked at her, and she lifted her eyebrows. The message was conveyed, because he dropped his head and had the decency to look cowed.

She wondered if he'd do the same if she confronted him about cheating on her. She just couldn't believe it. She'd never detected any dishonesty in Aaron, but the alarms in her head wailed at her that he'd been slipping out of the house late at night recently. She didn't stay every night with him, but he'd had to "go into work" twice when she had been with him. The most recent time had been two nights ago, on Friday night.

"I'll listen too, Bills," he said.

"You will?" she asked. "For real, Dad?"

"Yes," he said, taking a big pile of salad. "For real." He passed the bowl to Billie, who filled almost her whole plate.

"Okay," Billie said, passing the bowl to Eloise. Grace already had salad, so Eloise took as much as she wanted while Billie began her argument.

"First, Kara's parents are going to be there. You know Scott Pyre really well, Dad, and he's not going to take his eyes off of us. Kara's actually really worried about it."

Aaron took a square of lasagna, and helped Grace get one too while Billie continued.

"Second, there are only going to be three boys there. We're not going to pair off."

"How many girls?" Aaron asked.

"Five," she said.

"Is Jake going to be there?"

"No," Billie said. "And that's my third point. Jake isn't even going to be there, and he's the only one I like. Therefore, there's no reasonable explanation for why I shouldn't be able to go to the party on Friday night."

Eloise concealed her small smile as she cut herself a square of lasagna, which suddenly took all of her attention. Billie had gotten a lot better at her persuasive arguments, and Eloise didn't see how Aaron could tell her no.

She also couldn't see how a man as attentive to his daughters and their safety could lie to her, sneak around on her, and carry on another relationship with another woman. None of it made any sense.

"Who's driving you?" he asked.

"Okay, I've worked that out too," she said. "So Addie lives a couple of blocks over, right? I was thinking one of her parents could drive one way, and one of you—" She looked from Aaron to Eloise and back. "Could drive the other."

Eloise's whole soul expanded, as if she wasn't already as happy as she could be. After all, Aaron had just announced to his girls that he intended to marry her. Their reactions were wonderful and made her feel so loved and accepted.

And to now be included in the equation of driving Billie to or from her party, Eloise found the future she wanted just out of her reach.

Tonight. 11:30. I'll be there.

What was that about? Maybe Aaron had just asked Laurel to attend a class or a hearing.

She told herself not to be stupid. There weren't classes or hearings at 11:30 at night.

Maybe he'd given her someone to visit. It really could be anything; it didn't have to be a meeting between the two of them.

He wouldn't do that, Eloise thought. Not moments after he'd told his kids about marrying her.

"What do you think, El?" Aaron asked, forking up a bite of salad and lasagna together.

She didn't know how he ate the hot food with the cold, but she was growing more and more used to it now.

She blinked to get her thoughts aligned where they needed to be. She could deal with Aaron's texts to Laurel later. "I think your daughter is exceptionally bright," Eloise said. "She knows not to do anything she shouldn't with a boy, and she has a sound plan for getting to and from the party." She reached for her drink. "I wouldn't mind driving one of the ways."

Aaron nodded and looked at Billie. "I wouldn't either. I suppose you can go."

Billie stared at her father, and then burst out of her seat, knocking into the table as she did.

"Oh okay," Eloise said, reaching to straighten her plate.

"Thank you, Dad," Billie said, throwing her arms around his neck. He chuckled at he patted her back.

"Love you, Bills." He held onto her one arm as she drew back and they looked into one another's eyes. "Don't make Eloise a liar, okay? She said you're a bright girl who knows not to do anything she shouldn't."

"I won't, Dad." Billie met Eloise's eyes as she took the quick steps back to her chair. "Thank you, Eloise."

Eloise just nodded, because she wanted to tell the girl she loved her the way Aaron had, but she didn't quite know how.

———

LATER THAT NIGHT, ELOISE LAY IN AARON'S ARMS, breathing in the scent of his skin as he traced a pattern on her bare upper arm. She loved being with him, as no one made her feel as loved or as comfortable as he did. They'd just finished making love, and while Eloise had tried to prolong bedtime and then take an extra-long time being intimate with him, she knew it wasn't eleven-thirty yet.

He finally sighed and slipped his arm out from under her head. "Be right back, baby," he whispered, pressing a kiss to her temple.

She kept her eyes closed until she heard his footsteps in the bathroom, and then she opened them and watched him check his phone. The blue light basked his face in eerie shadows, and she saw the frown as it pulled down his eyebrows. "I have to go into work, El," he said.

She moaned and said, "Really? Again?"

"It'll be fast," he said, tossing his phone on the corner of the bed as he started to get dressed. "I'll be back before you know it."

Eloise sat up, determined not to let him go without making sure she was in the forefront of his mind. "Aaron," she said. "Is this something I should get used to? You slipping away to your mistress in the middle of the night?"

He laughed and came around to her side of the bed. "My mistress?"

"Your job," she said.

He pressed his mouth to hers and kissed her fiercely for a few moments. "No," he said. "I rarely get called into work at night. There's just someone new on the graveyard shift right now, and I like to keep my night crew on their toes."

"Who texted?" she asked.

"Laurel," he said, stepping away. He sat on her corner of the bed and pulled on his boots. "If you're still awake when I get back, I'll sing you to sleep." He grinned at her, and Eloise watched helplessly as he twisted to grab his phone and then left the bedroom.

"Well, he didn't lie to you," she said. Laurel *had* been the one to text him earlier, and perhaps she really was going to do something at eleven-thirty but now needed his help.

Eloise thought about setting an alarm for herself but decided against it. She couldn't sleep anyway, and her imagination went wild in Aaron's absence.

He returned in under an hour's time, and Eloise was still awake, on her side of the bed, just as he'd left her.

She kept her eyes closed though, and Aaron made minimal noise as he changed out of his clothes, used the bathroom, and slipped back into bed with her.

Eloise rolled over then, her fingers seeking the hard ridges along Aaron's chest. "You're awake," he whispered.

"Mm." Eloise kissed him, desperately trying to taste another woman on his lips. She had to know, and even the best cheaters couldn't keep every scent and every clue hidden.

He tasted like himself, though, and as Eloise's hands wandered south down his body, he tensed. He broke their kiss, quickly moving his lips to her neck. "I might not be able to do that," he whispered. "I've only been gone for forty minutes, and we've already done it tonight."

Eloise was aware of what they'd done. She also knew what a male's body could and couldn't do, and he surely couldn't have made love to another woman so soon after her.

"You're so sexy," he whispered. She did enjoy it when he called her sexy, but a hint of embarrassment sliced through her when he rolled and took her into his arms, kissing her like perhaps he could make love to her again.

What she knew was that Aaron had not snuck off to have sex with Laurel, and strong guilt struck her right behind the lungs as she felt his love for her in his soft, insistent touch. She could hear it in the way he told her to how beautiful she was. He said it in words with, "I'm so in love with you, El."

He wasn't cheating on her. He couldn't be. No man could put on such a convincing performance if he was sleeping with someone else.

CHAPTER TWENTY-THREE

Robin looked out the windshield at her mother's house, a sense of dread filling her.

"It'll be fine," Duke said. "Remember, girls." He looked into the rear-view mirror at their two teenage daughters. "We're trying to show love to Grandma, not argue with her or get annoyed with everything she says."

"We know, Dad," Jamie said, but Robin needed the reminder.

Her mother picked at everyone, not just her, and Mandie particularly had a hard time with Jennifer Golden, as she wasn't the thinnest girl in the cove and had quite a few insecurities about it.

"I'll be on my best behavior," Robin said, reaching for her door handle. "Mandie, grab the cake, would you?"

"Got it, Mom."

They all piled out of the car, and Robin carried the

compound butter. She'd purposely placed herself in her office when Matthew Hymas had come to her house to pick up AJ, and he really was a gorgeous man.

He was sweet and nervous around AJ, and Robin found that so endearing. AJ had called her out of the office to say hello, and of course Robin remembered Matt. They'd shook hands, and AJ had taken his hand and followed him out the front door, a glow about her that Robin hadn't seen in a while.

She needed some of that glow right now, as she led the way up the sidewalk between the perfect flowerbeds to the front door.

She rang the doorbell and waited a couple of beats before opening the door. "Mom," she called. "We're here."

Duke's hand, warm and heavy, on her lower back gave her the support and comfort she needed, and she appreciated him so much in that moment.

"Come on back," her mom called, and once again, Robin led the way.

Her mother wore a light blue blouse the billowed around her aging, slight frame like a kite, paired with a pair of white shorts that went tastefully to mid-thigh.

That was another thing she always zeroed in on—what Robin and the girls wore. Duke, however, existed in a class all his own. He seemed dipped in gold, and all of his decisions were the right ones, and he always laughed at appropriate times and "dressed for success."

Whatever that meant.

He was a fisherman. What, exactly, did they wear to show the fish they were serious about catching them that day?

Robin mentally shook her head, trying to clear the thoughts. She couldn't go into dinner with a poor attitude, or they'd leave upset the moment they could.

She longed for the type of relationship where she wasn't counting down the minutes until she could escape. Where she and her mother lingered over coffee and scones, chatting about everything and nothing, and just enjoying one another's company. Where she could be her authentic self, and her mother would accept her for who she was, and not who she should be.

"Hey, Mom." Robin smiled as she approached her mother, who stood at the island, where her stove had been built-in. She had the grills on today, with hamburgers and hotdogs sizzling away.

"Robin," her mom said pleasantly, and they embraced. It was a quick hug—nothing like the hugs she got from Kristen or even Alice—and Robin stepped out of the way so her kids could say hello.

Duke rounded them all out, and her mother's smile grew when she saw him. "You look well, Duke. Alaska must have something special in the air."

"It's a great place," Duke said. "I hope to get the whole family up there next year."

Robin stiffened, because that was the very first time

she'd heard that. Mandie's face turned to stone, and Robin's annoyance soared.

"Oh, heavens," Robin's mom said. "Can you imagine Robin in Alaska?" She chuckled as she nudged a hamburger patty up on the grill an inch or two.

"I think I'd like it," Robin said, if only to argue with her mother. She coached herself through her thought processes. She did not need to argue with her mother. It wasn't required or necessary, and she shrugged.

"But I might hate it. I've heard the sun never sets in the summer."

"Yeah," Duke said, throwing his arm around her. "Then you can run morning, noon, or night, babe." He smiled at her, and sometimes she wondered what went on inside his head.

"I thought we were having crab legs, Grandma," Mandie said, picking up a pair of tongs. She'd worn a black sweater with an array of colorful stripes on it, because Robin's mother had once said it made her look slimmer. With her cutoff shorts, Robin thought she was a very cute girl, and she'd told her so before they'd left the house. She did not want to have the same kind of relationship with her daughters that she'd had with her mother, and Robin worked very hard to talk to them about real things, but maintain her role as matriarch of the family.

"They ran out," Robin's mom said. "So we're having an indoor roast instead."

Robin opened the fridge and put the compound

butter inside. She wished her mother had texted or called to tell her about the change in menu, because then she wouldn't have had to make the compound butter at all. Surely she'd gone to the store last night, as Robin knew her mother hated leaving the house on Sundays.

She called it her one day of rest, though Robin wasn't sure why she couldn't rest on Mondays or Tuesdays—or any other day of the week too.

Her mother didn't work. The Goldens had generational money, as Todd Golden had been one of the first to come to Five Island Cove and open up a housing development. They owned real estate on all five islands, and Jennifer Golden had managed their properties, investments, and rentals for thirty years before retiring.

Robin's oldest brother, Fisher, did that now, and Robin benefitted by living in one of those properties for practically free.

She didn't want to be more involved than she was, and sometimes she and Duke talked about getting out of the house and into something without apron strings that led back to Robin's mother.

But the truth was, Duke was just a fisherman, and while it provided a good living for them, they weren't rich by any means.

"I made that macaroni salad you love so much," her mom said. "And cowboy caviar."

"I love that stuff," Jamie said excitedly.

"Can I help with anything, Grandma?" Mandie asked, and Robin relaxed a little more. Things were going well.

Mandie helped get out the sides Jennifer had made, and soon enough, they all sat down to eat. The porch off the back of the house had two fans to circulate the air, and now that September was a week or two old, the temperatures around the cove had started to drop.

Duke kept them entertained with stories from Alaska, and Robin legitimately started to enjoy herself. She'd started to wonder if such a thing was even possible, and relief filled her that it was. Sometimes being on her best behavior was so dang *hard*, but she told herself that every relationship worth having took hard work.

"Let's call Eva," Jennifer said only a few minutes after the last mouthful of food was swallowed. "They're an hour behind us, and I know they want to have a family dinner too."

Robin stacked her plate with Duke's, and he picked them both up. With everyone helping, they got all the dishes and utensils back inside while Jennifer went to get her laptop.

She positioned it on the dining room table and said, "Everyone get a chair and gather 'round."

"How old is Eva now?" Duke asked. "Eighteen?"

"Seventeen," Robin said. Her younger brother lived in Virginia, and he had three kids—Eva, the oldest, and two boys that were younger. His wife owned a jewelry store, and Robin had never seen the woman without gems and diamonds dripping from every finger, earlobe, and both wrists.

The line rang, and there Anna-Maria appeared. She had three piercings in each earlobe, and somehow that was perfectly fine with Jennifer Golden. But when Mandie had gotten her second hole last year, she'd frowned at Robin's daughter and said it made her look like she was trying too hard.

Mandie had taken them out for a while after that, but holes never really grew in, and she wore her second pair of earrings on occasion now.

"Jennifer," Anna-Maria said. "And Robin's family. How wonderful."

"We have a cake," Jennifer chirped. "Are you ready for us?"

"Let me get the boys." She disappeared from the frame, and Jennifer patted Robin's leg.

"Go get the candles, dear. Let's get them lit. We'll sing and say hello."

Robin did what her mother said, and in the tiny picture at the top of the screen, her applesauce cake glowed with seventeen candles, brightly lit and flickering.

Robin stared into the fire, seeing different sides of her mother with each twisting, licking flame. She could be sweet and caring. She took care of a neighbor down the street when her shingles flared up. But some of her remarks came with poison on the tongue, almost like she was aiming to hurt when she spoke.

"Here they are," Anna-Maria finally said, and Jennifer held up one hand.

Everyone shuffled on Stu's end of the line, and finally Eva settled in the front, a wide smile on her face.

Beside her, Mandie dug her fingers into Robin's thigh, but Robin didn't flinch. She knew how Mandie felt about her cousin, and Robin could only agree.

Eva wore a tank top with such thin straps she looked nude on top. A large, bright blue stone hung from a pendant around her neck, with matching earrings dangling from her lobes.

"One...two...three," Robin's mom said, and all five of them started singing. During the thirty-second song, Robin told herself this was a blip in time. Barely worth remembering, and therefore barely worth thinking about or being annoyed about.

The song finished, and Robin's mother squealed and giggled while she clapped. Everyone else gave a good effort, and Robin appreciated them so much.

"Thank you, Grandma," Eva said, and that was something, as Robin wasn't sure she'd ever heard the girl express appreciation for anything. "What kind of cake is it?"

"Applesauce," Jennifer said. "With that cinnamon cream cheese frosting you love."

Robin kept her painted smile in place, feeling vindicated when Stu said, "Robin must've made that."

Her mother's demeanor fell, and she admitted, "Yes,

she did," in a near-mutter. "Happy birthday, my lovely," she said in a much louder, higher voice. "What have you been doing today for your special day?"

As Eva droned on about her special pecan waffle breakfast, and then lunch out with her boyfriend—which was a perfectly acceptable activity for her, but definitely not for Mandie—Robin glanced at Duke.

She could tell he was doing the same thing she was—counting down the minutes already. Mandie had actually pulled out her phone, but Robin didn't have the heart to tell her to put it away.

Finally, Eva wrapped up, and Jennifer leaned toward the screen. "Well, we love you, dear. Happy birthday."

Choruses of the same sentiment came from Robin's family, and the call ended.

Jennifer sat back with a satisfied sigh, and she simply gazed at the computer with a look of adoration on her face.

Robin wondered if her mother had ever looked at her like that, or even one of her kids. It felt like because they lived so close and saw her so often, that she simply didn't think they were that special.

"Well," Duke said, exhaling as he stood. "My boat's arriving nice and early in the morning, and I need to be at the dock by four a.m."

Robin rose to her feet too, never more grateful for Duke and his early-morning job. "Thank you, Mom." She waited for her mother to rise, and she hugged her extra-tight. "Dinner was great."

"You're not going to have any cake?"

Jamie looked like she might cry at the thought of leaving the cake behind, her eyes wide and afraid. Mandie just looked at Robin with an edge in her eye that said, *Save us, Mom.*

"I have another one at home," Robin said. "I can't eat anything right now anyway." She patted her stomach. "I ate so much at dinner."

"You always do that," Jennifer said. "I don't know why you do it. You know there's dessert."

"I can't help it," Robin said with a smile. She imagined herself to be a duck, with water-resistant feathers and a round back, where all her mother's criticism would just slide right off her. "Especially when you make that cowboy caviar."

She grinned at her mom and nodded toward the front door. "Do you want me to leave the compound butter? You can have it next time you get your hands on some crab legs."

"No, it's fine." Jennifer started for the kitchen, and she opened the fridge. As she leaned down inside, Mandie gasped. Robin's gaze flew to hers, asking plenty of silent questions.

"Where is it?" Jennifer grumbled, because she wasn't leaning over far enough to see it on the top shelf where Robin had placed it.

"I'll get it, Grandma," Mandie said, stepping next to her grandmother. "It was...hey, look. You have crab legs right there." When she straightened, she held a large bag of crab legs. She looked at Jennifer, and then back to Robin.

Her heart started to pound in her chest. It leapt around, because what was she supposed to do now? She glared at Mandie, because the gasp made sense now, but she hadn't had to step over there and call her grandmother on her lies.

No one said anything, and Robin put her arm around Jamie. "Leave the butter for her," she said to Mandie. "She likes it, and she already has the crab legs."

She started for the front door, noting that only Jamie came with her. "Duke," she said over her shoulder, and her husband jolted into motion.

"Robin," Jennifer called after her, and Robin let her family flow around her and out the front door before she turned back.

Her mom stood at the corner of the wall that separated the hallway from the kitchen, an unreadable look on her face.

In that moment, Robin saw all the human frailties of her mother. She was a good person, with a lot of good qualities, but she wasn't perfect. Robin would want someone to see the good in her, instead of focusing on every little fault.

Wasn't that all she wanted from her mother right this moment?

"I love you, Mom," Robin said, walking back to her.

"Thanks for having us for dinner." She embraced her again, glad when her mom patted her back. "I'll call you this week, and maybe we can go to lunch."

With that, Robin turned and went back down the hall, out the front door, and to the passenger seat.

She buckled her seatbelt calmly, silently. Duke backed out of the driveway, and they drove halfway across the island to their house.

"I'm sorry, Mom," Mandie finally said, her voice full of tears.

"It's fine," Robin said, twisting to look at her daughter. "I promise you I won't lie to you like that, okay?"

"Why did she do that?" Mandie asked. "I don't understand her."

"No one does," Duke said, pulling their minivan into the garage. "You still didn't need to pull those crab legs out of the fridge like that."

Mandie nodded, still looking like she might cry. "It made me mad, Mom. Why does she treat you like that?"

Robin loved her daughter fiercely in that moment. "We have a long history, honey." She got out of the car and turned back to wait for Jamie. "I'll make us another applesauce cake, okay? I have all the ingredients."

And this one she'd actually enjoy making and serving, because it was for her family.

She looked over the hood of the van as Duke and Mandie rounded it. "And hey, I lied to her too, when I said we had another applesauce cake here at home."

Duke started to chuckle, and that lifted Robin's spirits. He took her hand and kissed it, then said, "Seeing Mandie hold up those crab legs was amazing."

Robin couldn't hold back her smile, and before she knew it, all four of them were laughing. They went into the house together, and Robin pulled them all together by saying, "Family hug. Come on, right now."

She didn't have to convince Duke or Jamie, and though Mandie took an extra moment, she too stepped into the family huddle-hug pretty easily.

"I love all of you with my whole heart," she said, her voice turning thick. "We're not perfect, but we belong to each other. It doesn't really matter what my mother does or doesn't do, okay? We'll always have each other."

"What your mother said," Duke said, because while he was very good at showing and telling Robin how much he loved her, he struggled with the girls, especially as they turned into teenagers.

"I love you, Mom," Jamie said. "And you too, Dad." She hugged them both tightly, and as Robin stroked her hair, she wondered what she'd done to get such a sweet girl.

Mandie looked at Duke and Robin and said, "You guys are good parents."

"I might fall down dead," Duke joked, and in the next moment, he pulled their almost-sixteen-year-old into a hug. "Love you, Mandie-moo."

"Okay, Dad," she said. "No. Just no." They laughed together, and the family huddle broke up.

On the way into the kitchen, Mandie said, "Mom?"

She turned back and caught the anxiety on her daughter's face. "What is it, Mandie?" she asked.

Mandie looked over her shoulder to where Duke and Jamie were going into the kitchen, and then she looked at Robin again.

"Something happened at Alice's yesterday, and I need your advice."

Robin's stomach swooped and slid around inside her, and she was instantly grateful she hadn't had any cake at her mother's. "Sure," she said as bravely as she could. "Do we need to get Dad?"

"No," Mandie said.

"Let's go in my office," Robin said, and she led the way in there, though she was sure the floor would vanish beneath her feet at any moment. With the door closed, she faced her daughter again. "Do I need to be worried?"

"I just didn't know how to handle a situation," Mandie said. "Charlie and Ginny had some friends over, and we were all vibing in the pool, having fun. Then one of his friends—some doofus named Dalton—pulled out a joint." She pressed her palms together, clearly nervous.

Robin wanted to gather her into a tight hug and tell her everything would be okay. "Did you smoke it?"

"No," Mandie said. "But he wanted me to."

"What did Charlie do?" Robin did *not* want to call Alice and even be thinking the words *pot* or *marijuana*.

"He just let him smoke it near the back fence."

"Did he smoke any?"

"No," Mandie said.

"Did anyone else?"

"No," Mandie said. "Then Ginny came out, and she was livid. She told Dalton to leave and that he couldn't come back if he brought weed with him again. And I wondered...I should've done that."

"You did fine," Robin said, doing what she wanted to do—take her daughter into her arms and shelter her from the bad things of the world. "Next time, if something like that happens, you can decide if you want to be more like Ginny, or if you want to let Dalton do what Dalton wants to do."

Mandie nodded against Robin's shoulder, and they stood together for several moments. It sure was nice, and Robin was glad her daughter trusted her enough to confide in her.

"Now, let's go bake a cake," Robin said, shifting her feet. "Otherwise, your sister will stage a riot, and I know at least one other person who'll be on her side."

Mandie laughed, and they said, "Dad," together as they left the office.

Robin needed to focus on her family today. She could call Alice about the pot tomorrow.

CHAPTER TWENTY-FOUR

Alice pulled up to the Cliffside Inn with a plate of mint-frosted brownies. Two plates, actually. One for the group to share, and one specifically for Robin, as her best friend had called that morning and told Alice about the marijuana consumption that had happened on her property over the weekend.

Charlie had already been at school, and now Alice was at the inn, so she wouldn't see him until later that night. She had texted him with *Dalton. Marijuana by the pool. We need to talk.*

He'd sent her no less than a dozen messages, most of them paragraphs long about how sorry he was, and he didn't know, and Dalton had gone down by the fence until Ginny chased him away.

Alice still needed to talk to him—and Ginny—and go over an exit plan for when situations like that arose.

Anything they weren't comfortable with, they needed to know how to handle. Right now, it was marijuana use. Tomorrow it could be a girl sending him naked pictures, and next week, he could find himself in a situation that could land him in jail.

As a lawyer, Alice knew how quickly things could escalate, and how easily good people could make bad decisions, and how devastating the consequences could be for years to come.

Robin must've been watching for her, because the petite blonde came out of the front door as Alice shouldered her purse and balanced the two plates of brownies in her hand.

"One of these if for you," Alice said.

Robin smiled and took the plate, her eyes never leaving Alice's. "How are you?"

"Good," Alice said, and it was only a partial lie. "You?"

"Good," Robin said, and at least Alice wasn't the only one using four-letter words to hide the truth. "Eloise has some news, and we want the low-down on Frank."

"I'm prepared to share," Alice said, smiling. "No special group codes required."

"All the kids will be here on the three-fifty ferry," she said. "Up to the inn by four-twenty, Mandie thinks, and AJ is buying dinner for everyone."

"Feels like what we did this summer," Alice said, her grin widening. She'd *loved* this summer and having all of her friends and their families in her house. It was exactly what she'd needed after she'd finally found the courage to cut ties with Frank.

"So let's get the adult conversation out of the way," Robin said, turning toward the front door.

"Something's different about the inn," Alice said, sweeping the majestic front of it.

"Eloise had the windows cleaned today," Robin said. "Doesn't it look great?"

Inside, Alice said, "Yes, it's amazing. She's making such good progress on it."

"That's all us, honey," Robin said, laughing afterward.

Alice laughed too, because she and Robin had been working on the inn with Eloise for a couple of weeks now. With AJ in town, and Aaron and Duke coming to help, the work really was getting done quickly.

"She tried staining the floor this morning," Robin said. "So that's the smell. We're actually in the caretaker's suite." She led the way through the inn to the back door. Across the patio they went, and Robin opened the door to the caretaker's suite and held it for Alice to enter first.

"She brought the mint brownies," Eloise said. "Praise the Lord."

AJ laughed, but Alice thought that might have more to do with whatever text she'd just gotten and less with what Eloise had said. She handed the plate to Eloise, who put it on the breakfast bar beside a plate of cream cheese squares —those were Eloise's mother's recipe—and half an apple-sauce cake. That came from Robin.

A store-bought plastic container of pink-iced cookies sat next to that, and it hadn't been opened. At least AJ knew where a grocery store was, bless her heart.

"Who are you texting?" Alice asked. "Your goldfish?"

AJ looked up, pure joy in her eyes. "I shouldn't have lied about that," she said, some of that emotion fading.

"Hey, you don't answer to me," Alice said. "I'm thinking of getting a fish too, if they're good kissers." She smiled at AJ and put her arm around the other woman's shoulders.

"They're not," AJ said with a giggle. "But you know who is?" She tilted her phone toward Alice, who read the name Matty.

Her brain fired, trying to figure out who that was. All at once, she knew. "Oh, my goodness," she said, somehow speaking and gasping at the same time. "Matt Hymas?"

"She went out with him last night," Robin said from the other side of the room. "Got home *very* late. Stood on the porch kissing him for a *very* long time."

"I did not," AJ said, turning toward Robin. "Get home that late."

All four of them burst out laughing, even Alice, though she was very aware that of the four women there, she was the only one without someone wonderful to kiss.

She told herself she didn't even want that. Over the years, she'd grown used to taking care of herself and the twins alone, and she actually thrived doing it.

"He knows you live in Brooklynn, right?" Eloise asked, sobering first.

"Yes," AJ said, practically floating as she moved over to the couch. "We're reconnecting."

"I bet," Alice said.

"No," AJ said. "Not that way."

"Not yet," Robin said.

"Not at all," AJ said. "I'm only going to be here for seven more days, and..."

"And what?" Alice asked, taking the middle cushion on the couch."

"And I don't know," AJ admitted. "But we're not here to talk about me. Eloise said she talked to her brother." AJ was a master at changing the subject, and this time was no exception.

"I talked to him this morning," Eloise said. "He said he can't tell me anything over the phone, and he's got a ticket out of Portland on Wednesday morning." She wore her nerves on her face, and Alice wanted to comfort her. She had a brownie in her hand as she took the armchair next to the couch. "I talked to all three banks this morning, and the money is still there. There have been no deposits or withdrawals in seventeen years, and the amount of money I suddenly find myself with is staggering."

Warmth filled Alice's soul. She didn't want to ask, but her curiosity pricked at her. Thankfully, it was Robin who said, "How much, Eloise?"

"A little over three million," she said, frowning.

"Why are you upset about this?" AJ demanded. "I'd be thrilled if my no-good father left me three million dollars."

"Would you?" Alice asked quietly, and the room fell silent. She looked around at everyone, wishing Kelli was there with them. Kristen was supposed to come too, and Alice remembered that the two of them were coming together after Kelli got off work.

"I suspect that Eloise is torn about actually accepting the money," Alice said into the void. "It's a lot of money, but it feels tainted by her father's gambling habit. She worries that if she takes it, she'll be hurting someone else." Alice watched Eloise as she spoke, and tears gathered in the other woman's eyes.

"She doesn't want to think of her father as a benevolent, caring man, who left her a fortune, because that is not who she knows her father to be. He was a violent, cruel man who drank too much and abandoned her and her mother when they needed him most."

"Alice," Robin said.

Alice flicked her gaze to Robin, and nodded. "Sorry, I'll stop."

"No," Eloise said, a sob slipping from her mouth in the next moment. Alice quickly got off the couch and knelt in front of her, accepting her into a tight hug.

"You're right, Alice. That's all exactly right." Eloise cried openly, and Alice wasn't surprised when Robin went to her shoulder and started patting it, nor when AJ positioned herself behind Alice, as if she needed help holding up Eloise.

Alice did, because most of the time, she felt one breath away from a complete collapse herself, and offering a helping hand or shoulder to cry on for someone else was difficult.

Alice felt a closeness with these women she'd experienced a few times in the past several months, and she knew she wouldn't even be here without Robin's foresight and strength.

She wouldn't weigh what she did without Eloise, and she wouldn't be practicing law without AJ's confidence in her. She wouldn't realize her own strength by seeing it in other women without Kelli.

Alice's own emotions surged, and before she knew it, she was crying too.

"Alice," Eloise said, pulling back. "You never cry."

Alice swiped quickly at her eyes. "I just love you, El, and I hate that you have these conflicting feelings to deal with." She stood and straightened her blouse, taking a moment to breathe as she brushed something invisible from it. "I know exactly what they feel like, and it is not fun." She retook her seat on the couch and crossed her legs, wishing she could contain all she felt as easily.

"What's the news with Frank?" Robin asked, still standing beside Eloise.

"I spoke with him," Alice said, finding a deep well of strength inside her that had somehow not been emptied yet. "He's agreed to continue to pay as much as possible through a payment app. He is actively looking for another job, and he assured me he is not going to file for bankruptcy." Alice delivered her news with as little emotion as possible. She didn't believe anything Frank said, but she could convey his message to her friends.

She'd made a checklist yesterday while the twins slept late, and then as Ginny cooked up sausage and a batch of strawberry pancakes.

Alice could trade in her expensive vehicles for cheaper models to make the payments doable for herself. She could sell the house and move to a more practical location for her and the twins to ensure she could pay the mortgage herself.

With dedication and tenacity and the ability to think outside the box, she could build her practice here in Five Island Cove.

She was going to start there, and hopefully steadily increase her own income so she wasn't so reliant on Frank to pay for things. The cars and house were things she'd do as last resorts, because right now, Frank was still able to pay as per the terms of their divorce.

Robin wore questions in her eyes as she came to sit beside Alice again, but she didn't vocalize any of them. "And Ginny?"

"Still dating Robbie," Alice said with a sigh. "I think it's harder to have your daughter be dating a boy." She looked at Robin. "I'm not sure how you've done this. I trust

Ginny; it's Robbie I don't trust. I find myself wanting to look at his phone or call his mother every five minutes."

Robin smiled at her and linked her arm through Alice's. "I'd be going nuts if I didn't have you to check with about everything."

Alice leaned her head back and looked at the ceiling. "If he wasn't two years older than her, I think I'd feel differently about it."

"She's smart," Eloise said, and Alice nodded. Ginny was smart. Hopefully, she'd know what to do if a situation arose she didn't want to be in. Heaven knew Alice had spent enough time telling her what to say, what to do, and to just call. Alice would drop everything and get to her as fast as she could.

"We had dinner at my mother's last night," Robin said, and Alice was grateful she'd taken the spotlight. "She said she'd make crab legs, and she asked me to prepare my garlic-parsley compound butter." She sighed, the sound heavy and long. "Then she lied and said they didn't have crab legs, so we had hamburgers and hot dogs. But you should've seen Mandie pull out this big bag of crab legs and ask my mother why she'd lied to us."

Alice turned and looked at Robin, surprise filling her. Robin started to laugh, and that broke the mood in the room.

AJ started talking about her date with Matt, and Alice enjoyed the enthusiasm in her. After all these years, and all the broken and disastrous relationships she'd had, AJ still possessed a healthy amount of hope.

Alice fed off of it, because she needed some of that. She was tired of feeling jaded and lied to, and as she listened to AJ detail how chivalrous and sweet Matt Hymas was, Alice felt like perhaps she could find someone else to be happy with.

Life didn't have to end just because her marriage to Frank had. She didn't have to live the rest of her life unhappy and alone, even if she craved solitude sometimes.

AJ had never been married, and she spoke with hope and excitement about the prospect of finally finding the just-right man that she could love and who would love her unconditionally.

Alice wanted that too, and while she wasn't going to rush into the dating pool, for the first time, it was a possibility.

The door opened, and Kelli arrived with Parker on one side and Kristen on the other. The twins followed, and Alice stood to greet them. She drew them both to her in a double hug as Robin did the same with Mandie and Jamie.

"I'm sorry, Mom," Charlie said, and Alice believed him. For how mature he was, she sometimes forgot how sweet and kind he was. He never wanted to disappoint her, and Alice appreciated that.

He stepped back at the same time Ginny did, their twin timing sometimes uncanny. "I called Doctor

Michaels," he said. "And rescheduled for Thursday. I didn't see anything on the calendar."

"Okay," Alice said. "You didn't want to go tomorrow?"

"They're having basketball tryouts," Ginny said, rolling her eyes. "He's not tall enough to make the team. He's only trying out because Robbie is."

"Hey," Alice said, slicing a look in her direction while trying to gauge Charlie's reaction to what she'd said. "We don't put each other down." She reached out and pushed her son's hair off his forehead, smoothing it back so she could see his whole face. "You're a brilliant player. Not everyone has to be seven feet tall to make the team."

He wore a look between fear and resignation, but he nodded. "Thanks, Mom."

Ginny said, "Sorry, Charlie. I'm sure you'll do great at the tryouts," before heading into the kitchen with Kelli and Eloise and Parker to get an after-school treat.

Alice drew Charlie a little further out of the way. "I don't want Dalton at the house without me there again."

"Okay," he said.

"And you owe your girlfriend an apology for putting her in that situation. It made her extremely uncomfortable, and she didn't know what to do."

Charlie hung his head. "I know. I will."

"And you need to tell your sister thank you for handling it as well as she did."

Charlie looked up then, his irritation plain. "Really? Mom, she's so annoying. She's all over that school, signing up for everything. And everyone *loves* her, even *my* friends. I'm just the loser in her shadow." The darkness on his face didn't comfort Alice, as she'd seen it in Frank's eyes many times.

Alice looked over to the kitchen, where Ginny chatted with Eloise and Kelli as if she were one of them. She was mature, and capable, and smart. Charlie had existed in her shadow his entire life, though Alice had never tried to make him feel that way.

"I'll talk to her about that." She focused on Charlie again. "You're not a loser."

He sighed. "I know. I don't want to talk about this."

"But you'll talk about it on Thursday with Doctor Michaels," she said, not really asking but sort of.

"Yes," he said. "I'm going to get a brownie."

She let him go, because it never did any good for Alice to press an issue with Charlie. He didn't have to talk to her—that was why she paid for his therapy. As long as he spoke to someone about the dangerous, festering feelings inside him. That was all Alice wanted for him.

She was just about to go get a cheesecake square when someone knocked on Eloise's door. She veered that way, because she was the closest.

She wasn't sure who would be standing there, because the only people missing were Aaron and Duke, and they would've just walked in.

Alice opened the door and froze.

"Hello," the man there said, flashing a brilliant smile. "I believe my wife is here."

Alice remembered all of her prestige and proper manners from the years of living in the Hamptons. "Yes," she said, her voice cool and crisp. "Come in, Julian."

She stepped back, turning to the group behind her to find Kelli. She'd also frozen, the hand holding the plate with a slice of Robin's cake on it hovering in midair.

"Julian," she said, and the plate fell to the floor, shattering the silence as it broke into dozens of pieces.

CHAPTER TWENTY-FIVE

"**D**ad!" Parker abandoned his snack and ran toward Julian. Her husband laughed as he swooped the boy into his arms and held him on his hip. They spoke, but Kelli was distracted with the women around her, all of them trying to clean up the shards of porcelain that had come from the plate she'd dropped.

"I'm sorry," she said, standing still in the middle of the chaos. "I was just surprised." She watched Robin scurry around to get the bigger pieces. Eloise arrived with a broom and Alice with a wet paper towel to get all the tiny shards that the naked eye couldn't see and even the broom couldn't get.

"It's fine," Eloise said. "I broke two or three glasses just yesterday. No big deal."

AJ had taken up a position about halfway between Kelli and Julian, her feet shoulder-width apart as if she were expecting Julian to have to barge his way through her friends to get to Kelli. And AJ wasn't going to let that happen.

Kelli looked back to where her husband grinned at and talked with their son, and everything in her world shifted. How had she thought it would be a good idea to separate them? Parker adored his father, and while Julian worked long hours, he'd always loved Parker as much as she did.

Julian's eyes finally drifted toward her, and Kelli drew in a deep breath.

"Kel," Eloise said. "You don't have to talk to him."

"It's okay," Kelli said.

"Are you sure?" Alice asked.

Kelli looked at Alice, who'd always been the strongest of them all, at least in Kelli's eyes. AJ was a powerhouse too, but Kelli knew her deepest, darkest secrets and desires, and AJ was more real for Kelli. Softer, with real human emotions.

Alice was almost robotic in how she dealt with things, and Kelli had aspired to be more like that when it came to Julian. She wondered if she'd made the right decision or not.

"Yes," she said, hating the weakness inside her. "I can handle Julian."

"I'd like to meet him," Robin said.

"Okay." Kelli stepped out of the circle of her friends and led the way over to Julian. He put Parker down and said something to him in a soft voice that sent Parker back to the breakfast bar to get another treat.

"Julian," Kelli said, her voice steady. She was grateful for that. "These are my friends. Alice Kelton, who answered the door."

"So good to see you, Julian," Alice said smoothly, and she was perfectly poised and professional. They shook hands, and Alice stepped back.

"Robin Grover," Kelli said. They exchanged pleasantries, and she added, "Eloise Hall. She owns the inn."

After Eloise had said hello, Kelli linked her arm through AJ's. "And AJ Proctor."

"Yes, Kelli talks about you often," Julian said, and he was definitely acting like the attentive husband who knew all of his wife's friends as intimately as she did.

With the introductions out of the way, Kelli had no choice but to say, "Should we talk outside?"

Julian played his gentleman card and opened the door, even going so far as to put his hand on her back as she passed him, A spark flared within Kelli, and she tried to tamp it down.

The sun shone down brightly, and Kelli detoured toward the trees lining the back of the yard. She folded her arms and turned to face Julian. "You didn't say you were coming."

They'd interacted over the weekend, doing one of the rituals they did whenever Julian traveled. They hadn't spoken about anything but Parker, but Tiffany hadn't been there.

"I decided last-minute," Julian said. He tucked his hands in his pockets, something Kelli had seen him do while they were dating. Not much since. "I'm sorry, Kelli. I miss you desperately, and Parker, and I want you both to come home."

Kelli didn't know how to say yes. She also couldn't deny him outright either. "Julian, it's not that simple."

"I know that," he said. "But Kelli, we belong together."

"Do we?" She turned away from him and gazed out over the island.

"I think so," he said, coming to stand beside her. Without the weight of his gaze on her face, Kelli could think more clearly. "I love you, Kel. I've been in love with you for years, and I think I just...forgot."

Kelli wanted to scream at him, a new type of storm brewing inside her. "What if you forget again?"

"I'm not going to," he said, his fingertips touching hers. "I've learned a lot in the past few weeks since you left, and I'm going to do better."

"Tell me how," Kelli said, surprised at her boldness with Julian. He'd run everything in their marriage, and he'd probably been shocked that she hadn't just gone along with his plan to have two women living with him— sleeping with him.

"I'm going to come home from work," he said. "And spend real time with you and Parker."

That was a good start, and Kelli nodded but didn't say anything.

"I've been cleaning the house," he said.

Kelli couldn't help the giggle that burst from her mouth. "Wow," she said. "I didn't know you knew how to do that."

"I didn't either," he said, chuckling. He took her hand fully in his, and Kelli let him. "But I can, Kel. I make my own dinner, too. And I'm just miserable in that house without you. It's depressing."

Kelli didn't want to say she missed him too. She did, though, and she wondered if she could just step back into her New Jersey life. That townhome and the job where she taught other housewives yoga felt thousands of miles away. It existed outside her grasp, and standing there on the cliffs overlooking houses, and trees, and beaches, and the vast ocean, Kelli realized she didn't want to grab back onto that life.

"So much would be different," Kelli said.

"That's okay," Julian said.

"I'd want to go to counseling together," she said. "And by myself. You should go yourself too."

Julian didn't respond immediately, and Kelli felt herself mentally digging in her heels on this issue.

"I can do that," he said a few seconds later.

"I'd need my interests and life to be as important as yours."

"I really failed there, didn't I?"

Kelli wanted to take the blame, because she'd *let* him, his life, and his business become more important than anything else. But she didn't take the blame. Every marriage had at least a dozen different things that made it work or caused it to start to erode, but Kelli's devotion to Julian and their marriage had been absolute.

"Where's Tiffany?" Kelli asked, sucking in a breath afterward.

"I don't know," Julian said. "She doesn't work for me anymore."

"Did she quit or did you fire her?" There was a very big difference in Kelli's eyes, and it was so big that she turned and looked at her husband's face.

He was a handsome man, and she'd always thought so. His strong jaw flexed as he tightened it, and his throat constricted as he swallowed. He moved those dark, penetrating eyes to meet hers, and Kelli remembered all the reasons she'd fallen in love with him. Could she throw those away because he'd made a few mistakes?

"I asked her to go," Julian said.

"But you didn't want to."

"It was hard for me," he admitted. "But only because I'm no good alone, Kelli."

"Is that why you need two women, Julian?" She let go of his hand and put a few steps of space between them. "Because you made me feel like I wasn't good enough. I couldn't satisfy the great Julian Thompson, so he needed to get someone else to share his life with. His child. His bed." She shook now, every part of her. Perhaps she was angrier than she'd thought.

"I won't go through that again," she said. "I'm not going to return to New Jersey—pulling Parker from school here—and quit the job I have here, only for you to decide next month or even in six months that I'm not good enough for you."

"Kelli—"

"Because I *am* good enough," she said. "I am. I'm a good mother, and I was good at teaching yoga, and I'm good at working with the kids at the junior high too. I'm capable, and I'm strong, and I'm not going to let you—or anyone else—tell me directly or indirectly that I'm not."

She pulled in a breath through her nose, trying to calm herself. She hadn't felt this unsettled in a long time. She didn't let herself *feel* things like this at all, and she certainly never vocalized them.

Julian's eyes blazed too, and Kelli felt the same fire burning through her. She was not going to back down from this. She was *not*.

"If it was so hard for you to let her go, maybe you made a mistake."

"It's harder for me to let you go," he said. "You wanted me to choose, Kelli. I chose. I chose *you*."

She studied him, trying to find the dishonesty in his face, hidden in his words. She wasn't sure about anything right now, and she didn't know what to say or do.

"Kelli," Robin called from behind her, and Kelli turned toward her. "We're headed down to dinner."

"Okay," Kelli said. "I'll be two minutes."

Robin hesitated, and Kelli waved to her to let her know she was okay. She would've never stood up to Julian like she had without her experiences over the past few months.

She looked at him. "I think you should move here to see if we can work things out."

Julian opened his mouth but nothing came out.

"A change of scenery might be exactly what we need," she said. "You can manage the courier business via texts, videos, or calls."

"I don't know, Kelli."

Voices started to fill the air behind her, and Kelli hooked her thumb over her shoulder. "Come to dinner with us. You don't need to decide right now. But I think that's what I would want. My mother is here. Parker started school here. I have a job here. I'd like to see if we can make things work here before we just try to go back to New Jersey."

She felt like he was a drug addict, and if they stayed in the same neighborhood, doing all the same things, he'd simply fall back into his old habits. She wasn't willing to relocate herself and Parker only to come back in four or six months.

She realized how negative her thought process was, almost like she was dooming their second chance without even giving it the opportunity for success.

She needed to be cautious though, and if he'd agree to come here, she could get him out of the environment that had led them to the point where he had a girlfriend in their bed, and they could make a real attempt to reconnect and rebuild their life together.

"Okay," he said. "I can start with dinner."

"Great." Kelli turned and headed back toward the caretaker's suite, finding AJ waiting for her and Julian on the stoop.

"Ready?" she asked.

Kelli linked her arm through AJ's. "Yep. Is Matt meeting us there?"

"Yes, he's with Duke and Aaron already." AJ increased her pace. "I'm actually kind of nervous about what they'll say to him."

"Duke and Aaron?" Kelli laughed. "They're not going to grill him over his intentions," she said.

"You've met Aaron Sherman, right?" AJ asked, and they both laughed as they piled into the group RideShare.

"You're right," Kelli said, leaning forward. "Can you hurry? We've got a guy down there who might have to answer questions he's not comfortable with." She and AJ laughed again, and once Julian got in the passenger seat up front, the RideShare driver started down Cliffside Drive to the restaurant AJ had chosen for dinner.

Kelli didn't whisper, because she found that rude. She let the conversation between AJ and Kristen go on around her, and she participated when Eloise asked her something from the way back seat of the minivan.

She'd have to fill everyone in later, but right now, she just wanted to see how dinner went.

CHAPTER TWENTY-SIX

Laurel strode toward Aaron's cruiser, her temper on the verge of exploding. He'd caused problems between her and Paul, and she was so done being the Chief's gopher.

She yanked on the door handle, and slid into the seat. "Here you go," she said, practically throwing the folder of documents she'd collected over the past few days.

Aaron wanted her to work on things in her spare time, but he wasn't paying her. She disliked how she'd so readily jumped at the chance to work more closely with him, and now that she had a real relationship with another man, her crush on the Chief of Police had faded to nothing.

"What is wrong with you?" he asked.

"Maybe that I've been working on this nonstop for three days, just so you'd have this by tonight," she said. "I missed dinner with my boyfriend on Monday night, and I had to skip bowling tonight." She glared at Aaron.

He gaped back at her, resignation and realization finally dawning on his face. "I'm sorry, Laurel. I didn't realize."

The fight left her. "I know. I should've said something." She folded her arms and stared out the windshield. "I had to tell Paul that we were working on something off the books," she said, her voice more wooden. "He might ask you about it."

"I can handle Paul."

"If you've messed this up for me," Laurel said, but she didn't finish the threat. She didn't know how to complete it anyway. She couldn't actually do anything to the Chief of Police.

"I'll talk to him," Aaron said softly. "Make sure he knows what we've been doing, and that it's not what he thinks."

"Thank—" Before Laurel could finish saying "you," a loud, high-pitched rapping noise filled the cruiser. She yelped as she turned toward her window. A scream escaped when she saw a face there.

A moment passed, and she recognized the woman. Adrenaline spiked and surged, quickly dropping as she said, "It's Eloise."

Laurel reached for the door handle and got out of the car as Eloise backed up a couple of steps.

"Eloise," she said.

"What is happening here?" she demanded. She grabbed onto her jacket and pulled it closed with her hands, folding her arms over the unzipped pieces.

"Nothing," Laurel said at the same time Aaron said, "Eloise, what are you doing here?"

"What am *I* doing here?" She wiped at her eyes. "I didn't want to believe that you were sneaking off to see another woman. I was *sure* Laurel was just training a new cop." She swayed wildly, like she was on a ship pitching madly in the stormy sea.

"Sweetheart," Aaron said. "Nothing's happening here." He approached her, but Laurel wanted to tell him to back off. Eloise did not want to be touched right now, and sure enough, she swatted his hand away from her arm.

"Isn't that what you said? That you had a new guy on the graveyard shift, and you liked to drop by to make sure they all knew you saw everything in that blasted station?" She threw one arm out as if to indicate a building or a person.

"And I find you in this dark parking lot, with *her?*" Eloise tossed a glance at Laurel. "I'm sure she's great. A good cop, and someone you can talk your police shop with. Or whatever." Tears streamed down her face, and Laurel wanted to wrap her in a tight hug and assure her that absolutely nothing had happened between her and Aaron.

"Eloise," Aaron said, glancing at Laurel too. "Nothing is happening between me and Laurel."

Eloise sobbed, her anguish and pain pouring from her

in waves of sound and feeling that made Laurel's heart hurt.

"You can go, Laurel," Aaron said quietly. "I'm so sorry. I'll talk to Paul too."

Eloise looked up, her eyes wide. "Who's Paul?"

"My boyfriend," Laurel said. "Eloise, honestly, this isn't what you think." She took a step toward the other woman, thought better of it, and nodded to her boss.

Then she got the heck out of there before Eloise Hall clawed her face off.

She pounded her steering wheel in frustration as she drove out of the grocery store parking lot, and instead of turning right on Saltwater Way, she went left.

She seemed to make turns without thinking, and she pulled up to Paul's house a few minutes later. Without hesitating, she jumped from her car, not bothering to turn off the engine or the headlights, and jogged up to his front door.

"Paul." She used her fist to pound on the door, not caring that the sound echoed like gunshots in the stillness of this neighborhood. Several seconds passed, and she'd just raised her fist to knock again when he pulled the door open.

"Laurel?"

"There is nothing going on between me and Aaron Sherman," she said, her chest heaving. "Not only would that be inappropriate, but I have no feelings for him." She took in a huge breath and added, "He's been having me research some people for him, as a personal favor to him. People in the life of his girlfriend—his very serious girl-friend—and her friends. That's it. We meet in the parking lot behind the grocery store, and I give him the things I've found."

Paul just stared at her, his eyes wide and his hands down at his sides. In that moment, she realized he only wore a pair of sweatpants. No shirt. No shoes.

She calmed enough to take in his muscles and the soft, dressed-down version of the man she'd only seen in uniform or all decked out in polos and jeans, cologne on, and his hair swooped to the side just-so.

"I'm sorry," she said. "It was a secret, but not a secret relationship." She leaned forward, desperate for him to understand. "I would *never* do that to another person, because I know exactly how demoralizing and horrific it can feel."

"Laurel," Paul said.

"My last boyfriend abused me," she blurted. "Emo-tionally, verbally, physically. He cheated on me. I haven't dated in four years, and you—" Her voice shook, as did the breath she pulled in. "You are the best thing that's happened to me in longer than that, and I can't stand the thought of you thinking anything bad about me."

"Okay." He stepped forward and gathered her into his arms, and she easily melted into his embrace. His chest was warm, and she pressed her cheek to his heartbeat.

"Okay, Laurel. It's okay." He stroked her hair, and

Laurel felt loved and accepted for this moment in time. "You're okay."

She started to cry, hating the weakness inside of her that prompted it. At the same time, once the tears ended, she felt made of iron. Strong, and immovable, and ready to take on the world.

She pulled away and looked up at him. "Do you believe me?"

"Yes." He stepped back, welcoming her into his house. "Do you want to come in?"

"Yes." She went into his house and let him close the door behind her. When his hands landed on her waist and snaked around her, Laurel tipped her head sideways so he could kiss her neck.

"Do you want to stay?" he whispered. "No pressure, Laurel. I can put you in the guest bedroom."

Laurel acknowledged the feelings inside her, naming them out loud. "I'm scared," she whispered. "And excited to be here. But mostly scared."

"I won't do anything you don't want me to do," he said, stepping back. "Come on." He led her down the hall and into a bedroom that clearly wasn't his.

He turned down the bed and turned back to her. She let him unbutton her jeans, and she stepped out of them. She lifted her arms as he tugged her shirt over her head.

His expression was made of hunger and desire, but he simply swept her off her feet and laid her in the bed. As she made herself comfortable beneath the soft blanket, he got in bed beside her and just held her close until she fell asleep.

CHAPTER TWENTY-SEVEN

Eloise had finally calmed enough to listen to Aaron, and the low, deep, slow timbre of his voice had further settled her.

"It was Laurel that found everything about Zach," he said, finally closing the folder he'd shown her. "And all of this about Garrett."

She looked from the manila folder to his eyes. Foolishness filled her, but she didn't know how to go back in time and erase the last forty-five minutes of her life.

"I'm sorry," she said.

"Don't you dare apologize to me," Aaron said, his voice strong yet firm. "You don't need to do that. It's me who needs to apologize. I shouldn't have told you I was checking in on my graveyard cops, because that wasn't true." He sighed and raked his fingers through his hair.

"I've caused a lot of problems. *I'm* the one who needs to apologize."

He approached her timidly, reaching toward her as if she were a wounded animal he wanted to take care of. She didn't want to feel like that, so she reached out and took his hand in hers.

"Why couldn't she have just come to the house?"

"I don't know," Aaron said. "I thought you might be upset about me digging into your life. Your friends' lives." He hung his head again. "Are you?"

"A little," Eloise said truthfully.

"It's who I am," he said. "What I do. I *love* you, Eloise, and I want to make sure you're safe. I want to make sure Kelli is too. I want all of your friends to be protected and happy."

Eloise couldn't help smiling a little, though the action felt a little manic on her face. "I know," she said. "And I love you for that."

He raised his eyes to hers. "You sure?"

"Yes," she said. "But Aaron, you have to find a line between work and us."

"I'm not sure I know what you mean."

"The same thing I asked you about the other night, if your job was going to be the mistress between us."

A hard look crossed his face. "I don't want it to be."

"You're free to choose," she said as kindly as she could.

"I'm not sure I am, Eloise." Aaron sighed and paced away. "After Carol left, all I had left was the job. I had my office, one of the only spaces she hadn't touched. I had my guys. The station became my safe haven."

Eloise approached him, wishing this conversation was happening behind the closed doors in his house and not a dimly lit parking lot in the middle of the night. "So it was like the lighthouse."

"Yes," he said.

She threaded her hand through the crook of his elbow. They stood together for several moments, just breathing in and out with one another.

"I bought you a ring," he whispered. "Billie is going to kill me, because she's been planning this whole huge proposal." He looked at her and leaned down to press his lips to her forehead.

"I would never cheat on you, Eloise. You're everything I've ever wanted in my life, and I don't need anyone or anything else."

Eloise's throat closed up, and she didn't know what to say.

"Well, and the girls," he said. "I love them too. I love how you love them, and I love how they love you." He shifted his feet. "I'm not great at saying things, sweetheart. I'm much better at showing them. I hope you can forgive me. I really did just want to make sure I knew what we were going to get tomorrow afternoon when your brother shows up. It was my way of trying to show you how much I love you."

"You already show me that," Eloise said. "By letting

me eat dinner with you and the girls. By letting me love them. By your amazing performance in the bedroom." She grinned up at him, and when he looked at her, they both started laughing.

He pressed her hand to his side. "Amazing, huh?"

"Oh, come on," she said. "You know you're every woman's dream, right?"

"Am I?"

"Aaron," she said. "Really."

He chuckled and shook his head. "Come on, El. Let's go home."

She'd driven her own car, but Aaron told her he'd bring her back in the morning to get it. On the short drive from the grocery store to his house, Eloise stewed over a question she wanted to ask.

She held it beneath her tongue until he pulled into the driveway. "When might this proposal be happening?" she asked. "I want to make sure I pretend to be the right amount of surprised so Billie won't know you spilled the beans."

"Only heaven knows," Aaron said dryly. "She keeps telling me it has to be perfect, and I, apparently, keep messing it up."

Eloise laughed, and they got out of the car. She met him near the hood, where he paused and took her into his arms.

"I'm sorry," he said sincerely.

"I may have acted a little irrationally," she said. "Jumped to a conclusion or two."

"You did nothing wrong," he said, leaning down to kiss her. Eloise enjoyed the taste of his mouth and the way his lips matched up with hers perfectly.

"Just tell Billie that I'll say yes no matter what, and that you want to get it done soon," she whispered.

"I'll tell her," Aaron whispered back. "Now take me to bed, El."

THE NEXT DAY, ELOISE ARRANGED HER FOLDERS AND papers one more time. She'd asked Garrett to meet her at the inn, and she and Aaron had been ready to receive him for half an hour. At least.

Aaron had asked a teenage girl down the street to come stay with Billie and Grace, and they'd both gotten pictures of Billie getting her hair done. They made Eloise smile, but nothing erased the nerves for very long.

She'd just reached to straighten the corner when a loud, booming knock filled the room, followed closely by, "Eloise?" in her brother's voice.

Relief rushed through her, but Eloise wasn't sure why. She and Garrett hadn't been terribly close for years now, but she spoke to him from time to time. They'd gotten along reasonably well growing up, and she'd never had any concerns about him.

He filled the doorway as she stepped around the folding table Aaron had set up for her, and Eloise froze. He was much bigger than she remembered, and she was suddenly glad Aaron had insisted he be there for this meeting.

"Hey," she said, not sure what else to add. He didn't look good, not with that scruffy beard that had started turning gray. His hair was long and held back by a pair of sunglasses. He wore a shirt that looked like he'd spilled nacho cheese on it, and which was at least one size too small. He'd gained probably fifty pounds since she'd last seen him.

He carried an expandable file folder in his hand, and as he approached, he put a smile on his face.

Eloise had the distinct impression that he was the Big, Bad Wolf, and she was about to get eaten. Rather than embrace him or shake his hand, she went back around the table and sat down.

He sat on the other side of it, and Aaron came into the room. She nodded to him, and said "My boyfriend, Aaron Sherman."

Garrett chuckled as he stood up. "Of course. The Chief of Police." He shook Aaron's hand, and Aaron smiled and said hello. He and Garrett were closer in age, and Aaron had likely known her brother in high school. Aaron sat beside Eloise and sighed. "Ready?"

"Ready." Eloise took a deep breath and opened her first folder. "This is a document I found in the walls upstairs," she said, taking out the paper. She closed the folder and put the paper on top. She did not slide it closer to Garrett. For some reason, she thought he might rip it to shreds. She'd taken pictures of all of them, and sent PDFs to herself, but she still didn't want to take any chances.

She detailed what she and Aaron and her friends had been able to find out about the ranch in Montana. Then the distillery in Kentucky. One by one, she went through all seven properties. Lastly, she put their father's will on the pile.

"Dad left all of this to me," she said, looking up. Garrett had said nothing, not one word, during her speech. "*I* own all of these things, and yet, you're running them. I'm assuming you have been for years and have been profiting off of them. Is that true?"

"Yes," he said, not even trying to hide it. His dark eyes glittered dangerously, and Eloise could barely hold his gaze. Aaron did though, and that gave her the same strength. "And you're wrong, El. I own all of this stuff."

He lifted his file folder to the table and opened it. "First off, this wasn't an inn. It was a gentleman's club. I worked here for years after you stopped coming, and I learned from the best." He grinned fully, his words confusing to Eloise.

"Dad stopped running the inn when I was fifteen," she said. "And it *was* an inn. There were families who came here. Not just men."

"On select weekends," Garrett said, waving his hand

as if he'd concede to her. A fire lit in her stomach, and anger began to simmer in her veins. "But it was definitely a gentleman's club, and we ran it until the day Dad died."

He pulled out some papers and pushed them toward her. "This says that. It was a legally operated and licensed gentleman's club."

Eloise scanned the documents. Again, she wasn't a lawyer, but she could read. What he said seemed to be true. She put her palm on them and looked at Garrett. "Okay. Why did you close it then?"

"Dad died," Garrett said. "And I was finished with college. I didn't need it anymore. I had all of this." He indicated her folders and files. "I know what the will says." He actually chuckled again as he dug for another paper. "This one was an addendum to the will, and Dad wrote it the day before he died. It was only to be opened by me and the lawyer, and it canceled out any and all other gifts in the will. Everything Dad had became mine."

He passed her the paper, and she and Aaron peered at it together. Time seemed to stretch then, because Eloise couldn't keep track of it. She read the simple statements on the paper. Saw the signatures. Recorded the date.

Only when Aaron put his hand over hers did she snap out of the loop she'd fallen into.

She cleared her throat and added that paper to the pile. Her brother was smart; he'd have his own copies. "Okay," she said, glad she hadn't mentioned the bank accounts. "Now what?"

"Do you intend to fight me for ownership of all of this?"

"I have documents," Eloise said. "And a very good lawyer."

"Ah, yes," Garrett said, leaning back into his chair. It squealed under his weight, but he didn't seem to notice. "Alice Kelton. She is good, but I don't think she's quite cut out to take me on."

Eloise lifted her chin, her devotion to Alice unwavering. "Oh?"

"Her husband just lost his job, right?" Garrett took another item from his folder and set it on the table. "Shame, that is. Who knows how long it will take him to get another one, and I believe I hold the deed to Alice's house here in the cove." Another plucking from the folder, another swishing of paper, and another document landed on top of the picture Eloise couldn't look away from.

It had been Frank Kelton, his arm around another woman.

"Frank has *quite* the reputation with the women," Garrett said as if they were discussing how delicious their lunch was. "I'm *shocked* he hasn't been fired before this, honestly."

Eloise looked up from the paperwork that listed Alice's address on it. Garrett hadn't issued any outright threats, but she'd heard them nonetheless. Her throat was so dry, and Aaron had nothing to add to the conversation.

"You should be careful here," Garrett said, his smile

finally fading. He tapped his expandable file folder. "With one little pull of a string, I can make sure Julian and Kelli Thompson lose their courier business. I believe they just got a loan for over a million dollars to buy out their leading competitor." He clicked his tongue like he was her disapproving grandmother. "What a shame that would be."

"You've made your point," Aaron said, his voice ice cold.

"Have I?" Garrett asked. "Did you know your father was a regular at our club?" He started to open his folder again. "Wait. Maybe you don't want to see the pictures. I hear he's running for mayor."

Aaron turned as stiff as a board, and horror moved through Eloise.

"Of course, I could call Carol and let her know you want her back. She could be here by morning, and then maybe the two of you wouldn't *quite* make it to the altar." He looked between Eloise and Aaron, his eyebrows up as if asking if he should make the call to Aaron's ex-wife.

Eloise had never pegged her brother to be cruel. The only thing pouring from him was hatred, and Eloise felt sure she'd give him whatever he wanted. She couldn't embarrass Aaron's father just for a few properties she hadn't even known existed.

"I've got lots of other pictures of people who used to be quite familiar with our club." Garrett tossed a stack of photos on top of everything else on the table, but Eloise didn't even look at it.

"I believe Duke's boat *just* arrived back in port after a delay," Garrett said. "I hear there's been some vandals down there lately. What a tragedy that would be if he lost the only thing that paid their bills."

"Stop," Eloise said.

"And what about AJ? I hear she's having *such* a tough time getting an on-air spot." He shook his head, as if the news really made him sad.

"You leave them all alone," Eloise said. "None of them have done anything to you."

Garrett laughed then, and the sound was cruel and high. It echoed around near the ceiling, and Eloise cringed as it moved through her whole body.

He cut off the laugh as abruptly as he'd started, and he leaned forward, pure malice in his eyes. "Eloise," he said. "You're wrong if you think all of these women don't want something from you. Now that they know about these properties, they're all thinking of what they can do with them."

She shook her head and leaned away from him, keeping the distance between them. She felt wrung out, and she just wanted him to leave. "You're wrong."

"Alice needs money. So does Robin. And Kelli. Perhaps the only one who doesn't is AJ, but one small tragedy, and—" He snapped his fingers. "That three million they know you have? They'll all be vying for a piece of it."

"That's not true," she said, though her stomach had

started to vibrate. She didn't believe her brother.

"Everyone just watches out for themselves," he said, settling back into his chair again. "You're a fool if you believe otherwise."

"You should go," she said, standing up. Aaron joined her, and Eloise gathered all her papers and stuffed them into the same folder.

"I can't go yet," Garrett said, not moving. "Not before we come to an agreement."

"What agreement?"

"The way I see it, you have two choices. One, you leave all this be. Leave it alone. I have control of the properties, and I'll keep running them the way I have for the past seventeen years. You'll transfer all funds from any accounts you've found in Dad's name to this account." He plucked a paper from his folder and tossed it on the table. "I know you've found them. I tried to get Dad to tell me where they were, but he died before he could." Garrett stood then. "Once I have the money, you can go back to remodeling your...inn." He glanced around the room as if it were covered in slime and cobwebs. "And you'll never hear from me again."

"You'll never come visit Mom again?"

"Oh, sure," Garrett said easily. "I suppose we might run into each other at a family function of some sort." He shrugged one shoulder. "We'll just pretend like this conversation never happened."

Eloise's tears were dangerously close to falling, and she

pulled in a tight breath.

"Two," Garrett said. "You fight me on this, and I will ruin you, him, and everyone you know." He glared at Aaron and looked back to Eloise. "Your choice."

She couldn't believe the man standing in front of her was her brother. She didn't know him at all, and she never wanted to see him again.

Still, it felt like a piece of her flesh had been carved out of her back, and she didn't know how to deal with the feelings of betrayal and shock coursing through her.

"You have until Friday evening to wire me the money," he said, picking up his expandable file folder. "I suppose if I get it, I'll know what you chose. If I don't, well, I'll still know what you chose."

With that, he turned his back on her and Aaron and walked out of the Cliffside Inn. When the door closed, Eloise flinched from the slamming noise of it. She sank back into her folding chair and broke down crying.

"Shh," Aaron said, settling beside her again. "It's okay, Eloise. Shh."

How he could say that, she wasn't sure. Hadn't he heard Garrett literally threaten everyone she loved— including him?

She had so much to absorb and so much to think about that she really wished she didn't have anyone she loved or anyone who loved her. That would make this so much easier, because then Garrett wouldn't have anything to hang over her head.

CHAPTER TWENTY-EIGHT

Kristen took out the pitcher of iced tea and set it on the counter just as someone knocked on her front door. "Come in," she said needlessly, because Robin was already opening the door.

She entered, a happy smile on her face. Behind her walked Alice, Eloise, and AJ. Kelli would be done with work in five minutes, and then she'd come to Kristen's cottage too.

"How are you all?" Kristen asked, surveying them as they scattered to various places in the small house. Alice went to the couch with Eloise, and the two of them started to whisper as if Kristen hadn't even asked a question.

Robin and AJ—never the pairing Kristen would put together—came into the kitchen. AJ detoured to the small table, and Robin got down a glass and started filling it with water.

"Good," she said, and she actually sounded like she was. "Duke's boat finally arrived this week, and he's been gone all day." She grinned like this was a spectacular thing, and Kristen laughed.

"And she booked another wedding," AJ said from the table.

"That too." Robin drank from her glass and smiled at the two of them. "What about you? How's life on this rock?"

"Windy," Kristen said. She was oh-so-tired of the wind. She'd lived with it day-in and day-out for seventy years, and she'd started to wonder if perhaps the Lord could just turn it off for one day.

Robin laughed, and even AJ giggled. "One of the cons of island life," AJ said.

"What's with them?" Kristen asked, looking toward Alice and Eloise. She swung back to Robin in time to see the sourness on her face before she could wipe it away.

"Some legal stuff," she said, her tone definitely not as chipper as previously. So she was jealous. Kristen had seen that look on so many teenagers' faces in the past, including Robin's. She marveled that even after thirty years of friendship, there could be some jealousy between these women.

Surely their friendships had ebbed and flowed over the years, and she thought they'd have worked out their place with each other by now. She supposed that women simply never felt comfortable in their own skin, and while Robin

had been strong and confident as a teen—and she still was
—she still wanted to be liked and accepted. She'd never
liked being on the outside of something, that was for sure.

The door opened again, and Kelli bustled in. "I sent
Parker up to see Jean," she said. "I love you all, but I have
Julian to deal with, and so much to do." She put her purse
on the tiny table beside the door. "So let's talk quickly, if
we can." She looked around at everyone, and Kristen had
definitely noticed a change in her since her husband had
come to Five Island Cove. Kelli had always had multiple
sides, and Kristen had never seen the one labeled "wife."

"Duke's boat got here after a delay," Robin said. "My
life is finally getting back to normal."

"I'm leaving on Sunday," AJ said. "And my boss called
today and said he wants to meet with me on Monday
morning." She grinned. "I just *know* I'm going to get an
on-air spot—*finally*."

Kristen smiled along with the others as they congratu-
lated her. She lifted her teacup to her lips, because she
didn't have any news. She knew her girls had been
through a few hard weeks, and she was glad the sun
appeared to be coming out again.

"Frank has an interview on Monday morning," Alice
said. "So Monday might be a good day for all of us." She
smiled as she stood up. She embraced Kristen and started
pouring herself a glass of iced tea. "Oh, and I just signed
another client."

"I booked a wedding," Robin added.

"Julian and I found a house on Pearl," Kelli said, pushing her hair off her face. "It's far for me and Parker, but I think we should live together and do our counseling together and all of that, so I'm willing to commute." She sighed and reached for a piece of the banana bread Kristen had made that morning. "I loathe the idea of moving again, but it is what it is."

"Any news on Zach?" AJ asked.

"Oh, yes." Kelli quickly finished her bite of bread and swallowed. "Aaron told me this morning that he's moved out of that apartment above the Chinese restaurant. We found out he had a one-way ticket for New Hampshire."

"So it's over." Alice looked so hopeful.

"Hopefully," Kelli said, and she certainly seemed to be carrying less of a load. That made Kristen's heart happy, and she reached over and squeezed Kelli's hand.

All eyes turned to Eloise, who hadn't moved from the couch. Her eyes scanned the group, but she never let her gaze settle on any one of them. She finally looked at Alice, who nodded slightly.

"I have something," Eloise said. She got up and approached the kitchen area, where most of them were loitering. "It's not good news." She pulled a sheaf of papers from her bag and started laying them on the table one by one.

"My brother is not a nice person," she said. "He got my father to sign some paper to cancel out the will, and he owns all the properties." She didn't look up at any of them.

"The inn wasn't an inn, but a gentleman's club. Joel attended regularly." She tossed a photograph onto the pile on the kitchen table.

Everyone had gathered around by this time, and Kristen's heart squeezed terribly tight at the image of her husband on the arm of some woman. A drink rested on the table in front of him, and the air was obviously thick with smoke.

"And Guy." Another picture landed on top of Joel's. Kristen's pulse pounded in her chest, and she just wanted all of this to stop.

"Aaron's father. Principal Drake. Peter Springfield." All prominent men in the cove, and while Kristen might have believed Peter Springfield would go to a gentlemen's club to be entertained by scantily clad women, she never would've put John Sherman in that group.

The man had just announced his intentions to run for mayor next year.

"And your mother, Alice." A handful of pictures got dropped over the others, splaying out like a fan. Denise Williams smiled broadly in all the ones Kristen could see. She sat on some men's laps, danced in other photos, and looked to always have a drink in her hand.

Alice sucked in a breath, and she was the first to move at all. She reached toward the pictures, her fingertips hovering just over them.

"Garrett knows you're nearly broke," Eloise said. "He owns your house, Alice, and he can take it in a second.

Robin, he knew Duke's boat was delayed, and he said it would be a shame if it got damaged at the dock. Kelli, he knows you and Julian just bought out your biggest competitor and owe millions on your loans. AJ, he suggested that the reason you haven't gotten your spot on the air yet is because of me."

Her voice faded to almost nothing, and she kept her head down, her spirit completely broken. "He made fun of me for wanting to restart the Cliffside Inn, and he even insinuated that he could get Aaron's ex-wife to come back to Five Island Cove and break us up."

She sniffed, but she didn't sniffle. "It was a terrible meeting."

Silence descended, and Kristen's heartbeat would not settle. She finally managed to tear her gaze from the pile on the table to look at the others gathered around. Kelli was already crying, and AJ's jaw was clenched so tightly, it looked like it might break. Anger rode in her expression as well.

Kristen was used to finding out the people she'd thought she knew were actually only a version of themselves, but she was still shocked to see her husband with other women. That would never be easy for her, as she simply hadn't known that side of him at all.

Alice's face had turned white, and Robin looked one moment away from a complete panic attack. It was she who said, "Is he going to do all of that?" She stepped in front of Eloise and grabbed her by the shoulders. "Is he going to sink my husband's boat?"

Tears slid down Eloise's face. "I don't know."

"Oh, dear Lord," Robin said, her voice stunned and hushed now. She spun in a circle, looking around wildly. "I have to call Duke."

"What did he want?" Alice asked, her voice stalling Robin's frantic movements.

"He wants the money," Eloise said. "In the accounts I found in the wall. He said Dad—" She sobbed and shook her head. "He said my dad was going to turn them over to him too, but he died before Garrett could get it in writing."

"So give him the money," AJ said, her voice low and tight.

"It's not that easy," Eloise said.

"Yes, it is," AJ said, and Alice started nodding too.

"Give him the money, Eloise," Alice said.

"*You* need the money," Eloise exploded, her voice growing so loud Kristen actually fell back a step. "You all need the money! Robin doesn't live in a house she owns. Kelli's up to her eyeballs in debt. Frank has no job—which he also knew about, Alice. In fact, he said that it was so *strange* how Frank has slept with so many clients, and yet *this one* cost him his job."

"This isn't happening," Alice said, rubbing both hands down her face. "Eloise, tell me this isn't happening."

"How can he know all of this stuff about us?" Robin asked.

"Did he send Zach here?" Kelli demanded, her voice suddenly much stronger than the tears on her face would suggest.

"He didn't mention Zach at all," Eloise said. "But honestly? Anything is possible. That's one thing Aaron and I agree on. Anything is possible."

"I don't need the money," AJ said. "How do I get out of this?"

"You can't," Eloise said. "Because you're too tied to me. You're all too tied to me." She looked around at all of them. "I'm sorry." Tears streamed down her face now. "I'm so sorry." She turned and started for the door, making it all the way there before Robin jogged after her.

"Eloise, wait," she said, blocking her exit. "You're going to give him the money, aren't you?" She searched Eloise's face, pure panic in her eyes. Kristen could feel it lilting through the air, and it was the strongest scent in the room.

"I don't know," Eloise said. "I'll let you know." She left, and Robin stared through the open doorway, her eyes as round as dinner plates. She turned back to the group, opened her mouth, and screamed.

Kristen flinched away from the sound of it, and when it stopped, she found Robin snatching her purse from where she'd laid it on the counter. She stomped toward the open door too.

"Where are you going?" Alice asked.

"To the dock," she said. "I am not going to let someone

ruin my husband's only way to make money." She walked out too, and Kristen wondered if her departure had just signaled the end of this friendship.

"I need to go call Frank," Alice said, reaching into her back pocket for her phone. "Find out who he slept with and how she's connected to Garrett Hall." She too left the cottage, and Kristen felt some of her own life go with Alice.

Kelli looked at AJ, and they both looked at Kristen. "I don't know what to say," she said, her voice weak and aged, just like how she suddenly felt.

"What am I supposed to tell Julian?" Kelli asked.

"This is unbelievable," AJ bit out. "I'm going to see if I can switch my flight and get off this stupid island." She strode out of Kristen's cottage too, no goodbye coming from her mouth.

"Kelli," Kristen said.

"I have to go," she said, hurrying to her purse. "I guess I got what I wanted—a quick conversation." She turned and looked over her shoulder. "It's amazing how fast some-thing can go up in flames, isn't it?" She didn't wait for Kristen to answer before she walked out, pulling the door closed behind her.

Kristen found she couldn't stand, and she quickly pulled out one of the table's chairs and collapsed into it. She didn't want to believe any of the things Eloise had said, but the proof of it was all right there, on her dining room table.

She sifted through the pictures, finally getting to the one of Joel. "Why did you do this?" she whispered to the horrifying image. "Was life here with me really that bad?"

He was dead and gone now, and he'd never been able to answer any of her questions. Fury and fear rose within her, and they were not good playmates.

She was more used to shocking news than the others, and they'd all rallied around her in her greatest need. She wanted to help them too, but when she finally looked up from the picture, she felt the keen sense of emptiness in her cottage.

They'd all left.

They'd all left in various stages of anger, disbelief, horror, and fear.

"Please don't let them end like this," she whispered. She'd spent many a night praying for her Seafaring Girls, and not just this group of them, though these five girls had meant more to her than any of her others.

This just couldn't be the end of them.

CHAPTER TWENTY-NINE

Robin finally left the dock when Duke agreed to talk to the head of security. He'd gone to do that, though he didn't fully understand her hysteria. She wanted to get together with someone to talk about this. Her first thought was Alice, but she suddenly didn't trust her friendship with her anymore.

She didn't trust anything in her life to anyone anymore.

She choked on a sob and just let herself drive, making a turn here or there. Before she knew it, she pulled to a stop in front of her mother's house. If she couldn't talk to Alice or Eloise, where could she go?

If she couldn't tell AJ or Kelli her worst fears and hopeful dreams, who could she confide in?

If she couldn't go to the lighthouse and get Kristen's advice, who was left?

Her mother.

She got out of the van and crossed the lawn, though if her mom could see her, she wouldn't be happy. Her mother loved her emerald green grass and worked daily on the yard to make it beautiful.

Robin took the cement steps two at a time and opened the front door without knocking or ringing the doorbell. "Mom?" Her voice cracked, and for the first time in her life, she didn't know how to contain it.

Her mother didn't answer, and Robin quickly ducked into the formal living room off the main entrance. She wasn't there.

Robin went into the kitchen, the scent of something toasty in the air. Through the windows on the back wall, she caught movement, and she practically sprinted toward the back door. "Mom," she said as she went onto the back deck.

Her mother raised her head out of a flowerbed, surprise etched on her face. "Robin." She straightened, her gloved hands holding a couple of weeds she'd just plucked from the earth.

"Mom." Robin ran across the deck and down the steps. She was sobbing by the time she reached her mom, who grunted as she enveloped Robin into her arms.

"What in the world?" her mom murmured, but she held onto Robin tightly.

Robin didn't cry very often, but right now, she felt as if she could sob and sob for hours. She couldn't believe

Eloise hadn't already transferred the money to her brother's accounts. She didn't even want the money.

But somehow she'd thought the rest of them did.

"What's going on, dear?" her mom asked. "Come on, let's go inside and get something to drink."

Robin stepped back and nodded. She let her mom lead her inside. She accepted the cool cloth her mom gave her, and she wiped her tears away as her mom got out a couple of cans of soda. They settled in the living room, and Robin pressed her unopened can of diet cola to her forehead.

The cold burned her flushed skin, and she found she couldn't look at her mother. The pop and hiss from her mother's soda helped Robin focus. "Mom, why did you get after me so much as a teenager?"

Her mother drank and let out a long exhale. "I don't honestly know, Robin."

"You like to argue," she said.

"My mother has said it would serve me well and haunt me," her mom said. "And haunt me, it does."

"How so?"

"Well, for starters, you're the only one of my children who speaks to me on a regular basis, and I'm surprised you still do that."

Robin looked at her mother then, having never heard her mother admit any faults before.

"I didn't know what I was doing when you kids were teenagers," she said, leaning forward to put her soda on the table in front of her. "And girls and boys are so different.

By the time you reached that age, I figured I knew what I was doing, as Fisher had helped me cut my teeth. But nothing that worked with him worked with you."

She shook her head, her sadness palpable. "I'm sorry, Robin. I tried the best way I knew how at the time."

"I know you did, Mom." Robin's tears leaked down her face as she reached over and squeezed her mother's hand.

"You have always been so strong," her mom said. "So sure of yourself. You've always known what you wanted and haven't been afraid to go out there and get it. You haven't needed me the way I hoped you would, because you have Duke." Her smile wobbled on her face, and while she had tears in her eyes, they didn't spill down her face. "And Kristen, and all of your friends."

Robin ducked her head, pure regret filling her. Not for how her relationship with her mother had gone over the years, but because she'd walked out on her friends.

Her friends had been there when no one else had been. Alice, especially, and Robin couldn't just walk away from her.

"You need your friends," her mom said. "You always have, and it took me a long time to realize that I wasn't competing with them. Took me even longer to get to that point with Kristen Shields, but I did it." She offered Robin another weak smile, and this time, Robin got up and hugged her mother.

"I love you, Mom."

"I love you too, sweetheart. I don't know what

happened today, but if you can do anything to make it better, you should."

"I'll try," Robin said. She'd yelled at Eloise, and she'd screamed and stomped out of the cottage. Embarrassment ran through her like a fast-moving stream, and she hated her passionate emotions in that moment.

"I'll call you later, okay?" Robin headed for the front door. She had to find Alice and get on the same page with her. They needed Eloise to transfer the money to Garrett, and the only way they were going to achieve that was together.

CHAPTER THIRTY

Kelli couldn't go back to the beach house and face her husband and son. She left Kristen's, but she didn't go back down to the parking lot where she'd asked the RideShare driver to wait.

She couldn't stop crying, and she couldn't keep walking. She made it to the picnic table and sank onto the bench there. Overlooking the ocean, Kelli just told herself to breathe in and out. As long as she kept doing that, she could find a solution.

She'd sat at this table to shell peas with the Seafaring Girls. They'd done sand dollar crafts, and threaded seashells they'd collected, cleaned, and dried onto fishing line to make necklaces.

Kristen had stood near the head of the table and quizzed them on how to sail a catamaran, how to survive in the ocean for hours at a time, and how to administer CPR.

Right now, she felt like she needed someone to breathe for her. Press their palms over her heart in a steady rhythm to keep it beating.

Humiliation lived where her pulse should be, and she couldn't swallow it away. She couldn't cry it away. The agony simply went on and on, and Kelli kept looking out into the sky and over the water, waiting for the calm peacefulness from the blue sky and smudge of the water on the horizon to flow into her.

She hadn't told her friends that she and Julian had gotten the largest loans they could. They knew they'd bought another company, but not that they were literally living hand-to-mouth, with the threat of complete ruin hanging only an inch above their heads.

She exhaled, her breath stuttering on the way out. Garrett Hall knew, and it felt like such a simple thing for him to flip a switch and ruin her life.

She heard Parker laughing, and she looked down toward the beach. Her son ran with a kite in his hand, trying to get the wind to pick it up. Jean stood down the beach a ways, her arms folded as she watched him. Gratitude filled Kelli, and just the simple act of watching her son and Jean reminded her that Kelli had never done anything or gone very far by herself.

She needed other people.

She'd needed Julian for many years—and she still did.

She'd needed her friends to help her in the past several months. She'd needed her mother to take Parker when she'd first moved back here. She'd needed Kristen as a teenager—and she still did now.

She couldn't sit at this picnic table until time stopped, no matter how much she wanted to.

She had one place she escaped to when she felt like the world was about to end, and she pulled out her phone and called her husband.

"Hey," he said, his voice happy, which was completely foreign to her in that moment. "Are you on your way back?"

"I'm wondering if I can send Parker on the ferry to you," she said. "He's old enough, and if you'll meet him at the station, he'll be fine."

"Where are you going?" Julian asked, confusion in his tone.

"I have to go to Bell Island for a little bit," she said. "See my mother. I might be there for a couple of hours, but I should be home later tonight. I'll keep you updated."

"I could meet you at your mother's," Julian said, and that alone testified about how much he wanted their marriage to work. He'd never cared about getting to know her mother before. In fact, he'd always preferred that Kelli go to visit her mom alone.

"Thank you," she said. "But I need to go myself. Can I text you when I put Parker on the ferry? It's only a nineteen minute ride; you wouldn't need to leave the house until I text."

"I can meet our son, Kelli," he said. "I can leave right now."

Kelli stood up, her decision made. "Thank you, Julian," she said, and she hung up. On her way back to the parking lot, she texted Jean, and a few minutes later, she and Parker crested the path.

"Thank you," Kelli called to her. "I'll send you some money."

"You don't need to do that," Jean called back, one hand on the doorknob. "I love seeing Parker." She smiled and went inside the lighthouse, and Kelli received her son into her arms.

"Get in the car, baby," she said. "I'm going to put you on the ferry, and your dad is going to meet you at the station on Sanctuary."

"What?" Parker asked. "Where are you going?"

"I have to go see my mom," she said.

"I want to go see Grandma," Parker said, buckling his seatbelt.

"I have to go alone." Kelli looked out the window, disliking the tiny fib she'd told her son and husband. She likely wouldn't see her mother that day, but she did need to go to Bell Island—and the house on Seabreeze Shore.

An hour later, Kelli got out of another RideShare, thanked the driver, and faced the house where she'd grown up. The stained glass window smiled down on her, and Kelli couldn't help smiling back.

She hadn't been here since returning to the cove, but she'd come in June for half a day and made sure things were still clean. She'd restocked her bottled water in the fridge, along with a few snacks.

She didn't want to find herself in another situation like the one she'd been in when she'd come for Joel's funeral. This house needed to be her safe haven, and that required chocolate chip granola bars and microwave popcorn.

They'd never used the front door as kids, and Kelli didn't head that way tonight either. She went to the garage and entered the code. She kept the key to the side entrance in a small, handwoven basket, and she pulled it from the shelf.

The basket was empty.

She pulled in a breath, her heartbeat suddenly fast and shallow, like a hummingbird's.

"Looking for this?"

Kelli yelped and jumped away from the sound of a woman's voice.

AJ stood at the top of the steps, holding the silver key pinched between two fingers. Relief filled Kelli, but she still pressed her palm over her pulse. "AJ. You scared me."

"I knew you'd come here." She jumped down from the steps, which surprised Kelli. The woman was forty-five years old, and Kelli had started holding onto handrails a lot more recently. She didn't want to fall and get hurt.

That had always been a big difference between her and AJ. Kelli didn't like confrontation or hard conversations, and she was terrified of getting hurt—in any way possible, not just physically.

AJ had lived life on the edge, and in many ways still did.

AJ sighed as she sat on the steps, and as Kelli did too, she said, "I hoped you'd be here."

"We must've been on consecutive ferries," she said. "I've only been here twenty minutes."

"I had to put Parker on one to Sanctuary," Kelli said.

"What are we going to do?" AJ asked.

"I don't know," Kelli said. "Part of me wants Eloise to fight, because I am just so sick and tired of rolling over and letting people do whatever they want." She sighed, thinking of the house she and Julian had just rented. They were still paying for their townhome in New Jersey too. Her husband was going to try to run his business from three hundred miles away, and guilt pulled through Kelli.

"But if she just gives him the money, this will all be over."

"Yeah." AJ fell silent for a few moments. "I just want it to be over."

"Me too," Kelli whispered.

"Do you think what she said is true?"

"Which part?" Eloise had said so much that Kelli was sure she'd already forgotten some of it.

"The part where she said the only way we'll be safe is if we're not associated with her."

Kelli didn't answer, because she didn't want to believe that. She couldn't imagine their group without Eloise, as she'd always been the quiet, steady one. The woman who knew what she wanted, and wasn't afraid to go after it, even if it wasn't proper or popular.

She was much quieter in the way she did things than say, Robin, but nonetheless, she'd shown Kelli how to be brave and how to be confident all the same.

"Even if she's right," Kelli said. "I don't want to not be associated with her." She stood up and extended her hand toward AJ. "Let's go talk to her."

AJ shook her head. "Let's have microwave popcorn first. I noticed you have the key lime sea salt, and I need it to get my courage up."

"Your courage?" Kelli couldn't help smiling at her as she went up the three steps and into the house. "AJ, you've always had the most courage out of all of us."

"Yeah, right." AJ scoffed and let the door slam behind her. "I almost quit my job before I came here," she said. "I don't really care that I'm not on-air. I *act* like I care, because everyone expects me to care."

Surprise darted through Kelli. "Really?" She set her purse down and picked up the bag of key lime sea salt popcorn AJ had already gotten out of the cupboard.

"Really," AJ said. "I hate doing the research and all the interviews and having someone else deliver the story.

So maybe I do want to be on-air again. Maybe I'd be happier."

"Maybe," Kelli said, sticking the bag into the microwave and pressing the popcorn button. She turned back to AJ and found her squinting at her. "What?"

"Do you need money, Kel?"

Her defenses flew into place, and Kelli's first reaction was to say no, of course not. Instead, she gave herself a moment to think, and then she shrugged. "We get along, month by month."

AJ nodded and said, "Okay."

That was that, and Kelli loved AJ for not being Robin and pressing the issue. Their snack finished, and Kelli shook the bag to get the flavor on every piece. "Come on," she said. "We can't eat this if we're not in the popcorn nook."

AJ burst out laughing, and she followed Kelli upstairs to the tiny closet with a tall, skinny window that looked out over the wilderness preserve behind the house. Plenty of light shone through the glass, and Kelli sank onto the beanbag that had been there for years.

A sigh pulled through her body, but she opened the popcorn, took out a handful, and offered it to AJ.

They didn't speak, and Kelli appreciated that. AJ had always respected Kelli's need for peace and quiet when she came to the house on Seabreeze Shore. It seemed like AJ needed it too, and after they finished the bag of popcorn, AJ looked at Kelli.

"Should we go?"

"Yes," Kelli said. "And we'll take Eloise's favorite treat from Bell."

Their eyes met, and they said together, "Sour grapes," before dissolving into laughter. They linked arms as they left the closet and then the house. AJ put the key back, and Kelli made sure the door was locked.

They shared a car to the old general store almost in the surf on the beach, and they got Eloise's penny candy. If Kelli had to give up the people most important to her to save herself, she decided she couldn't do it.

She would not give up Eloise so she didn't have to admit her debt. *Let Garrett Hall do what he wants*, she thought as she and AJ boarded the ferry. Kelli was going to stick with her friends. After all, when the world came crashing down at Garrett's hand, who would be there for her?

Alice, Eloise, Robin, and AJ, that was who.

CHAPTER THIRTY-ONE

Eloise walked into the kitchen crying. She pulled the utility knife out of her pocket and sliced open one of the boxes that had been delivered to the inn that day. She pulled out a brand-new set of cookware and started putting it away.

She couldn't sit still, but nothing she did took enough brain power to make her stop thinking about the situation she was in. She pictured Robin's face, so full of fear and panic, and a fresh set of tears streamed down her face.

She wasn't sure why she was being so stubborn about transferring the money from the accounts she knew about to the one Garrett had given her. Perhaps her brother had simply ignited her stubborn streak. True to his word, he had not contacted her again, and the whole world seemed to be holding its breath while it waited for Eloise to make a decision.

She'd seen the horror on Alice's face. Heard the desperation in her voice. She'd witnessed Kelli's tears, and she'd felt Kristen's shock when Eloise had put down all the pictures and started naming the men who'd come to her father's version of an "inn."

Honestly, the whole thing felt tainted now. When the inn re-opened, would she have to deal with people who thought it was really something else? How did she make those explanations?

She shook her head and wiped her face, breaking down the box once all the pots and pans were put away. She opened another box and found clean, white kitchen towels inside. She'd been toying with the idea of monograming them, but everything felt ridiculous now. She didn't need to spend the money to get the towels embroidered with some cute logo she hadn't had designed yet.

She probably didn't even need a logo.

Helplessness filled Eloise, but she kept working. Always one to keep busy, she opened, unpacked, put away, and broke down. When she ran out of boxes, she looked around at the empty spots where the new industrial kitchen appliances would go once they were delivered.

Eloise felt those holes and spaces way down deep inside her soul. They multiplied while she stood there, and she finally strode out of the kitchen and back into the sunshine behind the inn. It was starting to weaken as autumn continued its perpetual march toward Five Island Cove, and soon enough the leafed trees would turn gold and crimson, and she'd have to rake the lawn clean for the first time in years.

Oddly, she was looking forward to it. So many things about what she was doing here were odd, and she wasn't sure why this building meant so much to her.

Then she'd remember how happy she was here, and the version of her father that she'd known here.

Her fingers fisted, and she wanted to shout her rage into the sky. How dare Garrett come here and shatter her good memories?

She tipped her head back and bellowed into the atmosphere, and among all the stillness, her voice sounded so loud. Her throat stung, and she quieted. Her chest heaved as she breathed, and she forced herself to open her fingers.

Aaron had promised to meet her at the ferry station whenever she texted him, and he had tomorrow off. He'd asked her to go away for the weekend with him, and Eloise honestly hadn't known what to say.

She hadn't been able to be excited, and Garrett had stolen that from her.

"Don't let him," she said out loud to herself. "He can only do what you let him do."

She felt foolish for thinking she could use her father's dirty money to help her friends, but her mind had started to make those plans. To have all of that taken away in a single conversation felt utterly unfair to Eloise, and she hadn't been able to let go of it yet.

She wanted to be excited when her boyfriend asked her to go away for the weekend, because maybe Aaron would propose. Maybe she'd come home with a diamond ring, and she could call her friends to come eat lunch with her so she could show them, tell them the whole story.

Eloise had lived for years telling herself she didn't care that she didn't have the same stories other women did. She'd been lying to herself, and she wanted to gather with Alice, Robin, Kelli, AJ, and Kristen and relate the most romantic way Aaron had asked her to be his wife.

"Go do it now," she told herself, and Eloise crossed the patio to the door that led to her suite. She'd put the folder and paperwork in the built-in bookcase, and she got it down quickly.

She dialed the first bank, and said, "Yes, hello, this is Eloise Hall, and I need to make a wire transfer. Can I do that over the phone?"

Ten minutes later, that account was empty.

Twenty, and so was the second.

She finished with the third and final bank account, stuffed the paper with her brother's handwriting on it inside the folder and took the whole thing outside. She'd hauled so much trash to the Dumpster, and this might have been the very first thing that was actual garbage.

She tossed the whole thing into the Dumpster with a primal yell and stood there while she listened to the thump and resulting echo when all that paper hit the bottom of the metal bin.

Drawing in a breath, she felt stronger than she'd ever felt before.

The sound of a car engine met her ears, and she turned as a silver sedan pulled into the driveway at the inn. The driver stopped, and Eloise shaded her eyes with her hand to see who'd arrived.

Both back doors opened, and the very best women in the world stood. Alice on the left, and Robin on the right.

Eloise sobbed and hung her head as her friends rushed toward her.

"We're here," Alice said, reaching her first. She wrapped Eloise up tight, and she was surprisingly strong for how thin she was. Robin hugged them both, and the three of them cried right there on the asphalt in front of the Dumpster.

"Whatever you want to do is fine," Alice said. "We're here to help you."

"Let's talk it through," Robin said. "Come on, girls. Let's go inside and talk it through."

Eloise nodded and the three of them separated. She wiped her eyes, feeling withered and spent. She wasn't sure she could endure a lengthy conversation, and besides, one wasn't necessary.

Before she could find her voice, another car arrived in the driveway, and this time, Kelli and AJ emerged from it.

They'd come. They'd all come, and Eloise did not

know what she had done to deserve friends like the four of them.

AJ hugged her first and led with, "I'm sorry, Eloise. I was mad at Kristen's, and I didn't handle the situation well."

Kelli said nothing, but the grip with which she held onto Eloise's shoulders spoke volumes.

"Come on," Robin said. "I know Eloise will have what we need to make cookies." She led the way to the caretaker's suite, and Eloise allowed everyone to enter before her.

When she stepped inside, she closed the door and said, "I transferred the money."

At least two of them gasped, and they all turned to look at her. Alice looked the most hopeful, followed by Robin.

"Really?" Alice asked, taking one step back toward her. She glanced at Robin. "What made you decide to do that?"

"You guys," Eloise said, pressing her palms to her outer thighs. "Maybe a little bit of Aaron. But mostly you guys."

"I thought..." Robin let her sentence hang there, and Eloise stepped down into the suite.

"I'd started thinking about how I could use the money to help you," she said. "I could pay off Alice's house, and then she wouldn't have to worry if Frank couldn't pay. I could help Kelli so she wasn't so stressed about being single and starting over here in the cove. I could pay for AJ to fly back and forth every weekend, because I miss her so much."

Her voice broke, and she reached for AJ, who came to her side instantly. She squeezed her hand, and while AJ rarely cried, Eloise found glistening tears in her eyes.

"I thought I could maybe get a new boat for Duke, and then I could buy the lot next door to this one and have more space for the inn." She shook her head. "They were fantasies, but they were real too, and I just...wanted to help."

None of them said anything, and Eloise wasn't sure what she wanted them to say. Maybe nothing was just fine.

"So I decided to help—and that meant I had to do what Garrett wanted me to do. Then he wouldn't make things worse, and we can try to put this behind us and move forward."

"Thank you, Eloise," Kelli said. "I came to say that I would support whatever decision you made, because you're the smartest woman I know, and whatever you thought was right probably was."

Eloise shook her head. "That's just not true, Kelli. But thank you."

"We are not going to let money come between us," Robin said. "Or the past." She walked over to Eloise too and faced everyone. "Right, ladies? Even if Garrett had come at us with everything he had, we would've been fine, because we would've had each other."

"That's right," AJ said.

"I still want cookies," Alice said, smiling at Eloise. Somehow, that statement broke the tension that had been stretched tightly through Eloise for so long, and she giggled. Robin did too, and then AJ burst out laughing.

Everyone joined in, and the five of them piled into Eloise's kitchen to make chocolate chip cookies, just like they used to do in Kristen's kitchen at the lighthouse.

While the first batch baked, Eloise snuck away and texted her brother. *It's done. Did you get it?*

He immediately sent a thumbs-up emoji, and Eloise simply stared at her phone screen, wondering if that was really how a sibling relationship died.

Obviously, she thought, and she shoved her phone in her back pocket, her chest constricting in such a painful way, she thought it would never expand properly again.

ELOISE LOOKED OVER TO WHERE AARON STILL STOOD at the check-in desk. He still didn't have the key to their room, and Eloise wondered what the problem was. He'd brought her to a boutique hotel on Pearl Island, and Eloise had been impressed with the charming gardens and high-end finishes in the lobby. It also boasted a private beach, and a personal hot tub on the deck of each suite.

But Aaron hadn't seemed to be able to get them checked in, and fifteen minutes had passed. He hadn't texted, and Eloise wondered if she needed to go over there and see if she could help. Just as she started to stand, he turned from the counter, a wide smile on his face.

She returned it, and she wheeled her suitcase across the marble floor toward him. He wore a simple pair of jeans and a pale blue shirt, open at the throat with the top couple of buttons undone. He was gorgeous and sexy, and Eloise could hardly believe she was with him.

"Got it?" she asked as he reached his hand toward hers.

"Yep." He slipped his fingers between hers and squeezed. "Sorry that took forever. First he couldn't find the registration, and you know how it's so hard to search your email on your phone?"

She laughed, because it really was difficult. "It's ridiculous how hard it is."

"Then, he couldn't get his key maker to work. He had to go to the next station over, and then the next one. So he decided to switch rooms, but that one didn't have the ocean view, and I paid for that."

"Good call," she said. "The ocean view is important." She grinned at him as he touched the button for the elevator.

"It is," he said. "The hot tub faces the ocean, and I want to sit in the hot water and watch the sun rise in the morning."

"I'm hoping to be asleep with the sun rises," she said.

He laughed as the elevator doors opened, and he

touched the eleven.

"Ooh, top floor."

"Nothing but the best for this weekend," he said. "Our first alone." He nuzzled her neck, and she giggled as he growled and kissed her. His phone buzzed, and he pulled away to send a quick text.

The elevator wasn't of the fast variety, and by the time they arrived on the eleventh floor, Eloise was ready to be in a room with air conditioning. Aaron led the way down the hall, telling her about the clawfoot tub in the bathroom, and that he wanted to take her to a new crepe shop for breakfast that had just opened on this island.

He touched the keycard to the sensor on the last door in the hallway, and Eloise was aware it was a corner suite. How Aaron had the money to pay for this, she wasn't sure. The door unlatched, and he looked over his shoulder to smile at her. "Ready?"

"Yes," she said. "Let's hope this suite has an amazing air conditioner. This hotel is hot."

He went inside and held the door with his foot so it wouldn't swing shut in her face. She pulled her bag across the threshold and looked up to take in the grandeur of the room.

Aaron stepped out of the way, and a wall of windows expanded in front of her. She smiled, because she loved sunlight. It took her several seconds to realize there were bouquets of roses on every table and counter. Red ones, white ones, yellow ones, pink ones.

"Wow," she said. "This place is—" She cut off, because Aaron stepped back in front of her, crowding right into her space.

"I love you, Eloise," he said, his head down as he looked at something in his hand. She followed his gaze and saw the black box. Her lungs seized, and she automatically fell back a step.

"Aaron."

"My dad loves you so much," another voice said, and Eloise jerked her attention to Grace. She came out from behind the kitchen bar, and she held up a bracelet made of nearly clear, blue stones. "I love you too, Eloise, and I got you this bracelet so we'll match." She held up her skinny wrist, where she wore an identical bracelet.

"Oh, I love you too," Eloise said, taking Grace into a tight hug. She held out her arm and let Grace slip the bracelet on. "Thank you."

"My dad loves you more than his job," Billie said, and Eloise's emotion caught in her throat. She came from the other side of the room, and she looked so grown up and so confident. She held up a pendant that had a silver charm on it. "I got you this necklace, so we can always be together." She touched her collarbone. "I have one too, because I like to think about what you would tell me to do in some situations."

Eloise's eyes filled with tears that were so unlike the ones she'd cried and cried yesterday. These were happy tears, and this was the perfect proposal. "Thank you," she said, lifting her hair so Billie could clasp the necklace around her neck.

Once that was done, she took Billie into a hug and said, "I love you. I'm so lucky to get to be your stepmom."

"Really?" Billie asked, tilting her head back to look at Eloise. "You think you're lucky?"

"Yes," Eloise said. "Absolutely."

Billie looked so vulnerable, and Eloise reminded herself of just how much the girl needed to be loved.

"I do love you so much," Aaron said. "And more than my job. I want to spend the rest of my life with you, and I want to raise my girls with you, and I want you to be mine forever." He dropped to both knees and cracked open the ring box he'd been holding this whole time.

"Eloise, will you marry me?"

She let her tears spill out of her eyes as she nodded. "Yes," she said. "Yes, I'll marry you."

He slid the ring on her finger, rose to his feet, and kissed her while his girls cheered. Soon enough, though, Billie said, "Dad, stop it."

He laughed as he pulled away, and Eloise tucked herself into his chest as he said, "Stop what?"

"You looked like you were going to eat her face." Billie looked thoroughly disgusted, and both Aaron and Eloise burst out laughing.

"Kissing is super gross," Billie said, and Eloise couldn't help disagreeing.

"Keep that opinion," Aaron called after her as she

went back into the room where she'd been hiding. "And get your phone, because Tara will be here in five minutes."

"They're not staying?" Eloise asked.

"Absolutely not," Aaron whispered. "I want to eat your face off, and they can't be here while we do that." He grinned at her, and Eloise warmed from head to toe.

She looked down at her ring finger while Aaron made sure his girls had their backpacks and Billie had her phone, and then he kissed Eloise real quick and said, "I'm going to walk them down to the circle drive. Be right back. Maybe go turn on that hot tub, and we can relax in there."

"Sure, okay," she said. He left, and she wandered out to the deck, which had an intimate hot tub for two, as well as the most amazing ocean view in the whole wide world. Eloise took a deep breath of the salty, sea air and let it brush through her hair before she turned to turn on the bubbles in the hot tub.

Then she pulled out her phone and sent a quick message on her friends' group text. *I'm engaged! Who can come to the inn for lunch on Monday? I want everyone there, because it's a great story.*

———

"THE CORN ON THE COB IS DIVINE," ROBIN SAID.

"Have you tried the corn and shrimp fritters?" AJ asked. "I can't even."

"There is nothing as good as Mort's blue crab," Alice

said.

"I just want a few bites of everything," Kelli said.

Eloise loved listening to her friends talk about the food. She wished she had made it, but her skill had never really been in the kitchen. She could order with the best of them, though, and she'd had practically the entire menu of Mort's delivered to the inn.

Her new picnic tables on the back patio were perfect, and she'd even put up the umbrellas by herself so they could eat in the shade.

They'd all come hungry, and while they'd all embraced and taken a moment to say hello, no one had asked to see Eloise's ring yet.

She didn't mind, because she'd be in the spotlight soon enough. She'd called her mother on Saturday morning and told her the good news, and then she'd called Kristen to tell her too.

Aaron had consulted with his parents as well, so they could find a date that worked for everyone. With his father doing his campaign next year, Aaron thought the earlier in the year, the better.

Eloise would marry the man tomorrow if he'd let her.

But he'd said, "No, El. You want this big, beautiful wedding, and you're going to get it."

She did want that, despite what she'd told Robin to the contrary, and she adored Aaron for reminding her that it was okay that her wedding be exactly what she wanted it to be.

"Okay, Eloise," Robin finally said when they'd slowed their eating. "I've got my calendar right here." She actually pulled a physical book out of her bag and spread it on the table in front of her. "Let's get a date on it."

"I can't believe you use a paper calendar," Alice said. "What is this? Nineteen-eighty-four?"

Robin threw her a dirty look while everyone else twittered. "This system works for me, I'll have you know. I never forget anything."

"My phone actually sends me reminders," Alice said, grinning.

"I'm so happy for you," Robin said dryly.

Eloise loved it when the two of them bickered. She wasn't even sure why, only that it brought her joy.

"You're not wearing your ring," Kelli said. "Where is it?"

"Oh, right." Eloise dug into her pocket and pulled out the ring, easily sliding it on her finger. She held out her hand the way she'd seen brides do and admired the shiny diamond.

"Holy cow." AJ grabbed her hand and asked, "Is this a Sadie Merchant?" She looked up with wide eyes. "These are like, twenty thousand dollars."

"That's not true," Alice said, but she ogled the ring too. "I had no idea Chief Sherman was pulling down that kind of salary though. Maybe I should go into law enforcement."

The idea of Alice in a police officer uniform struck Eloise as hilarious, and she burst out laughing.

"What?" Alice asked between her giggles. "You don't think I can take down the bad guys?"

"You can barely support your own weight," Kelli said, laughing too.

Once they'd quieted again, Kelli said, "It's a beautiful ring, Eloise." She reached across the table and patted her hand.

"It *is* a Sadie Merchant," AJ declared, turning her phone toward Eloise. "It's the Deep Sea model. I knew I'd seen it." She stared at the ring again, her expression unreadable. "I can't believe he can afford this."

"Who's Sadie Merchant?" Eloise asked. She'd bet the value of the ring Aaron didn't know who it was either.

"She's only the best jewelry designer on the Atlantic Seaboard," AJ said, obviously disgusted Eloise didn't know. "She has this pair of teardrop earrings that legit look like the ocean waves when light hits them." She tapped and swiped and showed her phone again a moment later. "Aren't they fabulous?"

"You'd look good wearing those on-air," Kelli said.

AJ lowered her phone then. "I called my boss this morning to say I'd missed my flight." It wasn't technically a lie, but AJ hadn't even tried to get on the flight, so maybe it was.

"And?" Robin prompted.

"And nothing. He said the meeting wasn't that important, and he'd catch up to me when he got back from Toronto."

"What's he doing in Toronto?" Alice asked.

"Something to do with hockey," AJ said. "I was probably supposed to go with him. I know a few of the players up there."

"None of this is important," Robin said, tapping her pen against her paper calendar. Eloise supposed it was a bit old-fashioned to make all of her appointments and tasks on paper, but it was also so Robin that Eloise couldn't imagine her doing it any other way.

"We need a date," she said. "What are you and Aaron thinking, El?"

"His father's running for mayor," Eloise said. "That will take almost the whole year, but Aaron and his parents agree that sooner in the year is better."

"How soon?" Robin's voice pitched up as she flipped back a few pages. "Are we talking January or February-soon? Or more like April or May?"

"April," Eloise said. "I want April, and Aaron said I could have anything I wanted." She smiled down at her ring, determined to ask him about Sadie Merchant and how much he'd really spent on this ring.

"We could do the tenth," Robin said. "It's sometimes pretty breezy and cold that early in April though." She looked up. "The seventeenth?"

"Either of those will be fine," Eloise said. "What's best for you, Robin?"

"Duke's already talking about going to Alaska again," she muttered, flipping a page. "Senior prom isn't until May eighth...I've got a fiftieth wedding anniversary on April third...let's do the seventeenth." She started to write it in—in ink—before Eloise had even confirmed.

"I'll text Aaron," she said, and she did, asking him to confirm that April seventeenth would work for him, the department, his parents, and the girls.

He took a few minutes to answer, during which AJ told how she didn't think she'd get an on-air spot, and she was actually coming to terms with it. She said, "And you guys, I want to get together at Christmas." She looked around at everyone. "The five of us. Right here." She met Eloise's eyes. "Will the inn be open?"

"I don't know," Eloise said. "We've made a lot of progress, but there's still miles to go."

"If it is, we could all stay here," AJ said. "And celebrate together. Husbands and kids welcome." She beamed around at everyone. "What do you think?"

"I think I'll book it," Eloise said. "It sounds wonderful."

"I'll talk to Duke," Robin said.

"I'll see if Frank wants the kids for the holidays," Alice said.

"I'll tell Julian what we're doing."

Eloise noted how Kelli hadn't put any wiggle room in her statement. She'd be there, plain and simple.

Her phone buzzed, and she said, "Oh, Aaron says the seventeenth is the 5K and ferry fundraiser."

"Oh, that's right." Robin sighed as she scrubbed out the words she'd already written in. "The tenth it is."

Eloise texted Aaron that date, and when she looked up, everyone was watching her. "I missed something. Sorry, I was texting Aaron."

"We just want the engagement story now," Alice said, smiling. She reached out and pinched off another tiny piece of a fritter.

A smile filled Eloise from top to bottom, inside and out, from here to the stars above. She held up her wrist, where Grace's bracelet dangled. "It was so sweet," she started. "The girls were there, and they said the cutest things about how much Aaron loved me, and how much they loved me."

She told the story, adding in some drama when Aaron had dropped to both knees. About that time in the story, her phone buzzed again, and he'd said, *The tenth is great.*

She showed her phone to Robin, who gave her a wide smile.

By the time she finished, Eloise felt like she was glowing. Silence descended on them, and she looked around at the women she loved so much.

"Thank you for not giving up on me," she said, her voice quiet. No, Garrett would not be at the wedding. Eloise wouldn't invite him. He'd know anyway, and she hoped he'd just stay away. She'd done what he'd wanted her to do, and surely he knew he wasn't welcome in her life anymore.

Alice put her hand in the middle of the table, and Eloise quickly put hers on top of it. Then Robin, and then Kelli, and finally AJ. They looked at their fingers, all in an array of different colors, and then they looked up and around at one another.

Eloise wasn't sure who started laughing first, but it didn't matter. In the end, they all joined in, and she experienced one of the happiest moments of her life—and none of that could happen without these four women at her side.

"Okay," she said, shushing them. "Here's the most important question. Really, two questions." She held up one finger. "First, will you all be my bridesmaids?"

Robin perked right up, as being a bridesmaid was probably one of her life dreams.

"And two," Eloise added once they'd all said yes to question one. "What color should the dresses be?"

Read on for the first couple chapters of Christmas at the Cove the next book in the Five Island Cove women's fiction series, for more secrets, more romance, and more great friendship and sisterhood fiction that brings women together and celebrates the female relationship.

AJ Proctor took off the red and white striped sweater with a muttered, "This makes you look like a chubby candy cane." She'd put on a few pounds since she'd quit her job at the sports network a couple of weeks ago.

Perhaps she'd quit a month ago, but she really had only gained about five pounds. She was happier than she'd been in a long time, and she knew it was because of a trifecta of things all combining together to increase her overall mood.

One, she was now seriously dating Matt Hymas. Yes, he still lived in Five Island Cove, and she still lived in New York, but he came to see her every chance he got, and she'd been back to the cove several times in the past few months since they'd reconnected.

Two, AJ had started seeing a therapist. She wasn't sure

why she'd been so resistant to meeting with a mental health professional, only that she'd once believed that admitting she needed help was the worst form of weakness she could exhibit.

She now knew her father was wrong. All of the coaches she'd had over the years were wrong. She herself had been wrong. There was nothing wrong with getting the help she needed to be the best, most whole, and healthiest version of her herself that she could be.

It was Dr. Genosie that had kept AJ in New York, actually. If not for the progress AJ had been making with her therapist, she strongly suspected she'd have already made the move back to the cove.

At the same time, AJ did not really want to move back to Five Island Cove. That was the topic of today's therapy session, and AJ pulled off her sweater and tossed it on her bed. She needed to make the right decisions for her about Five Island Cove, not because Matt lived there and she'd already fallen for him all over again.

He was precisely the kind of man she'd always wanted to look her way. Had she known he would respect her, show up on time, and hold her when she was uncertain, only providing suggestions if she asked for them, she'd have answered his telephone calls in the months following her departure from the cove.

He'd gone to college too—right here in New York City —and he'd tried calling her in Miami a few times. She'd had her roommate screen those calls, because she'd been running from the first eighteen years of her life.

Sometimes she still felt like she was.

AJ peered into her closet, which in the apartment she rented, was about the size of a kitchen cabinet and couldn't be called a closet at all, trying to find something else to wear. She reached for the same black, floral blouse she'd been wearing everywhere lately and tugged it over her head.

It at least lay so it wasn't obvious that she'd gained a few pounds. She needed to stop eating so much pasta, but she lived above The Noodle Factory, and it was so easy to stop there on her way back from the gym in the morning, and even easier at night when she finished writing her columns in the shared workspace she rented on the next block over.

That was the third reason she was so blissfully happy—her new career as a freelance sports columnist. She could finally get credit for all the contacts she had, all the stories she dug up, and all the knowledge of sports she'd acquired over the years. She'd had no problem selling her columns; as it was, she was booked out for the next three months, as the basketball regular season had just begun, and all football fans everywhere were gearing up for bowl games on the collegiate level, and then the Super Bowl in just six weeks.

Everyone wanted to know everything about their favorite athlete's training schedule, and what they did to stay mentally strong through playoffs and stressful games, and what they did to rejuvenate in their personal downtime.

AJ hadn't had to call in any personal favors yet, and she was making twice as much as she had writing the stories for the on-air talent at her network.

It's also a job you can do from the cove, she thought as she quickly stepped into her boots and reached for her coat. She wasn't sure why the thought was there; she had never wanted to return to the cove permanently. Just eight months ago, she'd only gone for Joel's funeral out of sheer obligation.

So much had changed since April, and AJ wasn't sorry about any of it. Down on the street, her stomach lurched as she lifted her arm to get a cab. She'd forgotten to eat again, but she reassured herself that Wendy, the woman who sat next to AJ in the shared workspace, would have snacks on her desk. She never minded sharing, and she even brought in the dried apricot and mango that AJ had sampled once and really enjoyed.

She'd head to the creative commons after her session, and she'd be able to eat then. She watched the city go by, seeing images of her life on the windows and walls of the tall buildings. College, which had been one big disappointment, though she'd graduated.

Her failure to make the Olympic track team. Her decline into more men for a year, until she cleaned herself up and got a job in sports.

Her return to college, this time with an emphasis on broadcasting and journalism. Her graduation. Her long relationships that led to dead-ends.

Robin. Alice, Eloise. Kelli. The women who never truly left her, and who'd always accepted her for exactly who she was.

A smile touched her face, and AJ blinked. The images disappeared, and the city became just the city again.

"Lexington building," the cab driver said, and AJ quickly tapped her watch to pay for the ride. Outside, she zipped her coat to her chin and started down the cleared sidewalk. Mother Nature had not been kind this first week of December, and she often felt like an insect bustling through paths with high walls of snow on either side.

Heat greeted her upon opening the door, bursting into her face with the scent of flames and vanilla. The receptionist at the front desk always burned candles, and AJ had started to purchase some of the brand for herself. They were all hand-created, with creative names and scents, from a female-owned business out of California.

"What's this variety?" she asked Raymond as she signed into the building.

"Take a chill," he said. "Vanilla bean ice cream, long naps, and marshmallow dreams." He grinned at her as he turned the jar toward her.

AJ read the same description, a smile crossing her face too. "I got the Boyfriend's Sweater one. I love it."

"Darby loves that one too," Ray said, taking the check-in clipboard and pressing the button to let her into the building.

AJ didn't immediately move toward the door, though if she didn't pass through it in the next sixty seconds, Ray would have to open it for her again. "She does, huh? And you two are...? Engaged yet?"

"I'm working on it," Ray said, not meeting AJ's eye.

"Are you?" AJ had loved getting to know Ray, and he made it very easy to do that, as he could talk the ear off a deaf man. "What's the hold-up?" She was at least a decade older than Ray and his girlfriend, but she'd heard a lot about the two of them in the past three months since she'd been coming to the Lexington Building and meeting with Dr. Genosie.

"The hold-up is Darby said she's not sure she wants to get married." Ray looked up then, and AJ's heart tore for him.

"Oh, no," she said. "Get on out here and hug me."

Ray shook his head, a small smile on his face as he did what AJ said. He was a sharp dresser, his hair always combed just-so. She'd thought him a good catch for someone lucky enough to find him, and she couldn't fathom why his girlfriend didn't want to marry him.

She wasn't going to be like Robin, though, and ask. A question did bounce through her mind, but she kept it silent. She'd been on the wrong end of it before, and she would not put another person through the emotional turmoil of wondering if Darby didn't want to get married in general, or if she simply didn't want to marry Raymond.

Nathan hadn't wanted to marry AJ, and that had been a painful, painful realization that she'd already worked through with her therapist.

"Thanks, AJ," Ray said, his voice muted and so unlike his own. He stepped back and kept his face turned away from hers as he returned to his desk. "Go on, so I don't have to open the door again."

"Okay," AJ said, stepping toward the door. She didn't move very fast, adding, "Ray, call me if you need to, okay?"

"Yep," he said, already back in his seat. AJ went through the door to the bank of elevators that led up to at least a dozen medical offices, knowing Ray wouldn't call her. They were friends, and they had exchanged numbers, but she saw him once a week. She didn't really *know* him.

AJ thought about the people who she did know, and who knew her. If she needed help, she didn't need to call Ray or Wendy. She'd call Kelli first, who'd probably alert Eloise or Robin, and the entire Seafaring Girls group would know within minutes.

She swiped on her phone as the elevator took her to the sixteenth floor and checked the group text string the five of them had started months ago. Nothing new, and Eloise's message about how the inn would be ready for them to spend Christmas together was the last one.

AJ had read it an hour ago, when it had come in, and she hadn't wanted to be the first to respond. Since no one else had either, she assumed she wasn't the only one who didn't want to be the first to confirm they'd be in the cove for the holidays.

She had no hesitation about going; her plane ticket was already booked, and she'd already made several plans with Matt.

Last time the five of them had gotten together over the summer, they'd assigned meals and planned activities together. Someone would need to spearhead all of that, and it shouldn't have to be Eloise just because they were all staying at the inn.

AJ could see herself doing it, because her articles for the college bowl games were already outlined. All she had to do was wait to see who won, get a couple of quotes, make some minor adjustments, and they'd be done.

As the elevator dinged her arrival, she quickly sent, *Thank you, El. I'll put together a meal schedule, okay? Unless anyone has any objections, I can do activities too, since Matt and I already looked into everything happening around the cove during the holidays.*

She'd barely given her name and sat down to wait before a flurry of texts arrived. *Thanks, AJ,* Alice had said. *With the move, I'm so scattered.*

No objections, Kelli had said. *We'll be a day early to the inn, Eloise, if that's okay.*

Take it away, AJ! Robin had said, ever the cheerleader of the group.

AJ smiled at all of them, wondering why no one

wanted to text first. She couldn't quite pinpoint why she hadn't wanted to either, and she looked up, trying to examine her feelings and make sense of them.

"AJ," Dr. Genosie said, and she looked toward the door where the woman stood. "I'm ready for you."

AJ smiled back at her, ready to do this too. She needed to determine whether or not she could return to the cove the way her other friends had, and if that was in *her* best interest and not because she felt left out.

A WEEK LATER, AJ DISEMBARKED FROM THE PLANE and hustled through the wind to get inside the airport on Diamond Island. At least it's not raining, she thought, because she'd been in the slanted, sideways rain that plagued Five Island Cove in the winter, and it wasn't pleasant. It could be as sharp as needles and as cold as ice, and a booming clap of thunder filled the sky as she stepped inside the airport.

Cries rose up, and AJ suspected the people in the waiting areas had been there for a while—and would be staying a while longer. Planes didn't take off in the driving rainstorms, and it was cold enough today to produce snow.

Sure enough, when she arrived at baggage claim, an announcement sounded through the whole airport. "All planes had been grounded for the next ninety minutes," a male voice said. He continued to talk over the groans of those who wanted to leave the cove, and the relieved conversations of those who'd made it in.

AJ wasn't sure how to feel. She'd come to the cove two weeks early, and not for a reason she wanted anyone to know about. She'd seen Dr. Genosie yesterday, but she'd already changed her plane ticket and packed her bag at that point. Meeting with the therapist had only confirmed what AJ knew to be right.

She hadn't told a single person she was coming today, not even the man she'd come to see. Her pulse fluttered in her throat, not strong enough to choke her. She'd been through that debilitating feeling of losing everything already, and it was time to *do* something about it.

After lifting her own bags from the belt, she went toward the RideShare line, hoping that wouldn't be too delayed, though she knew it would be.

Her mind raced, as it had been doing for the past three days, since she'd learned of her condition. She'd been working through so much since then. Flight changes. Laundry. Submitting a couple of articles early and pulling others. Packing. Flying.

"Ma'am," the attendant said, and she clued in. The man already stood at the back door of a sedan, waiting for her to take the RideShare.

"Thanks," she said.

He helped her with the bags, and gratitude filled AJ. She didn't want to lift them into the trunk, and she hoped the driver could help her once she arrived at her destination.

A woman sat behind the wheel, and AJ's hopes withered slightly. "Where to?" the driver asked, a pretty smile on her face. She eased away from the curb before AJ could comprehend the question.

"Oh, uh, Seventy-four Blue Lake Drive," she said, her stomach and chest rioting against what she was doing.

But it had to be done.

The drive didn't take long—or maybe AJ had zoned out again. She didn't need to take her luggage to the door, but she didn't have anywhere else to store it. She probably should've gone to the hotel first, but she hadn't allowed herself to even think of it. If she didn't just tell him, she was worried she'd chicken out.

The driver did help her with the bags, and then AJ faced the simple yet stylish house that sat only two blocks from the beach. The rain had definitely driven Matt indoors, and he'd told her once that he didn't stay at the clubhouse if he didn't have to.

"He'll be home," she whispered to herself as she towed her suitcases up his front sidewalk. She'd just stepped under the protection of the eaves when the rain started. She tugged her biggest suitcase out of the way and reached to knock.

He'd tried to replace the doorbell a month or so ago, but he'd ended up shorting out the whole assembly and hadn't gotten back to it yet.

AJ's knuckles against the door sounded like gunshots to her own ears, and she only rapped four times. With all the rain and thunder, perhaps Matt wouldn't hear her.

Her fingers shook, as did her chin, and she told herself it was just because of the cold temperatures in Five Island Cove.

Matt didn't answer, and AJ's thoughts scattered again. She'd tried, right? She could just go get warm in the hotel now.

"No." She shook her head and knocked again.

Only a few seconds later, the door opened, and Matt stood there. Handsome, tall, refined, mature Matthew Hymas. "AJ," he said, clearly surprised. A smile touched his mouth as he stepped back. "Come in out of the rain. Come in."

He didn't ask what she was doing there. He reached to help her with her luggage. He closed the door behind her and drew her into a tight embrace. "What a great surprise." His voice was soft and tender in her ear, his voice rumbling from his chest to hers. All of her fears evaporated, because he was so perfect. He could handle what she needed to tell him. "What are you doing here?"

AJ drew in a breath, realizing how shakily it entered her lungs. "I have to tell you something," she said. She stepped back, because she needed to see his face when she told him. All of her worries returned, because she and Matt had already spoken about this topic, and his desires were crystal clear.

"Uh, Matt, I don't know how to say this, so I guess I'll just say it." She looked him right in the eye and exhaled, the air sort of sounding like a nearly-silent machine gun. "I'm pregnant, Matt. The baby is yours."

A baby he didn't want. A baby he'd *told* her he didn't want.

When he just stood there, saying nothing, doing nothing—barely even breathing and blinking—extreme foolishness filled AJ. After all, she was forty-five years old, and she knew how to make sure this particular brand of unexpectedness didn't happen.

"I'm sorry," she said, tears filling her eyes. Everything inside her broke, and she realized then that Dr. Genosie had been right to be cautious. AJ had somehow created a fantasy out of Matt's reaction, and he hadn't given her what she'd conjured in her mind.

Her tears spilled down her face, and that was finally when Matt wrapped her up in his arms again and let her cry against his shoulder. He still didn't say anything, though, and AJ really hated reality in that moment.

Finally, he whispered, "Shh, AvaJane. Don't be sorry," and those were the best words AJ had ever heard in her entire life.

Robin Grover added the red cooking dye to the chocolate cake batter and got the mixer going again. Her husband, Duke, loved red velvet cake, and it was his birthday today. The girls would be home from school in an hour, about the same time the cake came out of the oven.

Mandie, her oldest, would frost the cake once it cooled, and together, they'd decorate the house for the party they'd have once Duke came home from fishing.

He didn't go out every day in the winter, because the seas could be rough, and his boat was starting to get up there in age. He used her relentlessly, and she'd gone all the way to Alaska and back this summer.

Robin thought of Garrett Hall and his threats from a few months ago. He had a way of creeping into her mind at the most inopportune times, but she hadn't been able to shake him completely. To her knowledge, AJ had not been fired or lost her job. She'd quit of her own volition, and she claimed to be doing better with her freelance writing than her job at the station. She'd never gotten an on-air position, but Robin had no idea if Garrett had been responsible for that or not.

Duke's boat had not been sunk or vandalized. Kelli hadn't heard from or seen Zach again. Alice had not lost her home. Eloise was still engaged and finishing up all the finer details at the inn. The five Seafaring Girls and their families would be staying there over the holidays, to test out the rooms, the systems, the kitchen, all of it. It would be a good trial run for Eloise, and everyone else would have somewhere magical to spend Christmas.

She put her fears out of her mind, because there was nothing she could do about them anyway. She poured the cake batter into the greased and floured cake pans and slid them into the oven.

With a timer set, Robin got busy cleaning up the mess she'd made. She didn't work nearly as much in the winter either, though her spring wedding prep would start the moment the holidays ended. She had five brides who wanted the perfect wedding, Eloise being one of them. Robin would do everything in her power to make every event memorable and as easy as possible for the people who'd hired her.

But she still had time to bake a cake for her husband's birthday. The girls had picked out simple presents for him, and Robin had wrapped them after he'd taken them to school and continued on to the dock.

They sat on the dining room table, and once the kitchen was clean, Robin went to get her gift for him from her office. Mandie had bought his favorite candy—dark chocolate covered almonds—in bulk, and Jamie had used some of her babysitting money to get him a gift card from the polish dog food truck that frequented the docks as the fishermen came in off their boats. Duke actually liked their breakfast dog the best, and his weakness was getting breakfast on the way out for a day of trawling.

Robin had purchased a new pair of gloves for him, along with a brand new set of walkie talkies. He loved his radios to communicate with his friends on the other boats, as they usually went out in groups to the best fishing grounds. Bryan Reynolds and Duke were good friends, and Robin could always count on Bryan to have her husband's back.

She quickly wrapped the gloves and the walkie talkies, put them beside the other gifts, and got the cream cheese out of the fridge so it could start to soften.

Her phone rang, and her mother's name sat on the screen. Robin's heart dipped down to her stomach, but she answered the call anyway. "Mom, hey," she said, hoping she sounded reasonably normal.

"Robin, dear, I have a gift for Duke."

"Oh, of course." Robin had not invited her mother to their family celebration. She had been trying to improve things with her mother, and for the first time in her life, Robin had what she'd classify as a real relationship with her mom.

It certainly wasn't perfect, but they'd both been trying. There had been apologies and honest conversations, and while Robin didn't choose her mother as the person she wanted to spend the most time with, they definitely got along better.

"You can just bring it to the party on Sunday," she said.

"I'm not going to be here on Sunday," her mother said. "I'm just going to drop it by right now. I won't stay."

Robin had her doubts about that, but there was a bigger issue at play now. "Where will you be on Sunday?"

"Oh, there's a senior holiday cruise leaving from Rocky Ridge on Saturday morning." She gave a light laugh. "I bought myself a ticket on a whim."

Robin had fallen still, her mind trying to work through what her mother had said. "Senior holiday cruise?"

"Yes, for men and women above age sixty-five," her mother said, her voice full of forced importance. "It's going to Nantucket for a few days. Then over to the Hamptons, then down to New York City."

"You'll be gone for Christmas?"

"It's a fourteen-day cruise," her mother said. "So no, I won't be back until the twenty-seventh."

"Wow." Robin exhaled, not quite sure what to think. "I can't believe I'm just hearing about this now."

"I just decided today," her mom said. "I'll be by in about ten minutes."

"Okay." Robin turned as the timer on the oven went off. "Bye, Mom." She set her phone on the counter and reached for the oven mitts.

The cake was done, and she slid it onto the stovetop just as the front door opened and Jamie's and Mandie's voices filled the air.

"...is all I mean," Mandie said. "You have to be careful with girls like that, Jamsey."

"Don't call me that," Jamie said. "I'm not a baby."

Robin held very still once more, listening to her daughters.

"I'm just saying," Mandie said, her voice purposefully quiet. "She's not a nice person, and she's probably using you."

"Whatever," Jamie said, and her footsteps went down the hall that led to the bedrooms in the house. Mandie came around the corner and met Robin's eye.

Robin's eyebrows lifted of their own accord. "What's going on?"

"Oh, there's this mean girl who's befriended Jamie." Mandie sighed as she put her backpack on the built-in desk and joined Robin in the kitchen. She opened a drawer and tied an apron around her neck and waist. "I tried to tell her to be careful. Sarah-Elizabeth is *not* anyone's friend."

"How do you know?" Robin got out of the kitchen as

Mandie started puling together the rest of the frosting ingredients. Jamie was in eighth grade at the junior high, and Robin had just started her junior year at the high school.

"Everyone knows about those Phillips girls," Mandie said. "The queen bee at the high school is Carrie. She's the exact same way." She shrugged. "I just steer clear of her, but I've heard stories. Apparently Sarah-Elizabeth is twice as snobby, and twice as cruel."

Robin looked toward the hallway, hoping Jamie would reappear and they could talk. Her mama bear instincts wanted to keep Jamie safe from mean girls and boys and bad grades and anything disappointing at all.

In reality, she knew she couldn't do that. She didn't even want to do that. People learned a lot from the disappointing things in their lives, and she didn't want to rob her girls of those learning experiences. She just wanted them to have the softest consequences possible.

"Should I talk to her?"

"No," Mandie said. "I'll keep my eye on her." She put the cake in the fridge before she whipped up the frosting. "I'll get her to come help decorate."

"Oh, right." Robin jumped from the stool and went down the hall to her office. She took the huge bouquet of balloons she'd picked up that morning into the kitchen and returned to the office to get the streamers and tape.

Jamie had come into the kitchen, and the three of them worked together to turn the common area at the back of the house into party central. Mandie didn't say anything about Sarah-Elizabeth, and Robin followed her lead.

The time passed quickly, and Mandie had just finished the peaks in the cake frosting when the garage door opened. "He's here," Robin said, her heart beating faster now. "Come over here."

The girls hurried to her side, and the moment Duke appeared at the end of the hall, they started singing. He lifted his head, a smile spreading across his whole face. Robin could still tell something was wrong—terribly wrong.

She kept singing though, and when they finished, Duke clapped for them and stepped into all three of them to hug them. "Ah, my girls," he said, his voice not nearly as jovial as usual. "Thank you. What a great surprise."

Robin wasn't sure how he could be surprised, unless he'd forgotten it was his birthday. She made sure he had cake and dinner and decorations every year.

"Presents first," Jamie said, her normal, smiling self. She handed them out and Duke gave the proper performance for each one, even kissing Robin after he opened the walkie talkies.

"Okay, let's eat," she said. "We can have cake now or later. Doesn't matter to me." She met Duke's eye, and he's sobered again already. He was usually so fun-loving, with bad jokes about the ocean and the types of fish it held, loud laughter, and serious-but-not-serious questions about Charlie, Mandie's boyfriend.

Tonight, there was none of that.

Robin pulled four plates from the cupboard and set them next to the slow cooker. "It's your favorite, baby," she said. "Barbecue meatball subs."

"Thanks, babe." His smile lit the house, and he perked up after that. The girls talked about school, and Robin spoke up about her weddings, and Duke said he saw a couple of whales that day.

Dinner ended quickly, and Mandie put the candles in the cake for her father. They sang Happy Birthday for a second time, and Duke actually paused, closed his eyes, and waited a moment before blowing out the candles.

Had he actually made a wish? And if so, what for?

Mandie served the cake, and Robin got out the vanilla ice cream. They spent the evening together, and finally, the girls went down the hall to finish their homework and go to bed.

"Come on, Mister Grover," Robin said, smiling at her husband. She stood and extended her hand to him. "It's time to put you to bed too."

Duke smiled at her, put his hand in hers, and let her lead him down the hall to their master suite. She hadn't cleaned up after dinner, something she always did. Tonight, though, she didn't care.

With the door locked, she turned toward her handsome husband. "What's wrong?"

Duke hung his head. "I didn't want to say anything during the party."

"You're not great at hiding how you feel," she sad. "I knew something was wrong the moment you came into the house."

Duke nodded and started unbuttoning his jeans. "The boat got damaged in the storm today."

Robin paused in the middle of changing into her pajamas. "How bad is it?" His boat had been damaged before, and he'd come home with a positive attitude. He'd been working on a fishing boat for decades, and the man could fix almost anything.

"I couldn't stay to see how bad," he said. "It was dark already, and we barely made it back to the dock."

"Barely made it back?" That didn't sound good at all.

"Bryan said he'd help me tomorrow if he can't go out. The weather is supposed to be wicked for the next couple of days." He stripped his shirt off and, wearing only his boxer shorts, went into the bathroom.

Robin slipped into her silk pajamas and sat up in bed, waiting for him to return.

He did only a few minutes later, and he looked a decade older instead of just one year. He ran one hand down his face and crawled into bed with her. He laid his head in her lap, and Robin liked the way such a simple gesture made her feel powerful and strong.

She stroked his hair, wondering if he wanted to be intimate that night. He sure seemed to be in a bad place, and perhaps he was too tired though it was his birthday, and he'd always told her she was the best and only present he needed each year.

Duke rarely worried, and that made Robin's concern double. She was the one who obsessed over every little thing. It made her a great wedding and event planner, but brought a lot of stress into other aspects of her life.

"Duke?" she finally asked.

"Hmm?"

"How bad is it?"

"Bad, babe," he said.

"Like, so bad we need a new boat? So bad we can't afford to fix it?"

"I won't know until tomorrow." He lifted his head and looked at her with those dark, deep, delicious eyes she'd fallen in love with the very moment she'd seen them.

"We need a Christmas miracle then," Robin said, thinking she better start praying for exactly that.

"I just need you," he whispered, lifting himself up so he could kiss her. Robin felt his usual passion for her in his touch, and as they made love, she tried to be as present as possible.

But really, the worry about how they'd pay for a new boat if the damage was really that bad lingered in the back of her mind.

Please, please, she thought as she lay in her husband's embrace after they'd finished. Everything she'd feared Garrett Hall would do seemed to be coming true, and Robin told herself that even Garrett, though he'd seemed all-powerful last fall, couldn't influence the weather in the Atlantic.

She simply needed a Christmas miracle, and she pressed her eyes closed, inhaled the scent of her husband's skin, and prayed for that miracle.

BOOKS IN THE FIVE ISLAND COVE SERIES

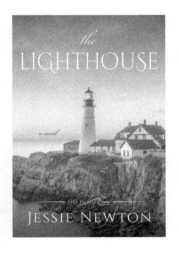

The Lighthouse, Book 1: As these 5 best friends work together to find the truth, they learn to let go of what doesn't matter and cling to what does: faith, family, and most of all, friendship.

Secrets, safety, and sisterhood...it all happens at the lighthouse on Five Island Cove.

The Summer Sand Pact, Book 2: These five best friends made a Summer Sand Pact as teens and have only kept it once or twice—until they reunite decades later and renew their agreement to meet in Five Island Cove every summer.

BOOKS IN THE FIVE ISLAND COVE SERIES

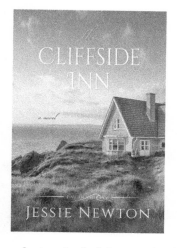

The Cliffside Inn, Book 3:
Spend another month in Five Island Cove and experience an amazing adventure between five best friends, the challenges they face, the secrets threatening to come between them, and their undying support of each other.

Christmas at the Cove, Book 4: Secrets are never discovered during the holidays, right? That's what these five best friends are banking on as they gather once again to Five Island Cove for what they hope will be a Christmas to remember.

BOOKS IN THE FIVE ISLAND COVE SERIES

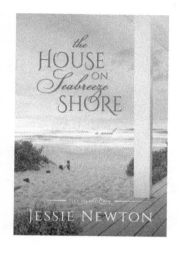

The House on Seabreeze Shore, Book 5: One last trip to Five Island Cove...this time to face a fresh future and leave all the secrets and fears in the past.

ABOUT JESSIE

Jessie Newton is a saleswoman during the day and escapes into romance and women's fiction in the evening, usually with a cat and a cup of tea nearby. The Lighthouse is her first women's fiction novel. Find out more at www.authorjessienewton.com.